# Rescue Me

# Janet Wallace

# Rescue Me

 Published by Obacle, LLC

Copyright© 2016 Janet Wallace

Dedication

This book is dedicated to all the horses that survived the cruelty of humans and endured the unthinkable. These are the lucky ones. Sadly, the horses that traveled over the rainbow bridge who couldn't endure or not allowed to live. This book was written to enlighten those who never experienced the lives of these beautiful, regal and loving creatures.

Those who volunteer to save horses, who give their heart and soul, have to make a better life for them. Hopefully this will help to understand the struggle and the heart felt pain when the battle to survive is lost. It is the wish of volunteers to help and support, for they give their all to save horses.

My best friend and husband Brad with his eternal optimism for me to complete this book. My children, grandchildren who are the support and encouragement for everything I believe and attempt to accomplish. All of you are remembered and without you I couldn't do this. I love you all.

My old childhood friends, many of you never knew at the time, but thank you for staying in touch after many years. You were my happy distraction with your memories and an equalizer.

Julie, Obie, Miracle and I thank you. Because of you and your idea you made me enthusiastic to write and understand nothing is impossible

My editor James Olivier, thank you for your guidance. Madelyn Stone for encouragement

Especially Obie and Miracle who wanted me to tell readers that horses need humans to rescue them. They are all worth saving.

IF YOU SAVE ONE YOU CAN SAVE THEM ALL

# Chapter 1

Speeding down the canopied tree two-lane highway in her 1980 SUV, Her long salt and pepper hair was blowing madly around her head and face. Dressed in patchwork worn jeans, a baseball cap and horse-faced tee shirt, the sixty year-old woman looking more in her early fifties with the energy of a twenty year old. That particular morning old rock n' roll music blasted out of her cracked speaker. The first light of the day was starting to peek through the morning fog with the warm breeze on her face. She inhaled the fresh, crisp air with a hint of orange blossom of her sunrise drive. Most people were not eager to get to the drudgery of their job every day. Debbie was in a select class of employees; she smiled every day on her way to her job as barn manager of a horse rescue. Her morning thoughts of how happy she was since she had left her job of twenty-two years at the real estate office. She hated her job, showing homes to people who couldn't afford the mortgage. Haggling the overpriced ugly homes. Smiling and dealing with people thinking they owned golden mansions. Spending hours on many Sunday afternoons in empty houses with strangers. Mostly they had nothing better to do then visit open houses. To nose around their neighbors home. For the most part, it was a lonely time wasting a Sunday afternoon.

When the financial market collapsed there were more homes being foreclosed upon then selling. Jumping at the opportunity, she decided to get out. This gave her time to return to her love of horses.

The past ten years of saving unwanted, neglected and abused horses had become more than a replacement for a job that she hated. It became a full-time passion. Her dream job of doing something every day that made an impact on animals who couldn't speak for themselves.

Putting her heart and soul into making it succeed gave her a sense of accomplishment. The Rescue Me facility was her baby like a protective mother of her vulnerable children she shielded it. Her thoughts everyday were always about securing a better quality of life for the horses she had under her care.

Making the final curve on the dirt road approaching her destination she started slowing down, turning into the long gravel drive. She reached for the radio knob it went silent. Lowering her driver's window to tap the secret code opening the security gates, Debbie slowly drove in. The only sound heard were the tires crunching on the gravel driveway as she approached the huge barn surrounded by forty-six acres. A light beam sneaking between the clouds glistened on the low-lying fog hovering over the pastures covered in heavy morning dew.

Debbie swung open her car door and hoped out of her vehicle. The car engine chugged after she turned off the key. Once the vehicle shook quiet she walked away. With a proud sigh and looking around she admitted to herself that she had found her paradise. She smiled knowing how lucky she was to have a job taking care of horses. It was her same routine every morning.

The grey weather worn clap board barn showing the years it withstood the test of time. Walking into the twenty-seven stall barn Debbie gave her morning greeting. "Good morning ladies and gentlemen, time to rise and shine." A sweet mixture of horse, manure and hay was the best aromatherapy for her. All twenty two horses poked their heads over their stall doors. Some answered with a mumble, whinny or a kick on their stall doors. She immediately set in motion her routine of gathering each individual horse's feed and placing it into a wheelbarrow. Each of the horses had a story of either abuse, neglect or both. Here at the rescue they had been given a second chance in life. Living here they were protected and secure. They had special feed, needs, and medical problems. She knew exactly what each one needed. While walking into each stall she quickly examined each horse. She knew every inch of them. If they were different for some reason, Debbie investigated it until she was satisfied that they were happy and healthy.

Each horse was greeted by name while she dumped into buckets for their morning feed. As they ate Debbie opened up her office and started the morning coffee. Quickly glancing over the detailed nightly notes from Hank the night watchman. Hank knew an important part of his job was to make reports on each horse throughout the night. If they were quiet or pacing he kept a keen eye on each one. He made notes if there were any changes in behavior or diet, like a nurse in a hospital documenting patients.

Returning the nightly report to where it hung on the wall from horseshoe nail. She mumbled to herself while looking around. "Good job Hank and nice quiet night." The coffee gurgled signaling it was done. Pouring herself a tall cup, she walked out of the office to deliver the morning hay. It was a practice for Debbie; once they all finished eating to walk them out to the pastures for the day. Some had to stay in for one reason or another. Slowly she opened the individual stall doors. Each horse knew its own pasture and a few didn't have to use a halter to be led. There were a few anxious to get to their green grassy pasture. Once they reached the barn opening they trotted out and the others padded along as they walk to their specific pasture. A few others had to be escorted; they were escape artists and couldn't be trusted to walk freely. Debbie's pet peeve was chasing a horse around, it was a losing game. Their long legs could travel much faster than her long, thin, mature legs. A tedious part of her morning ritual was to administer medication to the horses. Many were on antibiotics due their poor health, others needed bandaging or salve rubbed on open sores. Reaching her medicine shelf she sorted through the medications placed them in a leather bag. Slinging the bag over her shoulder she walked to each horse and administered their individual special treatments. Debbie called to the horses, "Come and get it kids." All the horse raised their heads to see her walking toward them and sloshing with her mid-calf neon pink polka-dot rubber boots through the heavy dew grass toward the horses. They knew what she was coming to do and did not want any part of Debbie and her medicine. In unison they all turned to walk in the other direction. With a snicker Debbie hollered, "You can run but I will get to you sooner or later. Please don't make it later." Each time she got close to the group they walked away and some even ran to the other end of the pasture."Oh come on you guys, don't make me chase you." Debbie continued the cat and mouse game. She walked toward the group and the group walked away from her. Laughing to herself as she stood in the middle of the pasture, Debbie stooped down, resting on the calves of her legs. It caught all of their attention and they watched her as she squatted in the wet field. It didn't take long for the horse's curiosity to get the best of them. They had to know why she was sitting on the ground. Once they got within reach she was able to administer their treatment. A few of the horse tried to avoid the medication, the others just took it all in stride. There were the difficult few, they were not going to have anything to do with her and her medicine. They usually took extra time of chasing, walking and ignoring them. Eventually they all gave in. She always thought it was a game they played and with the difficult life they'd had the game was ok to play. It amazed her how every horse had its own special personality. Each one special in their own way. Some were shy, others proved to be dominant among the herd. She found the older geldings appeared to be laid back yet set in their ways when it came to daily schedules or food. She enjoyed watching the younger horses running and playing. It was her stress reducer watching while they grazed. Eventually returning to the barn, Debbie sat down at her desk and documented on each horse and what medication was administered. Knowing this would be the last time for the entire day that she would have the opportunity to sit down, she checked her email, medical inventory, and made notes on what needed to be ordered or scheduled. Today the vet would be coming out to re-examine the new horses. They were in quarantine to avoid passing any contagions to the others. Rescue horses weakened immune systems could be fragile due to their poor living conditions. As hard as they all tried to build a beneficial environment, a few horses were easily susceptible to infections. All precautions were taken to avoid problems. Recently brother and sister Quarter horses Cleo and Clyde were brought in by the Sherriff. A neighbor had reported that they were locked inside their stalls without food or water for weeks. The lady said that she could hear the horses crying at night. She and her husband sneaked over to investigate. They were horrified with the condition the horses were living. The smell of manure and urine burned their eyes. Both horses were knee-deep in manure, malnourished and had several open sores from fly bites. Their eyes were encased in crust and fur was missing all through their bodies. The stalls were blacked out by tarps covering the openings, leaving the horses in the dark all day and night. Sheriff Ed was a large man, over six foot, six inches tall and weighed about three hundred and twenty five muscular pounds. He was not a man to contend with when it came to abused animals. He had little to no compassion for any abusers and treated them as criminals. The word was if Ed was coming to your door he was taking the horse or horses. You would either go to jail or face the courts. He had managed to convince the local authorities and judges to impose a legal restriction upon a person having a horse or animal removed from the property. Additionally they would be prohibited from owning another animal. He developed a website that posted names and pictures of the animal abusers who were convicted of neglect or abuse of any animal. He felt that if it was done for sexual predators it could be done for animal abusers. Often he had received feedback from people who researched his site and refused to sell their pets to the abusers. People could anonymously inform him of neglect or abuse without fear of repercussion, from the criminal. It was successful many times in saving the lives of animals. Over the years Ed and Debbie became great friends. They spent holidays and children birthdays with their spouses and families. As friends they spent a lot of their work hours together. Usually the conversation would always turn to the world of animal abuse. Their circles of friends were all somehow associated with animals, either as Vet Techs, Animal Control or working in Shelters. Debbie's husband, Lee, had a full time job as an operations manager for a metal distributer. He helped with property repairs. Numerous times he had companies donate their time, manpower and supplies. This helped with the low budget Debbie had to work with. Completing her office work, she returned to the pasture with the two new horses Cleo and Clyde. They had extra special needs so she had to take special care. Both still showed signs of being malnourished. She understood the dangers when an animal is starved. When the body is kept from nourishment it will start to feed off itself. Feeding can become a slow process due to the damage to their weakened bodies. They were kept on a special diet of hay and additionally they had parasites in their system. The vet prescribed eye medication to be applied three times a day and an antibiotic cream for the open sores. Both horses could not be separated from one another. They both would scream and as weak as they were they would stomp and panic. Both horses would be escorted to the pasture together, one always followed the other. Debbie treated both horses and left them alone. They allowed her to give them the medicine but they didn't trust her with anything else. Understanding this she knew they would eventually warm up and start to learn basic trust. As part of her job Debbie assigned volunteers to each of the horses and one lady, June, offered to take on both horses. She had patience and let them determine when to approach her. The trio seemed to have a good start. Debbie had confidence in June. All the volunteers were matched up with horses according to personality of the horse and knowledge of the volunteer. With each horse having special needs, all volunteers were required to have training dealing with horses with their individual issues. Some volunteers were exceptional with the care of horses and others who lacked enough knowledge were best to deal with horses that were not in the immediate and intense stage of care. Debbie felt it was important for every volunteer to protect the horses. One wrong move with any horse and it could prove to be dangerous to the point of being fatal for the horse or volunteer. Debbie's biggest problem with some of the volunteers was dealing with egos. There were a few who thought they were expects in the equine field. Others wanted to play with the horses and not do the grunts work. They thought they were above doing what they thought was menial chores. It was one of the first things they all learned when they began the volunteer process. It was required for everyone to have a volunteer orientation class. Rule number one was that every volunteer was important, nobody was better than anyone else. Everyone had to pull their weight with barn chores. Debbie never had a problem asking a volunteer to leave if they couldn't follow the rules. First and foremost the main rule was that the horses came first and they should leave the sense of self-imposed importance at home.  After every horse was taken care of for the morning, Debbie had more chores to tend to at the barn. Slipping on her purple and gold rubber knee-high mucking boots, she grabbed a fork out of the supply room. The stalls needed to be cleaned every morning and afternoon. As she skipped to the first stall she turned on the radio. An old rock and roll song echoed the barn. The music put Debbie in a good working mood. She slid open the stall door and began shuffling the shavings as she found manure and raked them into the bucket. She continued mucking the stalls and when her favorite song came on the radio she started to dance. Debbie danced her way around the stall, side-stepping the manure and shavings around with her feet. Startled she looked to her side she saw Kate the barn coordinator and good friend dancing along side of her. They both boot scooted and boogied to the song, and when it ended both laughed and high-fived each other.  Debbie and Kate had a long history with their friendship. In high school they both dated the same guy who they discovered was cheating on them with the other girl. Instead of being angry with each other they devised a revenge plan on the unsuspecting cheater. Kate invited him over for a secret dinner when her parents left for the weekend. Debbie and Kate made him a special dinner of fried spicy dog food along with a salad laced with bird seeds. Watching the dinner date from the pantry closet Debbie appeared to surprise the boy. Blood drained from his face when he knew he was caught by both girls. He didn't have an escape plan until both girls enlightened him about the ingredients of his dinner. His ash-colored face turned a lovely shade of green as he fled through the front door. That escapade began a lasting friendship between the two women.

Debbie gave Kate a hug. "Good morning Kate, how are you? How's your mom doing?"

"She's great and I love the idea that she has moved in with Jack and I. She still has her days when she misses Dad. But the grandkids keep her busy."

Debbie smiled. "Good! Glad to hear it. Can she come out and work on the books again? She really cleaned up my mess with all the figures and our new budget". Debbie crossed her fingers.

"Debbie she loves it out here. The more busy she is the more she feels needed the better for her". Kate grinned.

"Wonderful. Anytime she wants she is welcome."

Kate laughed. "Hey, you do know that you're not supposed to county line dance to Rock and Roll.' Debbie put her finger to her lips and in a whisper "Keep my secret".

"No problem, girlfriend, you're always safe with me." Kate reached for a rake and walked to the next stall to be cleaned.

Both ladies worked until noon cleaning stalls. Putting everything away they sat down to have lunch. While eating they discussed what was on the agenda for the day and who would do what job.

Kate was the expert on training the horses and new volunteers. They had an hour before the volunteers started to arrive. Debbie and Kate worked on the daily assignments for them. A few would show up early to help with the barn chores but it wasn't every day. They couldn't rely on them. The job was always left up to Debbie and Kate

Kate raised her hand. "Oh Debbie I have a new volunteer coming in later this afternoon. She's an expert in Public Relations and I thought we could have her on the fund raising committee."

"Sounds rally good to me. We need someone who can put special events together, how is she with horses?" Debbie asked.

Shrugging her shoulders, Kate said "Not sure how experienced she is. Guess we will find out because here she is and early. Talk to you later about this."

Kate was a few months younger than Debbie and pencil thin. She kept her hair short with the tips of her sun-washed hair Kool-Aid dyed different colors. She had many years of horse experience and feared nothing. Debbie loved and admired that about her. Both had a silly sense of humor which at times could and would be sarcastic.

Kate and Debbie had originally worked at another rescue. The lady running it turned out to be a horse hoarder. She accepted donations and never spent any of it on the horses. Both Kate and Debbie ended up running the barn.

Finally one day uniformed IRS agents walked into the barn to ask questions along with a government employee who issued 501c charity licenses. They had questions for Lucy the owner, questions about her finances. It didn't take long to discover Lucy had been embezzling all the funds from the facility.

Lucy and her husband ended up spending time in jail and their property was seized to repay their very expensive debt. Debbie and Kate read in the paper the amount of money Lucy and her husband cheated the government out of was in excessive of 2.5 million dollars.

The incident, as they called it, left both Debbie and Kate with the responsibility of 18 horses and no funds. Scraping together their own money and borrowing from friends. Begged a few people who had previously made generous financial donations. They were able to keep the horses until they could find a place for them.

A small group of people from the thoroughbred race track came forward. They offered to form an equine rescue and help fund it. The group purchased an abandoned horse facility with ample room for twenty or more horses. They called in every favor from all over and other race tracks. Within a month they moved in and brought the horses. Once it was open and word was out the horse population exploded.

Debbie and Kate managed the rescue. Both ladies worked almost 24 hours, 7 days a week when it first opened. Having eighteen horses to care for and with some who needed around the clock care, Debbie and Kate worked hard. They were lucky to have husbands to help. Their kids also tried to help as much as they could but none of their children were horse people.

Debbie and Kate couldn't decide what to call the new operation so they just called it. Equine Rescue Me or just Rescue Me for short.

The local newspaper and television station reported on the operation and it brought in donations and much-needed volunteers.

Debbie never forgot that time in her life and was always grateful for Kate and their close friendship. She hated to think of what would have happened to all the horses if they failed and couldn't keep the place going. Her beautiful horses would have been left to either be euthanized or placed with people who would not care for them properly.

Turning to face her computer Debbie just nodded. She heard Kate directing the volunteers on what jobs needed to be done and what horses needed their attention. They all were talking in the barn, offering to do one thing or another. Standing up from her desk she walking to the door Debbie quietly closed it so she could think. The distractions outside her door made it hard to concentrate. They were short on money again this month. They needed more donations to keep the doors open. They were highly in debt to the feed store. Some of the supplies were running real low and the price of hay took another jump up.

Looking out the back window, she could watch the horses lazily graze. Talking to the window Debbie said. "We really need to either win the lottery, receive a generous contributions, or find forever homes for these guys." With a depressing sigh she went back to work.

The rest of the afternoon she spent trying to beg for donations from contributors.

Debbie snuck out back for a quick cigarette when Kate walked in. "Aha caught you. Put that thing out. I thought you quit?"

Bumping her shoulder on the screen door," Good gosh Kate you scared the crap out of me." Taking her last puff, she put the cigarette out. "And yes I did give them up but every once in a while I need one."

Kate followed Debbie into the office asking "What problem has you all worked up?"

Frowning at her, "M-O-N-E-Y" she spelled.

Kate put her hands on her good friend's shoulders, "Well my BFF, I think I have someone who might help with that and she likes wine" Kate winked. "I told you I had a lady coming in who worked in a Public Relations office. She wants to volunteer and has some great ideas. Her name is Carol and she said she will be back Saturday morning with a list of special event ideas."

Debbie leaned back on her desk. "WOW we do need someone like her, can't wait to see what ideas she has."

The day lingered on, Debbie spent most of her afternoon on the phone which included members on the Executive Board. They required monthly financial report and Debbie overspent on her budget with medical needs the past month. She was fortunate to have a generous board that supported her but they had to report to the Internal Revenue and other government agencies.

As the afternoon drifted into evening Debbie took a walk around the barn, checking on the horses and administering the afternoon medications. She started to shut down her computer and lock up the office when the phone rang."Equine Rescue Me, this is Debbie." A female voice on the phone was reporting a horse in danger. The excited female voice stated that she had seen a horse loose on an abandoned property and was concerned. Debbie took the information and location of the property.

Kate nodded back. "You going to be here much longer? It's going on 7 pm and Hank arrived for his night watch."

With a small yawn Debbie answered Kate "Yeah, I'm going soon, I didn't realize how late it was but I just got a call about a loose horse on an abandon property. I will take a ride on my way home and if I need help I'll call.

Debbie finished up in the office, took one last walk around checking on all the horses, and stopped to talk to Hank. They were all ok for the day.

# Chapter 2

Debbie jumped into her vehicle to drive home, but first she had to make to check on the report called in. Finding the property was easy and just as to see that it was abandoned. Debbie carried a taser in the event there was a problem. Walking the property she didn't see any loose horse. Reaching in the back of her SUV for the coffee can full of feed she pulled out a halter and lead rope. Calling out for the horse she shook the can to entice it. She found nothing, didn't hear anything except the wind blowing through the vacant property and a few distant birds. Debbie always felt edgy walking alone on deserted property. She walked around for a few minutes and out of the corner of her eye she saw tall grass moving way back in an overgrown pasture. Mumbling she said, "Sure enough, there you are kiddo. I knew you had to be somewhere". Walking quietly toward the horse she could see there was plenty of grass. She shook the feed can again, getting the horse's attention. Its head lurched up looking in her direction. Like a deer in the headlights, the horse froze. It didn't move a muscle only staring at her. Debbie could see the grey dapple horse. It was thin but not skeletal; the tall grass had kept it alive. With her hand outstretched she talked to the lone horse "Whoa boy, it's ok, look, I have some feed for you. Come on, come here I'm not going to hurt you. The grey horse continued to stare at Debbie like she was some sort of alien from outer space. Debbie was within an arm reach of the horse. Pouring feed into her hand, she offered it. The grey horse shied away, suspicious of her. Continuing to quietly talk to the horse, "I know sweetie, you have every reason to be guarded. Who would leave you all alone? I have a nice place for you with a lot of friends and plenty of food. Come on honey, let me get you closer." The horse warily stretched its neck to smell the food in her hand. It pulled back for an instant then moved closer again. Debbie's arm started to get tired from holding it out. Talking to the horse Debbie said. "We can take all the time you need. I wish I could convince you I'm not here to hurt you. Come on, just a few inches closer." The horse sniffed the food again only this time he nibbled a few crumbs, not trusting her fully to accept the generous offer. Debbie poured more into the palm of her hand and the horse welcomed the generous handout. Tenderly stepping closer to stroke the horse's neck, it accepted her touch. She offered more food and the horse ate it like a kid in a candy shop. With her hand on the horse's neck she continued to stroke it and with slyness she placed the halter over the horse's face. The horse figured out what she was doing, pulling back its head and spun and kicked up dirt running as it ran off. Debbie threw her hands up in the air. "Oh shit, so close. This is going to be a long night. Come on horse, I'm tired and hungry. Don't play hard to get with me. I guess I don't blame you. Look at all the tall grass and freedom. I would run away too." Debbie picked up the halter and followed the horse to the long back pasture. "Can we try this again? Here check the food out, how about apple treats?" The horse seemed willing to accept her this time. Just as she was about to put the halter on her cell phone rang. It startled the horse and he ran off again. Debbie answered the phone with an angry tone "What?" It was her husband, Lee. "Yeah, I'm late, I'm trying to catch a horse. Hey, as long as I have you, can you go get the truck and trailer. I have to bring this one in. I can't leave it here." Giving Lee directions she made another attempt at capturing the horse. The horse was not going to cooperate. Debbie decided to leave it alone for a few minutes. She had to wait for Lee anyway, so she went exploring the abandoned property. Walking the weathered and neglected barn she imagined how it could look with some care and repair. Opening every closed door she stumbled upon the tack room and it was full of horse equipment and tack in pretty good shape. Looking around she said to herself. "Hmm, finders keepers, we could use this stuff at the rescue." She found leather halters, bridles, saddles, stirrups, blankets, and saddle pads. Most of it was weathered but it could be salvaged. It was obvious the saddles were expensive. "I hit the mother lode and it's all mine or the rescues, these folks don't know it but they just made a bighearted donation. I wonder if I could get arrested for this? Who cares." Debbie walked to the SUV and backed it up to the barn. She packed up the tack room. Seeing a broom in the corner she giggled at how she could at least clean the room before she left. Just as she closed the door she said in the empty room, "Good thing the room was empty, I would hate to see someone steal things if it was full of nice stuff. I'm going to either jail or hell for doing this." Taking advantage of her freedom to nose around she walked to the house. The patio door was unlocked. She walked in and looked in every room. The home was very pretty, nice hardwood floors, stone fireplace. Every room was oversized. The master bathroom had an old claw- footed bathtub that included a whirlpool. Debbie climbed in and sank down. "I could handle this kind of life, with a nice glass of wine, a good book. It just doesn't get any better. Lottery gods look down on me with some favor, please." Pulling herself up, she moved on to the remainder of the tour. Leaving the same way she came in.

She headed back toward the horse to see if she could catch it again. For the next few minutes the horse refused to get close. It couldn't be bribed by food anymore. The horse was onto her tricks.

"Alright you want to ignore me, I can do the same to you," Debbie turned her back to the horse and pretended to chew on food. Horses are naturally curious. It walked over to see what she was doing. Just as the horse put its head over her shoulder Debbie flung the lead rope over the horse's neck. It stood perfectly still. It didn't fight, move or run away. it knew the cat and mouse game was over. She buckled the halter over its face. Being proud of herself she caught her horse. Debbie said "Why did you run and give me a hard time before? I will never figure you guys out at times.

She walked the horse around for the next hour wondering what was taking Lee so long. He finally showed up and they easily loaded the horse into the trailer.

With her hand resting on her hip, Debbie asked, "What took you so long?"

"It would be nice if you put gas in the truck when you're done using it. It was running on fumes." Lee slammed the truck door. He walked to the back of the trailer. He opened the rear doors. They both were silent.

Returning to the facility Hank helped unload the horse and walked it to the quarantine barn. They threw down some hay and the horse seemed to settle in. Hank said he would check on the horse every hour or more. He promised to call her if there was any sign of problems.

Lee parked the truck and trailer, walking to his car to go home. As he left he promised to stop for fast food because they had missed dinner again.

The ride home for Debbie didn't have the same energy as the drive in. Her days were long and she always stressed about how to keep the money flowing. The horses need so much, but there is only so much money to go around. She had to stretch it as far as it would go.

Walking into the house and straight to Lee, she gave him a thank you hug and quickly grabbed the food bag. Gobbling down her meal she dragged herself to the shower, sitting on the bed she ate a small portion of the leftover food. She could feel her bed enticing her and she was ready to sleep. She was satisfied with her successful save and thankful she didn't arrive too late.

Lee stood at the door of their bedroom. He knew what was bothering her. It was always the same thing. "I know someone will bestow a generous endowment or something. I got faith in you." Debbie gave a short smile and climbed into bed, she didn't want to discuss it.

The next morning she was up early at the barn to check on the new horse. Hank walked out and happily reported that the new addition had a restful night. He thought the horse's, which was a mare was running a fever. He called the Jerri the vet. Debbie walked to the stall and she agreed the horse felt warmer than normal. Hank hung around to help take the horses temperature, which was 101 degree. That is warm. He offered to wait for Jerri to show up in case they need help.

Hank stood outside the stall "Oh Debbie the horse is a mare. I named it Nola."

Debbie turned to Hank, that's fine, but why Nola?"

Shrugging his shoulders "I don't know, it sounded good at the time."

"Well Hank, Nola, I like the sound of it. Good choice."

Hank threw a paper surgical gown at Debbie with the paper booties. "You need to put these on in case Nola has something contagious." Unwrapping the paper gown and booties she covered herself. "Hank your on top of everything this morning as usual. I'm too tired to think."

The sound of a diesel engine could be heard in front of the barn. Jerri jumped out of the truck. She was in boxer shorts, tank top and flip-flops. "Good morning everyone. Where in the hell is the coffee? Where is the new patient?"

Debbie stood up facing the stall door. "Why are you so chipper this early in the morning? I can see you have your usual doctor uniform on. Here is your new patient. Hank named her Nola."

Jerri stepped into the stall. "Nola huh? I like that it's different. I haven't been to bed yet, I had a special delivery last night - really special. I delivered a set of twins. That's a first for me in a long time, and both are healthy and happy. What's with the surgical costume?"

Debbie rolled up the gown sleeves. Not sure if she has anything contagious, just precautionary. She has a fever of 101 and it hasn't dropped all night, Hank checked every hour. She hasn't touched much of her hay and only some water. No manure yet. You can do your doctor thing now."

Jerri opened her heavy medical box, the top flipped back against the stall dirt. "Now let me have a look at this kid." Jerri talked as she examined the horse. Eyes clear, nose clear, chest clear." Moving around the back end of the horse. Temperature is 101. With her stethoscope she listened to the mare's stomach. I can hear some sounds but not very loud. Gums are nice and pink. I'm going to take some blood and give her some fluids. Debbie give me a hand with her, I'm going to start an intravenous. Debbie held the horse while the vet inserted the needle into the horse's neck.

Debbie comforted the horse and she held very still for the vet as if she knew they were doing this to help her. "She just might be dehydrated but we will find out more with the results from the blood test. So what is her story? When did she come in?" Debbie told her the story about where she got the horse. Jerri looked at Debbie with a strange look on her face. "I know this horse. I thought she looked familiar. With a panic in her voice she said. "You have to go back to the property. There is another horse on that property. Nola is really Poppy and she has a colt named Charlie somewhere. I know the owners of the horses and property, the parents died and the kids were keeping the house. Apparently they didn't and left. What a bunch of jerks to leave horses behind like that. Now that I think of it there might be another horse there too. She was older I'm going to guess about in her late twenties. We have to go back and find the other horses. Debbie turned to Hank. With urgency in her voice. "Can you stay and babysit the gang here and call Kate, have her meet us at the property. Hank nodded as he pulled his cell phone out of his pocket. Debbie and Jerri took off in the rescue's truck and trailer. Taking about twenty minutes to get to the property, both ladies jumped out of the truck and one went left and the other right. They had whistles in their pockets to notify the other one in case they didn't have cell phone signals. Debbie could hear Jerri call to Charlie. The property went on for what seemed like forever. They had twenty-five tall and overgrown acres to search. The overgrowth was hard to find their way around and try to locate the small horse. Debbie's phone rang, it was Kate, "Where are you guys?"

"We're all the way in the back. Jerri went right and I went left. Do you have your whistle?" "Yes" Kate hung up the phone and she heard a whistle, she started to run toward the sound, she could hear Debbie calling out "Jerri found something." Kate and Debbie found Jerri about the same time. She was on her knees bending over a dark brown mud caked horse. Lying still, his eyes were glazed over looking toward the heavens. It was easy to see that there wasn't any life to the horse. Her ribs protruded, it was obvious she was starved. Jerri was crying. I know where the kids live. I'm calling the Sherriff and pressing charges on them. They killed this horse by letting her alone." Debbie touched Jerri's back and sat on the ground with her. Kate walked away. She had to find the colt. She wasn't going to lose another horse. Silently she walked around and inside a heavily treed area sitting was Charlie. Kate dropped down to her knees and called him. "Charlie, come on little boy. I'm going to take you to your momma." Charlie tried to get up but he fell backward. He made a few more tries to get up but he was caught on something. Kate gently whispered to him, "Charlie let me get you, just relax, shhhh little boy." Kate saw that his back leg was caught in old wire fencing. He sat quietly and let her take the fencing off. Getting up on his own he stood next to Kate and followed her to the trailer. He walked in and ate the small amount of hay on the floor. Jerri and Debbie walked up to the trailer, both had tear- soaked eyes. A few minutes later the Sheriff showed up, Jerri directed them to the dead horse. They had to take pictures and statements, treating it as a crime scene. Kate took Charlie to the rescue to be with his mom. Debbie and Jerri stood back until the Sheriff was done. Both ladies had nothing to say. As many times as they have witnessed the horror of abuse and neglect they just could never get over it. Silence was the best medicine right now. Over the next few days Charlie and Poppy became comfortable in their new home. Jerri came by daily to check on them. She was happy with their progress. Jerri filed a complaint on the owner's children for animal abandonment, neglect and abuse. She was going after these people with every legal means. The Sheriff's issued the citation to the people and they were ordered to appear in court. A few months later Jerri, Debbie, and Kate appeared to testify in court as to the condition of the horses and the dead horse. They came prepared with pictures and Jerri's professional medical testimony. All three of the owner's children had their chance to speak and they threw each other to the wolves, blaming each other for the neglect charges. The judge's finale order to the family was a stiff fine and court costs. Additionally they each had to pay the vet bill and donate five thousand dollars to the rescue. Plus they were banned from ever owning another horse or animal as long as they live in the county.

Debbie and Jerri added up the finale expense, totaling over five thousand dollars apiece. They wanted life in prison but they had to be satisfied with hitting them in the pocket. Debbie was happy with the six thousand dollar donation. She knew what she was going to use the found money for. Besides playing catch up with past due bills she wanted to put in new ceiling fans for each stall. With the court fiasco over Jerri decided to adopt Charlie and Poppy. Debbie was thrilled to have it happen. She knew both horses would have a wonderful life with Jerri and her family.

# Chapter 3

Over the next few months Debbie was busy with Kate and her new fund raising team leader, Lauren. Kate organized her team and having prepared a list of fund raising ideas they wanted to discuss with Debbie. Following the Executive Board's policy Debbie had to present the ideas to them for approval. Most of the time they agreed with all fund raising ideas. All except for the time Debbie wanted to use the board members as targets in a dunking booth. Then another time Debbie had an idea to have a private ladies night and auction off young men who were exotic dancers. Both ideas were highly discouraged even if some of the women on the board did have a good laugh at the ladies night idea.

In between rescues, adoptions, and barn business Debbie kept busy and everything seemed to be running well. They added the 4-H Kids to help around the barn and the Boy Scouts made saddle racks and halter hangers. They planned to use a few of the halter hangers and saddle racks in the next fund raiser and auction them off.

The first of six scheduled fund raisers of the year was the Formal Valentine Ball, catered dinner. The usual high rollers attended with each one trying to outdo the other on the amount of donations. Expensive bottles of wine, paintings, and jewelry were auctioned. Debbie, Kate, and a few of the volunteers had a stash of formal dress they purchased from the local thrift store. Other volunteers who attended the formal affairs donated their dresses, saving money for others who would not otherwise have a dress.

This particular night was always special for Debbie and Lee. They joked about it being their Senior Prom night. Debbie was just a bit too pregnant to fit into a formal dress their Senior year in High School. Every year was a romantic treat for Debbie she was able to enjoy the evening without having to run everything. They had the entire event catered with bartenders and waitress.

For all the other fund raisers Debbie with her family and Kate and her family along with volunteers were the cooks, organizers, and cleanup committee. The exception this year, Lauren coordinated and made all the arrangements for all the charity events. This way Debbie and Kate could schmooze the prospective contributors.

By the night's end they tallied up the total donations and after paying the bills they made twelve thousand dollars. This was the biggest amount in history of Equine Rescue Me. The downfall of this one was that the Executive Board took their cut from the proceeds first. However, Debbie took whatever they handed her. After everyone left, Debbie, Kate, Lauren and Hank did bed check with all the horses and everyone appeared to be fine. Hank stayed behind to do his security guard duties. It was almost three in the morning and Debbie had to be back at eight to go train a new volunteer who has joined the adoption committee.

Exhausted, Debbie arrived as usual. As she turned into the driveway her car careened to a stop. Climbing out of the SUV Debbie said, "Oh shit not again, who do we have here?"

Debbie walked to the gate and slowly approached a horse tied to the gate with a note. The horse was extremely calm. Debbie patted its neck and opened the letter, she read it out loud. "Please give Prince a good home, my dad lost his job and we have to move away. I couldn't let my Dad shoot him, he is fifteen years old. He can be ridden and loves going on trail rides. Loves to have his ears scratched. He had all his shots. His neck is wet because I cried. Please love him like I do."

With tears in her eyes Debbie untied the rope and walked the horse to the quarantine barn. As they walked the long driveway Debbie talked to the horse.

"I know you will miss your little human girl, Prince, but we will find you a good forever home. She was a brave young lady to walk you and leave you. This economy is breaking people and it's more than just losing jobs. It's breaking hearts." Debbie wiped her eyes, she shook her head and gave the horse a hug.

Arriving at the barn Hank greeted her. "Where did you find this one?"

Handing him the lead rope, "He was tied up at the gate with a note attached to his halter."

Hank tilted his head, "He was there when you drove in?"

"Uh huh," Debbie nodded "Why?"

"Debbie, I was just down there and this horse was not at the gate. You had to have seen someone walking the road."

Debbie turned and ran down the driveway, the length of a foot ball field. She reached the gate, opened it, and jumped into her car. Turning it around she drove down the road hoping to find someone. As she drove she saw a young blonde girl sitting on a tree stump on the side of the road, her head down resting on her arms. She could see the girl was crying. She pulled over and got out. Walking to the girl she sat down on the same tree stump and put her arm around her shoulder. The young blonde girl sobbed in Debbie's arms, she rocked her like a baby.

Soothing her, Debbie said. "It's ok, Prince will be fine. Maybe we could find another way without you giving him up. Come on, get in. We'll go back to the barn and see how we can work this out." The young girl continued to sob, "I can't go back and look at him. I can't say goodbye again."

Debbie pulled at the girls arm. "Come on get up, my name is Debbie. Besides if you don't get up I will go to the police and have you charged with animal abandonment."

The girl's cry turned into hysterical sobs. "Oh god no, please don't," Debbie pulled at her arm again. "Come on we need to work this out, get up. What's your name?" She didn't intentionally want to sound cruel, but she needed this young girl to get in her car.

"Dorothy, but they call me Dot. You gonna call the cops for sure? My dad will kill me, like things aren't bad enough for him."

Reaching over the girls shoulder, "No I'm not, I just want to talk. You won't even see Prince, he's in the quarantine barn."

"Why? He's not sick. I wrote that he had all his shots."

The two drove back to the barn. Debbie led the girl to her office, opened the refrigerator, and offered her a drink.

"Thanks," crying again. "I'm going to miss him so much. My Mom left us about a year ago and Dad got stuck with my two sisters and me. He lost his job about two weeks ago and he put the house up for sale. We're all moving to my Grandparent's house.

"Dot, where do your grandparents live?"

"Over in Riverton and they hate horses. They hate everyone including my Dad and us."

"Hmmm, that's less than ten minutes away from here", Debbie crossed her arms. "I could use some help around here, I'm always looking for volunteers. Ya wanna volunteer and you can keep Prince as long as you help here."

Dot's eyes dried up, she started to smile. "But I have to get a job and I don't have a car to get here." Debbie looked at her. "By the way how did you get here and how far did you come?"

Dot waved her hand, "About five miles down on Picos Road. I rode Prince here, our last ride together."

Debbie nudged Dot. "Come on take a walk with me." Debbie led Dot to the quarantine barn, "This barn needs a special person. You can come, when you're not working and I will get someone to pick you up."

Dot walked to the stall and opened the heavy sliding door. Prince was eating his hay. She walked in and hugged him. Tears flowed again and even Debbie started to cry as she walked away leaving the two alone. It broke her heart to see people grieve because they had lost their best friend. She never had the power to be strong when times like that occurred. She walked to her office and closed the door. Flopping in her heavy leather chair she bent over her lap, putting her hands to her face and sobbed. She needed to cry every now and then to release the sadness she saw so often. She didn't know if these were happy tears or tears of frustration. Didn't matter, she needed a good hard cry. Eventually Debbie calmed down, fixed herself her morning coffee. Turning on her computer, she glanced at her email. She poured herself a cup of coffee without sugar. She needed it straight and strong. Walking out of her office she saw Hank and Kate sitting on lawn chairs just outside the barn doors.

"Morning crybaby, Feel better?"

"Shut up Kate and yes I needed it"

Kate patted Hank on the shoulder. "Everyone is fed and I see we have a new visitor to Hotel Manure.

Debbie smiled at the two of them. "Thanks for the help. Not the best way to start a morning, but it ended up with happiness. Do either of you know anyone who lives over in Riverton they could pick the girl up to help out here?"

Kate stood up and walked past Debbie. "I'll check and see who can help. I know we have a few who live in that area. I don't know anyone who would object to picking her up. Let me work on it."

"Thanks, I need to do my meds." Turning to look at Hank, "You need to go home and get some sleep."

With his grandfatherly smile, he nodded in agreement. "Hey, don't forget I won't be here tonight. My night off and I go bowling with the boys."

Debbie snapped her fingers. "I almost forgot. I'll spend the night, thanks for reminding me. I'm going home for the day. Do you mind taking over Kate?"

"Not a problem. You need some down time, besides Lauren is coming in and we have to put the finishing touches on the Marti Gras party in two weeks. Have you seen the box of beads? Been searching for them for days."

"Kate are you going to put beads on those poor horses again?" Kate smiled. "Yup, they love it and so do the volunteers. This year we will actually have a float to decorate and throw beads at the people. I got a couple of the kids from the high school to let us use one of their homecoming floats."

"Ok I'm out of here, by way of the beach. I'll be back around six tonight." Debbie waved goodbye. Jumped into her SUV. Spitting dirt, she headed down the drive for a special day all to herself.

Dot walked out looking for Debbie and appearing a little lost herself.

"Hi I'm Kate and I will be your humble servant today? How long you gonna stay?"

Looking around Dot said, "As long as you let me. What can I do to help? Prince is taking a nap so I thought I would get started. Where is Debbie? She said I have to fill out some paper?"

Wiggling her finger at Dot. "Come with me my little sweetie. Be quick or I release the flying monkeys." For the first time in weeks Dot smiled.

Kate walked into the office, pulled out an application for Dot to complete. Dot followed her and sat down at Debbie's desk. Picking up a pen off the desk she began working on the form. "Hey Kate, it says I have to get my Dad's permission. I don't think he will go along with it, especially if he knows Prince is here. I plan on getting a car and job so I can get Prince back."

Turning toward Dot, "We'll let Debbie worry about that. She has a way with people, or by the way can you lie?"

Dot looked puzzled. "Why?'

"Cuz Debbie will make up some sort of BS. You might not know it but this will be a school project."

Dot laughed. "I can do that and I can BS too."

Kate walked toward the door. "Finish the form and leave it on the desk, then come out and you can work with some of the volunteers and learn to routine around here. Let them know that Prince is here and he is yours." Dot nodded her head. She was excited with her luck and turned back toward the paper on the desk.

# Chapter 4

Debbie drove into the parking lot of her favorite fast food business. At the drive-thru she ordered an extra large salad, fruit cup, and vanilla shake. She headed toward the beach to relax for a few hours. Let the sun burn off the stress.

At the beach she threw down her saddle pad and rolled a small lamb's wool pad to use as a pillow. She opened her food and ate like she hadn't eaten in a month. She could feel every muscle in her body start to unwind. Staring out at the ocean. Debbie watched the surf roll in and let her mind roll with it. She could feel herself loosen up, the sound of the waves were putting her in a trance. Lying down, she felt herself drifting off to sleep hoping to not dream the same dream.

But the dream came without warning. Debbie could see the orange groves and feel the hot wind blowing through the trees. Debbie was riding her horse Blu. He was a huge seventeen hands high, stocky appaloosa. He was her first rescue and she took him for herself. Blu and Debbie were on a trail. The orange groves were thick with the smell of orange blossom was heavy in the air. She and Blu just walking thru the groves, she had her music player and was serenading him. Her favorite song at the time was country western singer John Anderson's Seminole Wind. They both crossed a small creek where Debbie could reach the branches and grab a small blossom off the tree limb. She rubbed it along his long grey spotted appaloosa neck, making sure to hit his dark spots, and leaned over to give him a hug.

Throwing her leg across his back she slid off his back. Let him graze and offered him a few apples and carrots. Meanwhile, she opened herself a can of soda and both shared his apples. Slowly strolling through the grove they walked and talked. Blu was her best friend, he was her first horse. He taught her how to treat a horse. She taught him to trust people.

Blu was owned by a young man who thought the best way to train a horse was with whips and sticks. She always thought it was some sort of women. She was driving out in the country looking for the house of a lady who was selling her patio set to Debbie. She accidently turned into the wrong driveway when she saw a man beating Blu. She jumped out of her car yelling at him to stop. He yelled back at her to get off his property or he would beat her ass along with the stupid horse. Debbie picked up a large clump of mud and threw it at the guy. He was out of control angry, and he turned toward Debbie to come after her. Reaching into her pocket for her pepper spray as he approached her she blasted him with the spray directly in his face. He started cussing and screaming, "I'm blind, you bitch."

Debbie stood frozen, her legs locked waiting for him to come at her again. Taking another pre-attack stance she readied herself for him but he walked away rubbing his eyes and face. Debbie got back into her car and drove off, Thinking to herself, she had to go back to get the horse.

Driving out of the property she almost ran into an off-duty police officer. He turned on his lights and she stopped right away. Jumping out of the car she ran to the officer. She explained what had happened and go back and get the horse. He called in for extra officers to help. As they entered the property the young man was about to shoot the horse. He had a rifle raised, directly pointing it at the horse face. The officer stopped him, pulling out his weapon. Debbie ran toward the horse and led him away. The man argued with the officer. He had a right to shoot the horse on his own property. He knew the law but it didn't make it right. The Officer convinced him to give the horse to Debbie. Now he wanted money for the horse. Debbie spun around and spit cuss words out of her mouth that she didn't know what they meant. The officers standing around started to laugh at how ridiculous she sounded. However, the translation they knew that she meant business and it was best to get her and the horse off the property.

The off-duty officer led the man away to try and reason with him.

Standing almost nose to nose the officer said, "Look, I would suggest you give the horse to her. You don't want it or you never would have held a gun to its head. Let her deal with him. Come on man, do the right thing. The lady doesn't have any money to give you. Besides, I have a hunch that she will be back with her friends. I don't want my officers to have to come save you from a bunch of women who will kick your ass with just their mouths. How 'bout it, give him up. Let me ask you something? Are you married? Looking down he shook his head "No and don't ever wanna be."The officer gently placed his hand on the man's shoulder. "Buddy, let me educate you what I learned from being married. When you see a women cross her arms across her chest and put one leg out in front AND most importantly when a women says FINE, you're better off leaving town till she cools down. It's what we call around the squad as dead man walking." From where I'm standing she isn't going to let this thing go. Just do the right thing and get it over with."The young man nodded his head. "K, but I want her to sign some sort of letter that she won't come after me and sue me because that crazy horse put her in a wheelchair."  Extending his hand to the man, the officer smiled. "Good, you're the better man. I agree that she should sign something to protect you and you do the same to sign the horse over to her and we can all call it a day and go home." The young man shook the officer's hand in agreement. He walked into the barn for paper to write their contract that she won't sue him and he won't charge her anything and come back to take the horse. The animal control officers took Blu away. Debbie took him from the county animal rescue to a friend's barn temporarily until she could find a barn to board him.  Over the next five years Blu and Debbie were best friends. She never loved any animal more than she did Blu. In her dream she was lying on the ground with Blu lying over her leg. She was trapped beneath him.  She could see he was hurt and he couldn't get up. She could never remember how they landed on the ground but she will never forget when Lee and a few of his friends found her and Blu on the ground.  Debbie was screaming for Blu to get up. Lee was holding her, telling her that Blu was dead. The firefighters found them to help get Blu off of her leg. Once she was free. She laid over Blu, stroking his soft belly and face, his eyes were clouded. She tried to feel for his heart. Lee pulled her away. She was out of control with heartache.  Her leg was broken. They air lifted her to the hospital and arrangements were made to have Blu buried. Lee cut a part of his tail as a memory. He had a bracelet made for her. Debbie spent four days in the hospital. She was depressed and her leg was badly broken. The family was worried about her state of deep depression. With a shake Debbie woke up, looking around at the others at the beach to see if they noticed her crying in her sleep. She rolled over and lay still for a while. Just thinking about Blu and all the good times they had shared. Every time she had the dream she went into depression. Pushing herself to pack up. It was time to go home and get ready for her night at the barn. She felt refreshed enough to push on, thinking she would never get over the sadness of losing Blu. When her leg ached it was a reminder of the incident, it never allowed her to forget. Lee arrived at the barn with dinner for them, carried in a paper bag. They shared a beer while sitting on the back patio of the barn watching the sunset. The mosquitoes arrived as soon as the sun went down. They moved inside to watch a TV for awhile. When it got late Lee left for the night. He hated leaving her alone, worrying if something happened she wouldn't have any help. Debbie was resourceful enough and could handle anything. She had learned to shoot a hand gun after an incident with a few wild hogs that wandered into a pasture and chased some of the horses. After bed check she opened the couch in the office leaving the door to the barn open. Sleep evaded her most nights when she was at the barn. Every creak, crack, and mouse noise woke her up, concerned she would sleep through an emergency. She enjoyed her nightly strolls through the barns checking on the horses. Sometimes she had to administer medicines through the night but this time everyone was healthy. Waking up to her body clock, she turned on the coffee, went in to take a shower. She walked out to the same place to watch the sunrise as she had watched the sunset the night before turning her lawn chair in a different angle.

A second cup of coffee had to wait. It was time to feed her kids as she called the horses. Get them set for the day and wait for Kate and the volunteers to arrive. Same routine every morning, turning on the radio, lead the group out to the pasture. Chasing down the ones who needed supplements and daily medications. It was the perfect life for Debbie. She loved her life and her work at the facility.

Walking back to her office, Debbie mumbled to herself, "It's just too quiet, let's hope I didn't jinx myself." Opening up her email Debbie deleted most of the junk mail and answered the important one.

Hearing a diesel engine pull in, Debbie got up from her chair, wondering who was here. A black Mercedes parked blocking the front door. She thought, "Shit, Patricia". The snobbiest lady on the executive board. She constantly tried to change the rescue into a Polo Club for her and snobby friends. Debbie put on a happy face. "Patricia, what are you doing here? Nice to see you." Patricia leaned over toward Debbie and gave her an air kiss. Debbie returned the gesture."Now Debbie, I have a wonderful idea for a fund raiser. Let's go into your office to talk."Patricia walked past Debbie opening the door to her office and slamming it shut. Debbie turned and gave the door a military salute. Opening the door Debbie saw Patricia sitting in her chair at her desk. "Patricia would you like a cup of coffee?""No thank you dear, but if you would have some green tea?""Sorry, fresh out of green tea." Reaching for her oversized leather purse with a huge stack of papers, Patricia tapped the top of her fingers to her other hand as if that is all she could do for a clap. Patrice's excited voice carried on loud and clear."I want to have a Kentucky Derby cotillion, here are the people I want to invite and you get your workers to fix the place up and we can have them run the arena with the horses. We'll have those attending place bets on the horses. Wouldn't that be a hoot watching the volunteers run around with the horses? I will need a few of them to serve Mint Julep drinks, and if we have a few men who could be car hops with nice uniforms.'"You mean valets" Debbie rolled her eyes. Clapping her finger tops again. "Yes, then we will need people to place bets and take the money. You do have a few honest people to work that area? I have a gentleman who can play the trumpet at the start of the race. Here are the plans for you to work out and get back to me." "Patricia, have you cleared any of this with the Board members? Debbie asked. I have an awesome lady who is doing our entire fund raising. You might want to work with her on it. But I have a suspicion that the board won't allow this as we have rescues from the horse race tracks. I am thinking they wouldn't like to promote the exact thing they are trying to save. In addition, I will not make a fool out of my volunteers and have them run around the arena or be car hops as you call it for your friend's entertainment. Plus many of the horses can't run. You run the risk of getting someone hurt with the excitement. I do like the idea of maybe some sort of Kentucky Derby day. I will give Lauren your phone number, the two of you can work this out. Lauren can approach the board for you for approval."

With a huffy attitude, Patricia stood up and said. "I think not. I am on the board. I don't need anyone's permission to give this place money to survive. I have some very affluent friends. Your volunteers could swallow their pride and run around for fun. From what I see they could use the exercise."

Debbie walked to the door and opened it as Patricia walked out. Debbie slammed the door behind her. Walking to the phone, she called Carl the President of the Board.

"Hi Carl we need to talk". Her voice was stern. Debbie replayed the conversation with Patricia his sister. Carl was laughing. "Debbie, don't get your undies in a bundle. I'll talk to her and it will be all forgotten. You can't take her so serious, just do like everyone else. Nod your head and let her go on. She will forget the idea and move onto something else." Debbie sighed, "Carl you keep forgetting the monkeys she rescued and brought here. I had volunteers bitten, some got sick from the bites and then a few escaped, that would be monkeys and volunteers! The Sherriff had to round a few of them up and the fiasco brought the local TV stations. It wasn't very good press, not to mention the real monkey rescue people. That group saves primates for a living. We stepped on their toes. I was the one who had to publicly apologize and I couldn't blame for being mad. The only good thing out of it we managed to get a few extra donations and the Primate rescue facility made out also. But your sister gets with a reporter and makes it sound like we all screwed up. Oh and while I do have you, can you make it to a meeting with the Equine Anti-slaughter group? They are asking to form a group in the area. I am really interested to hear what they have to say."

Carl agreed and asked Debbie to text him date and time. She agreed

# Chapter 5

The door flew open, Kate yelled in "We gotta go! Now! A pregnant mare with its leg caught in fencing, she's been down for a while. "Gotta run." Debbie slammed the phone down and ran off, jumping in the truck. Kate drove like a crazy lady. She had an idea of where she was going. In a case like this every minute counted. A horse down too long can only mean one thing, with her caring a foal made matters worse. She could crush it and injure herself if she tried to thrash around.

"Debbie yelled at Kate, "slow down please, you're going to get us all killed. I can't see anything with the speed you're going. WAIT! STOP! I see something, pull over." The volunteers skidded to a stop behind them. The more help the better was the theory in every rescue. One volunteer waited on Jerri to show up. The rest jumped over the fence and started to work on the wire to get the mare's leg released. One volunteer, Judy, had a wire cutter. She was the strongest and she worked to cut it loose. The mare fought them. Debbie leaned her body over the horse's neck. They could see blood gushing out of her leg. Judy dodged every kick from the horse. Kate got the bandages while they were cutting the wire. Another volunteer, Amitola, but they called her Amy, tried to hold down the other leg so she wouldn't kick Judy. Amy was Native American and the smartest lady when it came to natural medical treatments. She would concoct some old inherent medicines and they worked on everyone every time. Everyone loved Amy, she had a calming effect on the barn. They all loved her old Native American stories passed down from her family. People would go to her for everything imaginable. One volunteer even asked for a special potion for her sister who had cancer. However, Amy couldn't help with that, but she was able to help her understand her sister was passing over to a better world without pain. Teaching her to rejoice the life they had with each other. When her sister passed away she was able to deal with her loss and was comforted about her pain being gone. Amy suggested that she put her extra energy into the horses now that she wasn't caring for her sick sibling and take her sister with her in her heart as she worked with the horses. Many times they heard her talk to her assigned horse telling him the silly things they did as kids. The old gelding listened to every word she spoke. Both horse and human needed encouragement. They both prospered from it.

Fighting the horse and her injury, the foal started to push through. Amy jumped over her and with her legs pressed against the back of the horse's hips she pulled the legs of the foal. With all her might she pulled and out it came. Blood gushed out of the horse. Amy was covered with blood and the foal lay on top of her. She dragged the foal to her mama, the two nuzzled at each other.

"Come on mama lady" Amy begged. "See your baby, he needs you." The mare rubbed her head on her new colt. Finally getting the leg free they quickly wrapped bandages on her.

Jerri worked on the leg when she yelled. "I've got too much blood coming from her. She's hemorrhaging. Judy, Amy pack her, we have to stop the bleeding." Following directions from Jerri, Kate saw the horses breathing become heavy, and her teeth began to grind, it was obvious that she was in pain.

Amy reached for the colt again. "Little guy make your mommy get well. Give her love." She kept the foal next to his mom as Jerri gave her a shot to end her pain. Quickly and quietly it was over. They all cried over the loss. The young horse stayed next to his mom as if he knew he had to. They heard him cry for her. He knew even at his young age he lost his mother.

The first one to speak was Amy. "I want him, please give him to me. I want to name him Halona. It means 'of happy fortune'. I want to make him happy and I am fortunate to have him. I'll call him Hal for short."

Debbie nodded. She couldn't speak. She never got used to losing any horse, especially one that had a baby that needed its mother.

Jerri sat back on her legs and fell back to the ground. She was soaked with sweat, blood, and mud. "I have one question, who in the hell let this horse loose and for how long?

Kate sat down between Debbie and Jerri.

Judy walked up and said, "You guys see that lady standing over there? All three looked over to see an older lady trying to hide behind a tree. She was watching them.

Jerri lifted her head to look, seeing a sweet fat lady. "Oh great. Tell me how she fits into the scheme of things? How did that lady kill this horse and leave an orphan? I just don't have the heart to bitch slap an old lady. Tell me something good."

Judy gave a slight wave to the lady and she just raised her hand and waved back with just the fingers. "The story she told me is this horse and a few others were set free because the owner had the horses transported from Texas. The guy he hired found out that the guy wasn't going to pay him and as revenge he let the horses go. A group tried to round up as many as they could but a few never got caught. She was running with a few of them. That's how she must have gotten pregnant. They had a stallion in the bunch."Debbie looked at them and said, "Oh yeah, I remember that, they called us but we were all full, as in no room at the inn. Some rescue from northern Florida came down and took them". They've been running loose for over a year. She spotted someone walking toward them. "Here's animal control, they will take the mare for us. Let's see if one of them can help Amy lift the colt in the back of your truck." Amy was still holding the colt next to his mother and she was crying. "Somebody help me. I'm not dealing with this much longer." Jerri stood up. One of the guys from animal control will help you and we will get him back to my place. "Looks like we're going to be barn mates for a few days, huh Amy?" Still holding the Colt, finally she was able to smile, "Yup this little guy is going home."Everyone started to get up and let the Animal Control Officers do their job. None of them wanted to watch them drag the mare's body to the truck. It wasn't a pretty to watch, and more painful because they all had a small attachment to the mare. The colt didn't need to see his Mommy being dragged off. He started to cry for his momma as they carried him away. He fought to go back to her. Everyone had tears in their eyes, having to pull him away. His little call almost sounded as if he was calling out "Mommy." She couldn't hear him. They all knew she wanted him but her body couldn't do it. Amy jumped in the back of Jerri's pick-up truck with the colt. Kate, Debbie, and Judy walked to the truck with Kate at the wheel. The whole trip back to the rescue was in total silence. There was nothing important or reassuring to say. Sadness filled the inside the cab of the truck. Kate was especially quiet. Losing her Dad recently made this all the worse for her. They were very close. She never accepted his illness. Kate held out that he would be fine. It wasn't until he passed away that she confronted the truth of what was happening. Then she had her mother and family to deal with. She never grieved for him until a few months later at the barn. Then the flood gates of tears flowed. Eventually she worked it out all by herself. But she still silently grieved for him.

After getting back to the barn, Debbie left to check up on Jerri and Amy. She wanted to spend a few minutes with the new colt. Walking into the clinic. She saw that Amy was feeding him with a bottle. Debbie smiled. "Looks like he is taking to it. Not to mention he looks hungry the way he is attacking the bottle." Looking like a proud new momma, Amy said." He is going after it. It's so good to see. Halona - Hal eating. Don't you wish you could read their minds just to know what they are thinking? I think they look at us like we're stupid. What's wrong Debbie?" Debbie sat down in the stall next to Amy and Hal, touching him with a light pat.

"Amy I don't know if it's starting to get to me or if I'm just overly tired. I'm sick and tired of the lack of compassion for these animals. We are supposed to be the thinking, rational creatures on earth. Instead we are mean, wicked and cruel. How does it work with humans? We have progressed to the point of being beyond the old west era, yet we are still shooting up the streets hurting innocent children. Destroy harmless animals as a form of entertainment. I think the world has gone crazy. It seems like we are only in it for ourselves instead of being for everyone. Why hurt animals? I was talking to an older woman one day about the older horses we have and she coldly said to put a bullet in him. I wanted to ask her if that is what we should do to older humans. Thinking this is a sweet old lady, I actually saw her as a cold-hearted bitch. This is what we teach our children. It's acceptable to be cruel to animals. I wanted to kick her cane out from under her. That makes me the same as her, but I would have felt better. Amy turned to her and said, "But you didn't and that's what makes you better than her. Trust me, she will have to see into her own mind's eye one day and face her own demons. I think most people do eventually."

Debbie reached over Amy's shoulder, giving her a hug. "I think it's time I go home, it's been a long day." Getting up from the ground, Debbie walked to her car turning up the volume on the radio. She sped off leaving an echo from her music behind.

# Chapter 6

The next few months were very busy for everyone. They prepared for the annual Barn Bash in between the rescues and adoptions. It took almost a year in advance to plan for this one affair. Normal everyday life ceased to exist. The number of fundraising committee volunteer's numbers dropped. Judy and her small group of four which dropped down from eleven were in high gear. Losing the people always hurt. Most left because of personal reasons or their own lives changed. Very seldom did a volunteer leave without a good reason. There were a few in the past who were asked to leave and then there were the freaks who managed to infiltrate. The one that stood out was the older gentleman who name nobody could recall. He was friendly. Good with the horses but he thought the barn was his own private dating service. He was approaching all the ladies as if he was the best catch. No one was off limits for him. He earned the name of Romeo without a Juliet. Then they discovered his heavy drinking habit. The final straw was when they found him passed out drunk in a stall. He was covered with manure and straw. He put a new meaning to the saying roll in the hay. They had to call in Bert, one of the male executive board members. Romeo had a bad temper when he had a hangover. He would cuss and get loud when he was hurting from his drinking binge. He was for the most part harmless however; he would come to the barn drunk and at times belligerent. Just about every female volunteer was ready to hang him up by the rafters. Debbie thought for sure he was going to catch hell from the women. They had talked about ganging up on him as they explained they wanted to set him straight. Once he left the next volunteer who was out of the ordinary thought he was going to run the show. Many times someone caught him trying to train one of the horses who had a physical problem thinking he could fix the problem. He almost got killed by one horse that had kicked him so hard it knocked him out. After the ambulance took him away Debbie left a text message on his phone that his services were no longer needed. Then there was "Crazy Carol". Everyone pretty much felt sorry for her because she was a lonely older lady. She would forget where she put the horses, forget to feed them, or put them in the wrong stalls. She talked to herself out loud and the worst part was she would talk in different dialects. One time she was Australian, another she was from Boston, and another time she talked in fork tongue as the girls called it. Except for the few weird ones, volunteers all had good hearts and were pretty much normal. Normal as normal could be. If you were a horse person you had quirks, most horse people did. That was normal.

 Judy's fund raising group was a small yet very functional troupe. They pulled it off every time. This was Judy's first year and everyone joined in to help. The "Barnyard Bash" was the biggest fundraiser of the year. It was also the biggest in the form of contributions. It was a two day event, the first day was a rummage sale with every kind of horse related equipment and an auction. The special instructional classes with a Ferrier, dentist, and veterinarians. Then the demonstrations with horses, special people came in to demonstrate the skills of a horse. One year they had a young man who thought that he would impress the crowd by shooting a gun from the back of one of the horses. This practically caused a stampede in the barn. Horses spooked and a few kicked boards in their stalls. Debbie quickly and tactfully ended his cowboy demonstration. This year they were including rides, such as two water slides, bounce house, rock climbing wall, and a vintage steeplechase ride. If the board gave their approval they were going to try and have a beer tent which opened only in the evening when the band started. The evening events started with country line dancing lessons and a special dinner served by the members of the executive board. The remainder of the evening was dancing to a fun country-western band. Sometimes they were able to have a celebrity come. But that wasn't always something they counted on. None the less when they did, they had celebrity football players, a singer and an actor or two would show up to sweeten the event. The local television stations attended and the country radio station broadcasted from the bash. The second day started out as an animal blessing. The local preacher came in and performed a special animal blessing, followed by a pancake breakfast. The event usually went over without much of an incident but every now and then someone would have too much to drink at the dance or a lovers' quarrel. There was the one year when the festivities were interrupted. They received a call in the middle of the evening about horses loose from a trailer tipped over in the middle of the expressway. They needed help before someone or something ran into an oncoming vehicle.

The Barn Bash was the single most successful event of the year with donations and contributions. People attending would always donate to the hay fund or bring in supplies. This year they had high hopes to get enough donations to put in a better security system, new roof with lightning rods on the quarantine barn, and a new small tractor. Debbie always thought big, and thinking big could bring in big assistance. Some years they made their goals and other, they fell short, but they were grateful for everything they received. In the beginning when she and Kate came to the barn, they lost a few of the horses. They had a few of the horses buried there. It became too much of an expense to bury them and special cremations was beyond the budget. She wanted a dignified area for people to come and visit with the horses. She named it "Horses Heaven Memorial". The first horse buried was her Blu. His ashes were in a bronze vase. She made a wooden sign with his name engraved on it and the date of his passing. She found a head stone maker and she would hunt their garbage for small stones to make makers or decorative stones. Most of the time she would use wood and she had them all face east because it is the direction the morning sun rises. Almost every memorial had a small plastic basket with apples and carrots.Finding an old wooden swing in the garbage, she repainted it and attached it on two wooden tree stumps. Debbie would work on her commemorative pasture for hours when she had the time. Often times she would be seen pushing an old fashioned lawnmower to keep the grass manicured. The small area was growing larger then she wanted. When an adopted horse passed away the owners would bring either their ashes or part of the horse's tail and place it in a spot of their choice. When a horse died on the property Debbie would arrange for a small memorial, most of the time the volunteer assigned to the horse was heartbroken. It helped to heal the pain and allowed for closure. It was never an easy time for anyone. Debbie wanted it to be a peaceful and respectful place because it was the only peace and respect many of the horses ever received until they reached the facility. She went to the thrift shop, picked up wood and decorative items used as memorials. Every horse that was buried or if a horse was adopted and died they were to be remembered. The first memorial she worked on was for Blu. The special plot was outlined with painted stones. Four of them spelled his name. Flowers and artificial flowers lined the parcel. Each horse that passed away had its own unique area with its name and information about him.

She taught herself wood burning and had their names engraved on a piece of treated barn board. On each board was a horse shoe painted gold with blue or pink stars depending if it was male or female. Lee built a small seat out of blocks for anyone to sit and visit. Many times Debbie would come out to visit with Blu and all the other residents. When times became too tough to handle she would walk out and sit. She would always think about the hard life many of them had endured. Then she realized that her life never seemed so bad after that. Some evenings when she worked the night shift she would come out when the moon was full. She would sit with a bottle of beer and talk to the horses. At times she could swear she heard hoof beats on the ground. She would sit next to Blu and cry. She would tell him how much she missed him. She asked him for a soft nuzzle to let her know he was around. But the sweet nuzzle never came. Occasionally she felt a cool breeze in her face and in her heart she knew it was him. Debbie wasn't a real religious person but she did believe there were horses in heaven. She imagined it was the perfect green pasture with a cool, clear current of air and plenty of open spaces to run free. Often time's volunteers or the owners of the lost horses would come out and visit the tranquil setting. There never was time, if anyone would watch, they would see the person crouch down on their knees, bent over with their head in their hands. Watching their bodies shudder with grief. Each person had their own sorrow and empty heart for the horse they loved. Even a person who didn't lose a horse would come and sit. They would be in the same position as the person before them who lost a loved one. They cried for the hurt, cruelty and abuse the majestic and regal horses suffered. The hidden guilt they couldn't fix the damage done. Some would pound the ground in anger at those who inflicted the pain and many vowed to carry on stopping the humiliation and damaging others caused. The Memorial Garden was a reminder to all who visited them. The Gardens were the reminder of the brutality and mercilessness humans wreaked on horses. They were abused as beasts of burden, worked until their bones couldn't carry or race anymore, and then left to live out their life in loneliness and most of the time hunger. Scars on their bodies were medals of honor and reminders of what was imposed upon them. Volunteers and rescues were passionate about repairing the damage done.

# Chapter 7

The other project Debbie took pride in was her volunteer appreciation day. It was a day for them to bring their families and enjoy being pampered. The Executive Board had to come in early and clean stalls, the barn and hand out appreciation gifts. It was all in fun and everyone enjoyed the day. The children and grandchildren were free to run around and play with some of the horses. The donkeys were the biggest attention for the kids. They were able to ride on them.

It was always the Sunday before Memorial Day. the special day arrived and Debbie had it all organized. Not a huge party but a nice comfortable day for everyone.

It was the only time Debbie's children and grandkids came out to the barn. Her family wasn't into horses, barns, and manure. She often would wonder where she went wrong, none of her kids liked horses. The oldest daughter, Amy, showed up first with her three kids. They had been to the facility plenty of times. Debbie heard "Grandma, Grandma, where are the horses, can we play with the donkeys, can we eat?" All three ran in different directions, one to the horses, one to the donkeys and the other to the food.

Debbie returned the "hi, hi and hi, walk don't run and where is my hug?" Waving her arm as they all took off, "Ok I'll get the hugs later I can see your busy." Walking up to her daughter she gave her a hug. "Hi Mom. It all looks good as usual. Introduce me to all the horses. I can't remember any of them."

With her arm around her daughter's waist. Debbie said. "Well why you don't come out more".

"Oh mom, I would but I really hate horse shit. It smells and I don't do bad smells. Where's Dad?"

Debbie pointed to the back of the barn "Follow the noise of your kids, they will be with him." The other two daughters, Jill and Jodie, drove up together with their children. Piling out of the car everyone ran up to Debbie and gave her a hug. The two older ones walked to the barn and sat down on the couch to text their friends and play video games. Debbie just stared at them and walked away shaking her head. The youngest of Jill's children walked out to where everyone else was and made friends.  She spotted a cute boy and wasted no time in introducing herself. Then ran off to get her sister Tiffani. Because she had a buffet of boys hanging around this time.

Finally, her son John and his kids. The same routine as the others, "Hi Grandma", gave quick hugs and ran off. John walked up to his mother and gave her a hug. His wife Erin came and everyone knew she wasn't into the barn, yet, she made the effort and it was appreciated. John's children, son Keagan and daughter Payton loved coming out to the barn but they lived so far away it was always hard to have them visit. Debbie watched as the games began, they had a potato race and a 3-legged burlap bag race. The adults played volleyball and relaxed in the warm sun.

Suddenly Debbie heard a hysterical scream, HELP, MOM, HELP. Debbie ran to the barn door and she saw Jodie's three children Bradley, Brookie and Brianna with John's children Keagan and Payton chasing Jill with one of the donkeys. The donkey was enjoying himself running with the kids after Jill. Her fancy sandals went flying off of her feet and she kept screaming for help. She jumped into the old wooden outhouse that was no longer in use. It was just a decoration piece on the property. Closing the door she kept telling the kids to get away. Take the killer donkey and put it away. Everyone was laughing at the scene. Jodie took the lead rope and tied the donkey to the outhouse door. Every time Jill opened the door the donkey was looking at her. She would slam the door close. Her voice was muffled behind the wooden door as she called for help. While this was going on one of the volunteer's dog grabbed her expensive sandal and ran away with it. John quietly walked up and untied the donkey from the door. He was laughing, looking at Debbie, "I wonder how long before she figures out the donkey is gone. Debbie mumbled to herself. "My kids put fun in dysfunction." She rolling her eyes and walked away. She knew that Jill would eventually figure it out and come out. The food was starting to be served and she joined her family for the meal. The executive board was all dressed as cowboys and cowgirls. Everyone was talking and having a good time. Debbie noticed that Keagan was missing. Getting up she went to look for him. He was not the kind of kid who missed a meal. He was thin and she never knew where he put all the food he ate. Walking thru the barn she saw him standing at a stall. The horse had been with the rescue for a few years. Keagan always found the horse interesting but he had a mean streak and couldn't be trusted. Debbie stood off to the side and watched Keagan and the horse named Thor. She could hear him talking to the horses but she couldn't make out what he was saying. Thor kept moving his head up and down as if he was agreeing with Keagan. Putting his arm up over his head Keagan reached for the huge horse. Thor reached down to take a smell of Keagan's open hand. It amazed Debbie how a horse as large as Thor could be gentle with a young boy, but mean as the devil with adults. He was a Morgan. He stood over seventeen hands high and was an angry horse but so gentle with the four foot boy. Debbie stood still as she didn't want to startle the horse or stop the communication. Both Keagan and Thor had a tough life. Keagan was sick baby. He was in and out of the hospital for the first years of his life and then he couldn't go out to play with the other kids. He lived in a semi-isolation because John and his wife couldn't take the chance of him getting sick. The whole family was concerned for him and very protective. Thor was a show horse and he was only brought out for work or shows. His owner wasn't kind to him. The only thing that mattered to her was winning blue ribbons and earning money. Thor spent most of his life in semi isolation. This is what made him an angry horse. He didn't understand how to be sociable with other horses. Both boy and horse somehow understood each other. His owner dropped him off at an auction and he was one of the horses the anti-slaughter group took from the kill buyer.

Keagan noticed Debbie standing there watching them. He waved Debbie to come closer. "Grandma, Thor is sad."Bending down at his side she put her arms around Keagan. "Yes he is. How did you figure that out?"

He shrugged his shoulders. "I don't know, he looks sad."Debbie stood up and stroked Thor's jaw. "Yes he is sad because he doesn't have any friends and his owner just left him and never loved him."

Reaching for the horse again "He said I can be his friend?"

"Keagan, he is a tough and unpredictable horse. I don't want him to hurt you. I know he has a good side to him. But sometimes the damage is done and we can't always fix it. Debbie stared into the horse's dark liquid eyes. She could see his soul. It was hurting and lonely. Turning to Keagan "How about you get your Dad to bring you out more and let's see if we can turn this tough cookie into a marshmallow".

Keagan's eyes lit up and agreed. Stepping on his tip-toes he reached up giving Thor a treat they walked back to the party.

"Let's go get your Aunt Jill out of the outhouse. She has to be hungry by now. Walking toward the outhouse they found it empty and walked to the party.

Debbie smiled as she looked down at her grandson and said. "I guess she found her way out."

Debbie went to the front of the party asking for their attention. It was time to present the volunteers with gifts and awards. One by one, Debbie and Kate handed gifts to everyone. Some received them for total amount of time they volunteered. Other received gifts for their participation with the committees. The last award and gift went to the Volunteer of the year. This was something everyone and the Executive Board voted on. This year it went to Tracy, she was at the barn every day. She worked the phones and she helped in the barn. She always offered her help in all of the committees. Everyone loved Tracy. She never asked for anything special. Her love and dedication to the horses was amazing and everyone loved her. For her dedication and service beyond she received a plaque and a weekend cruise for her and her husband. Everyone stood up giving her a standing ovation. Tearfully she accepted it, thanking everyone.

The Board also recognized a few people and for the first time in twelve years they honored Debbie. The volunteers all got together and had a picture of her and Blu professionally painted. It was magnificent. She was speechless and tearful. Admiring the beautiful picture she couldn't get over how well the artist had captured Blu. Every strong muscle, to his beautiful mane and tail. Forgetting she had a crowd watching her she couldn't take her eyes off the picture. Finally looking up all she could say was "Thank you, thank you, thank you. It's breathtaking. Thank you, thank you." Everyone laughed.

The party ended and everyone pitched in to help clean up and went home.

Debbie was staying the night, giving Hank the night off. The kids and Lee all stayed. There was enough food left over to have for dinner. The kids were able to ride some of the horses. Jill was the only one who just enjoyed everything from the side lines. Jodie, Amy and John left with Debbie and took a short trail ride. Lee watched the kids letting them ride the ponies and donkey. Jill eventually warmed up to the one donkey who she thought was a killer. They shared a bag of carrots. The only problem was Jill never did find her other sandal.

Eventually, it was getting late and everyone was ready to go home. A few of the grandkids, Bradley, Brookie, Brianna, Payten, Tiffani, and Trisha wanted to spend the night with Grandma. Debbie agreed and they all went into the office climbing into the fold out chair and two futon's. Turned on the TV and they all fell asleep. The older kids, Tyler had a part time job and had to work the next morning. Dana, Michael, and Angela didn't want to sleep in a barn this time. They had their turn few weeks ago with Grandma all to themselves. Keagan was coming back the next weekend to start his friendship with Thor. They all said their goodbyes. Lee and Debbie sat outside in the lawn chairs having a beer. Laughing at the antics of the day with the children. They did the last bed check on the horses and opened the sleeper couch and they fell asleep quickly.

# Chapter 8

As the Barn Bash date got closer Debbie was doing more on her own. She chased down every lead when a call came in. Amy and Doti became her biggest help. Kate ran the barn and had new volunteers to train. Amy was trained by Jerri as her assistant and she would come out to help when needed. Doti learned to be the second person with Kate. Tracy was promoted to Volunteer Liaison. She moved into the office to coordinates the volunteer schedules and new volunteer orientations. It was all running smoothly, as smoothly as a rescue facility could run. Nothing ever stayed the same, they had good weeks and bad weeks. The barn was filling up, they had only a few vacant stalls left. The volunteer barn was going to be used if they needed the room. Rearranging the horses and who was going in a different stall or pasture started to get confusing. They moved Tracy back out to the barn to manage and take charge of the horse's living arrangements.

The new ceiling fans for the stalls were being installed and the new roof to the volunteer barn was half done. Debbie's wish list for the property was starting to be filled. However, with every new improvement she found something new for her list. The annual budget was coming due and Debbie had not gotten to it. She knew it would be bad. The census of the barn was becoming more then the budget allowed. That only meant one thing. They would have to turn away horses. They could lose some and understand that they would have to walk away. It was not an option for Debbie but they were becoming over crowded. She could only hope that the board would be generous with her and that the Barn Bash would exceed their needs. Over previous years it had happen, however, not very often. The medical bills and maintenance alone was beyond the normal. They had more and more sick horses coming in.

Another call came in and Debbie went alone to investigate the complaint. When she first pulled up she could see a smaller horse in a pasture. It was grazing and didn't seem to be in trouble. Even so, it was thin. Ribs and bones were protruding. Debbie saw a woman walking toward her. She was smiling and her short round body had a jovial step. Outstretching her hand. She said "My name is Polly, can I help you?"

Accepting the hand shake, "I'm Debbie and I represent the Equine Rescue Me. I received a call about your horse. He is thin. Someone was concerned for him." Polly laughed. "He is thin, and he is thirty-three years old. He doesn't have any teeth and the few he does have are very soft and loose. Come on into the barn let me show you." Debbie could see fifty pound bags of senior feed, rice bran, alfalfa cubes soaking in the corner. Nodding her head with approval, she said to the lady. "I can see you have everything you need. He is an old guy and they can be hard to keep weight on. Hopefully you understand that when I saw how thin he was I was wondering how his condition was. Polly smiled. "Yes, I sure do and I would do the same thing, except I know the lady who called. She's my neighbor and we don't get along. She thinks I should put him down just because he is old." Wrinkling her mouth. "We've been together since he was six months old, and if I thought for one minute he was in pain, I would do the right thing. But he is fine. We walk everyday around the property, I massage his tired bones. Here let me prove something to you." They walked to the gate of the pasture, opening it. Putting her hand in front of Debbie, "Don't step in front of the gate opening, now watch this. The lady called to the horse, "Patch, time for dinner". The horse looked up and started to jog toward the two ladies. He jogged straight through the gate opening and directly to the barn. Following him they saw him stop in front of his stall door. Using his nose he pushed the door open and walked in. Debbie applauded the horse. "Well I can see he is doing just fine, you're doing a wonderful job. If you ever need any help let me know." She handed her a business card. "Give us a call please."Polly thanked her and dumped Patches' dinner into his bucket. Debbie made a mental note to stop and check on the two. Not sure what to worry about at the time but better safe than sorry. She started to head back to the facility but changed her mind. She was within five miles of the track rescue and was curious about what had been going on. She hadn't seen or heard from anyone in a long time. Plus, she thought she might be able to get in some riding time. Many of the thoroughbreds were still able to be ridden. They were rescued because they weren't money-makers who ran fast enough. The horse track people worked hard to prevent horses from being killed, dumped, or sold to a kill buyer. In spite of it there was always someone who didn't care. Debbie loved the speed and the smooth ride of a young thoroughbred. All they wanted was to run and run fast.

Turning her SUV into the drive way of the thoroughbred rescue she was greeted by Lois. "Debbie, well, if it ain't my eyes going bad, how the hell are ya? Oh no, don't tell me something bad. You can turn that ratty old vehicle around and get off my property."
Debbie grinned at her old friend, "Oh for God's sake Lois, shut up. I came to go for a ride on one of your ponies. Who ya got one for me?"
Lois grabbed Debbie's arm. Come in and sit down first. Tell me what's going on in your life. How's Lee doing, has he left you yet? He knows he can always come to me, I'll love him." Both ladies belly laughed, "Like always Lois your crazy. Is this what happens when you spend your life at a rescue. No luck finding a man yet? Come on, give me the ten cent tour". With her hands on her hip. Lois said. "Let me tell you something smartass, I did find a man and he's wonderful."
Debbie raised her arms above her head as if she was being held up by a robber "Oh yeah, two or four legged. I'm afraid to ask." Wiggling her hips, Six".
"Lois, where did you dig up a freak with six legs?"
"I got a real man with a horse and he is wonderful. Kind of sexy too" Lois blushed. "Come on I'll introduce you to him."
They walked into the thirty stall barn with a floor that anyone could eat off. The barn was a palace. It had air conditioning, hurricane resistant walls, grooms' quarters, a birthing barn which used to be a breeding barn and medical barn, exercise arena, and plenty of room for horses to run, all within one hundred acres of land. It was a dream barn for anyone who had horses. The thoroughbred rescue purchased it when the owner went bankrupt. Motioning to Debbie, "Come on in and meet the man of my life. Ronnie I want you to meet a good friend of mine. Debbie this is Ron Shellman."The grey-haired gentleman turned around in the big leather chair and stood up. Debbie looked up at the tall, thin man with his hand extended to her. "So you're the Debbie I've heard so much about. It's all good, don't worry, except the episode with the fourteen donkeys. Stealing fourteen donkeys and you both thought nobody would notice, as noble of an idea it was. You're both nuts. It's good to finally meet you."

Both ladies giggled, I didn't think you would tell anyone that story Lois. "Ronnie, did she tell you how she got caught in the barbed wire fence and had to take off her pants to get away. They were torn to shreds and she was running down a dark road with seven donkeys in tow in her pink undies glowing in the moon light."

Ron looked at Lois. "You left the panty part out. Wish I could have caught you at the time. My lady here is a wild one. The more I hear of her antics, the more I wonder what I have gotten myself into. Don't worry, Lois, I'm loving every minute of it."

Lois nudged Debbie, "'Come on, let's go for a ride, I still have Marty if you want to ride him?"

"I would love to ride. I can't believe he hasn't been adopted." Debbie looking for the horse.

" He's been adopted. I adopted him, said Lois. I adopted him, Chester, and another one."

The ladies saddled up the horses and took off for a ride. Debbie didn't ride too often anymore. "So tell me, Lois, how did you meet him? He seems like a wonderful guy."

Looking over her shoulder at her good friend. " Lois answered. I went back to Milwaukee to visit friends and was thinking of moving back. He was at a party and we struck up a conversation. He lost his wife around the time I lost Tom. We hit it off immediately. It's funny how some people go on vacation and bring back souvenirs. I brought back Ronnie. The funny thing was that he was moving to Florida to be closer to his kids. They're in Gainesville and they are great kids. My kids and his are good friends. It's like fate was looking kindly at me. I still miss Tom and he misses his wife but we help each other get through it."

"Well good for you both. So what else is new with you?" Debbie asked.

"Not much. How are Lee and the kids?"

"Everyone is great. John and his family moved back from California. Amy and her crew moved down last year. I have them all close to home and I'm loving it," Debbie proudly explained. The two ladies rode the back trail for over an hour and returned. Debbie hugged Lois. 'It's always good to see you, and love that man you have." Hugging Debbie. "As long as I have you, can I come out tomorrow for a visit? I have an idea to run by you."

"Sure, I'm always willing as long as I don't have to see you running down a road in your underpants," Debbie laughed. "I'll be there all day and most of the night. I don't even want to know what you're up to. See you tomorrow." Giving her another hug, Debbie left. The next morning Debbie arrived at work finding Sherriff Ed unloading two tall dark brown horses. "Morning Ed, what did you bring me? They look good." He points to the horses. "Take a closer look." Debbie could see both horse's shoulders and hips looked swollen and their tails were up in the air. Confused she looked back at Ed as he was putting both horses in the small round pen with hay. "Do you know a trainer named Mike Sipperton?"

Debbie shook her head no as she walked into the round pen to take a closer look at the horses. Both were calm as they ate the hay. Then Debbie noticed the problem, lifting the one horses tail. It was a raw, bleeding, open sore. "You have got to be kidding. Who in the hell did this?""I never thought I would see this again. They're Tennessee Walkers!" Debbie knew why the underside of their tails were raw. People would take steel wool and scrape the underside of the horse's tail raw, to make them hold their tails up. This old horse custom made them look better while they were in the performance ring. The horses were too sore to let their tails relax. It was extremely painful to the horse. The area under the tail is sensitive skin and taking anything abrasive is horribly painful. She looked at their shoulders and hips, she knew what was going on here. They placed heavy weights on the horse's legs so their legs would reach higher. making their gait more pronounced. When the weights came off the horses were able to raise their legs because of them being lighter to move. "Walking out of the round pen." This is the work of Sipperton?"As they walked away from the horses for Ed to sign the horses over to the barn and to be in protective custody. The owners lost the horses because they allowed the abuse. Ed explained. "One of my guys pulled Sipperton over, he was all over the road pulling a trailer with the horses. He was drunk behind the wheel. They arrested him and took a look at the horses. They knew they had a problem and called me. Sipperton won't be pulling any trailers any time soon. He had his driving privileges pulled over a year ago for drunk driving and it was his third offense. He will be in jail and charged with animal cruelty on top of the drunk driving, driving after suspension, no insurance, no health certificate with the horses. Plus his name will be ruined as a trainer around here. Whoever owns these horses won't come forward if they're smart because I will charge them with cruelty too.

 Debbie and Ed walked in the office to sign the legal papers and he left. Debbie called Jerri to come out to look at the horses. She wanted them to be comfortable. Both were very gentle. The allowed her to touch them even where they were hurting. Looking at them Debbie stroked their manes. "What do we call you? We'll see what happens and let someone give you names." She left them alone. Jerri careened in about an hour later, went straight back to examine the horses. Then walked into the office.

 "Debbie they both look good.  Feed them slowly, let them graze as much as possible. I took blood and will get back to you if there is a problem with the results. Don't touch the tails. Call if they turn green and slimy. Got to run, call ya later." She flew out as fast as she flew in.

 Debbie walked back out to check on the two and they were grazing and seemed fine. She would talk to a few of the volunteers to see who would take them on. They were to be kept together at all times. She had to think about which volunteer to take them on. Both horses appeared to be passive, however, once they felt better it could be a different story. When horses are sick they are like humans, they don't have the strength to fight, but once they feel better they can show their true colors. They also can get a bit feisty when they are feeling better, just because they are feeling good. She didn't know if it would be better for two volunteers to work together or have one work with both horses. She finally decided to let the horses make the choice. She would have Kate arrange to have a few volunteers to see who the horses wanted to work with. Sometimes the chemistry makes the choice. Not the human or animal. Debbie had to get home and as long as everything was quiet she made a quick escape.

# Chapter 9

The work increased with the horses. Kate assigned two volunteers to take on the new horses. She put up a notice for everyone to suggest a name for them. All the volunteers loved to name the horses. It was a fun competition and many times it became a game. The next step everyone voted. As it turned out everyone agreed on Elliot for the darker and larger of the two and Narnia for the other. As usual someone always disagreed but it was a friendly disagreement. Ironically, the same ladies who won the name contest also were assigned to the horses. Workers arrived to complete the construction on the barn. Lightning rods and stall windows were the first on the list. With all the amount of lightning in Florida it was always for the best to avoid getting struck. The new opening for windows replaced the sliding plastic panels. All the stalls would have shutters to open and close. It would protect the horses from the elements. Right from the beginning Debbie noticed a problem. All the shutters closed with a rope to make it easier to pull them shut. Horses are mimics and the first ones figured out how to close their window shutter by pulling the rope. This became a game for their entertainment. Opening and closing the windows, a few found it funny to pull the rope extra hard and it would slam shut. Debbie laughed telling the workers, "It doesn't surprise me they would figure out how to use them to their advantage. Could you somehow secure them so they can't grab the rope and stop the window slamming?"The young men working on the problem thought it was funny, taking videos with their cell phones. Debbie had to stop them because the horses were considered protected property and any photos or documentation of the horses were strictly prohibited. They both understood the situation and happily agreed. Neither man wanted to jeopardize any of the horses. As it was they loved to come out to work and didn't want to lose opportunity. Both young men always offered to help with other duties when they finished the work. And being young men they also found a few of the younger female volunteers interesting. Kate kept a close eye on them because a few of the girls were under eighteen years of age and they could fool everyone with their looks and appearances to seem older than they actually were. Kate had to play chaperone at times.

The other project donated to the quarantine barn was a medical exam room with a larger refrigerator, cabinets, shelves and included air conditioning. Additionally, a private shower with hot and cold water was installed. That was the biggest treat for everyone with the stifling heat in the summer. Mostly everyone who wanted to cool down had to go around the back and use the horse wash racks. This was important because periodically they had a few volunteers in the dead of the heated months fainting from heat exhaustion. Everyone joined in decorating the new rooms. Items related to horses garnished the walls, and floors. Small items sprinkled throughout were a nice bonus to the new rooms.

For the most part Rescue Me members were all good people with a very strong loyalty to the horses and the organization. Debbie could remember a while back that there was a group of ladies who came in and did nothing but upset everything. Volunteers were intimidated and quickly quit, others fought back the best way women know, gossip, and backstab. Debbie had to handle it with sensitivity. Some of the biggest trouble makers were friends and family members of the Executive Board. Debbie also snuck around behind the scenes thinking of ways to make their lives extremely uncomfortable. These members realized that they would have to do some real horse and barn work and moved on to make someone else life miserable. When a few of the board members heard of the trouble they almost voted out the ones who had connection to the trouble makers. New rules were born for Executive Board members and their families if they wanted to offer their services. An odd thing happened. They never had another Board member's friend or family volunteer again. Which was fine with everyone. Most of the Board members were wonderful people and it was sad to see associates ruin it for them. These were people who cared about horses and their survival. But they couldn't control certain people, nonetheless, it worked out for the best for everyone. New projects on the property were a constant item. If it wasn't fences to mend or fixed, it was one of the motor items like the tractor, manure spreader or lawn mower fizzled out. Luckily they usually had someone come to their rescue.

It was often heard from Debbie, "Our rescue needs to be rescued. Call a plumber, electrician, someone to rescue us."

Watching the construction work, an official looking car drove up. The driver pulled up to Debbie. The whirl of the electric windows lowered, his hand reached through with a paper and passed it to Debbie.

The young man, looking like he had an attitude as if he had been raised with money and catered to most of his life asked her, "You the Manager here? Well, Mom you've been served to cease any burials on this property by order of the health department. As far as I'm concerned take them to the glue factory or landfill."

In total disbelief she lowered her face to his window. Looked him straight in the eye. "Listen junior, I'm not your Mom and your concern is to get your ass off this property before I send you to the glue factory." Before she could stop herself she kicked the door making a good size dent with her heavy boots.

The vehicle backed up and thee tires spun spitting up gravel and dirt. Turning away before she was hit with the debris she jumped to the office door. Slamming it closed she reached for the phone to call Board director Carl.

Volunteers could hear her yelling into the phone. Everyone scattered to be anywhere other than the place they sat.

Debbie explained to him what had just happened. "What the hell, Carl? Who started this crap? What are you doing about it?"

"Calm down. I figured something was going on. A developer came in to make an offer to purchase the property. We turned them down and I thought that was the end of it. Apparently they think they can go over our heads and force us to sell. They can't purchase the land with dead animals buried in the ground. To tell you the truth, we're not supposed to bury them. It is supposed to be an actual licensed cemetery. It has to do with contaminated ground something or another. Again, calm down, I'll call our lawyers about this and if anyone comes onto the property without permission or wants to look around kick them off and you don't have to be polite about it."

With a loud sigh. "Thanks Carl. Sorry about the hysterics, please keep me informed."

Hanging up the phone she walked to the door. Leaning on it she stared up to the memorial. She didn't have any thoughts, it just made her mad. Debbie needed to keep herself together. The small piece of the property was a place for her to gather up strength and continue to fight for those who couldn't fight for themselves. It was special to everyone.

When others saw someone sitting in the pasture they would not bother them. They were given an unspoken respect. A few volunteers would have a picnic and reminisce about the good times with the horses. It was the only area on the property that was protected and only certain people were allowed to visit. When they had fund-raisers and the public was invited it was off limits for anyone not associated with the barn. The small piece of pasture was sacred ground and it was sheltered.

The most recent addition to the Memorial Gardens was a broodmare named April. She was a baby maker, for a breeder. She never recovered and died from anemia. The stupid man thought he could make money off mares. He tried to sell the urine of pregnant mares to the drug manufactures for female hormone replacement. Mares were bred and while they were pregnant they were tied up in a small stall with tubes attached to their urethra, their urine drained from them. Then when they had their foal they would be bred again and again and again. Their life sucked out of them as they reproduced and lived a life of abuse.

This one particular man thought he had a get rich scheme using pregnant mares and selling their urine to a female hormone manufacture. The property owner's children turned him in when they found out what he was doing to the mares. Whoever made the call, it was obvious his children didn't have much love for their father. One of the volunteers received the call and she rounded up the meanest ladies she knew at the rescue. Driving out to his property they were ready to take this guy down. Sheriff Ed got a 911 call from the man's friend telling him that a bunch of crazy women came out to his property to steal his horses. When Ed arrived he saw six angry women with rope halters draped over their shoulders standing at the horse owner's door. Two other women put halters on a few of the mares. The man saw Ed and started yelling to him to get these crazy women off his property. As Ed slowly walked to the front porch door he could see the guy was shaking out of fear. Ed turned to the ladies and motioned with his hand to the ladies for them to go back to their cars so he could straighten this out. The man introduced himself as Russ and he was confused why the women were there to take his horses. He loved his beloved animals and treated them like as he stated "golden angels".

Ed said, "Ok let me talk to these ladies and find out what is going on, looking toward the barn he saw a horse being led out. It was obvious that the horse was malnourished and pregnant.

Lilly walked up to Ed and told him her side of the story. "Ed, this man is a criminal and we want him. He needs to learn a lesson on women and bad hormones. We'll show him a hormone- stressed female."

Ed raised his hand and said. "Lilly I'll work this out. Where is Debbie?"

Looking toward the driveway, "I think she is on her way, someone called her."

Ed called Russ out and they walked to the barn. Russ stopped him and said "If you want to examine my property you better get yourself a search warrant."

Ed turned around and walked away. "Oh Russ, I have to go along with what you want. But, you see those ladies?" He pointed to the group of women with their arms crossed their chest. Giving him a real serious evil look.

Russ looked over Ed's shoulder and he nodded. "Let me ask you, have you ever heard of the Salem Witch hunts in Massachusetts? Ya know where they burned everyone in the center of towns?"Russ nodded.

"Well Russ, if I leave it's going to be a bitch hunt in Florida and you're going to be their bitch if I have to get a search warrant. Those women fight every day for horses. You're trying to make money from pregnant horse urine to make a hormone replacement that is proven to give women cancer. Yeah buddy, you are either really stupid or suicidal. Not sure which one but I can tell you that this will not turn out well for you if I leave". He turned his body in the direction of the property entrance . "Then to make matters worse their leader is just pulling into your driveway. Now you can take my advice and give up the horses, or face the consequences with those angry hormonal ladies. Cuz. I got to leave according to your orders."

Debbie walked up to Ed and Russ, "Hi Ed, this is mares' owner? What's he going to do?"

Russ looked down at Debbie's side and he could see she had a taser strapped to her belt. She raised her hand to shake his hand, "Hi I'm Debbie and I run Equine Rescue Me."

Russ shook her hand and smiled at her. "I'm Russ and I guess I was wrong, you need to do what's right for the horses."

With a sassy smirk on her face, Debbie walked away. Turning toward Ed she said, "I'll call off the posse." Looking back at Russ, "You need to thank Sheriff Ed. He just saved you from the unthinkable, and it's not death, but you would have wished it was. You have a nice day Russ." Watching Debbie walk away, he mumbled "Bitch" loud enough for her to hear. Without looking back she hollered over her shoulder, "Yes I am," and gave him the finger. Calling her band of merry ladies out of the truck and cars to go get the horses. They all circled around Debbie. One of them said "Can we get him now?" Another one said "Let me tie him up and put a tube to his meat?" They all were out to do damage to this guy. Debbie laughed at them. "I understand and agree with you. I want to hurt him just like you do but we'll let Ed have him. Now go do your thing ladies. Let's get them out of here. Load them up and would someone call Jerri to meet us at the barn?" Promptly the group walked to the barn and loaded the six mares on two trailers and quickly they exited the property. Ed stayed to give Russ a citation to appear in court for animal abuse charges. Russ slumped down on his top porch step and stared at the ground. "Yeah, you have a nice day, asshole." They all met back at the barn to unload the horses. Jerri drove in behind them. As the horses were unloaded one small mare collapsed on the ramp. Her legs gave out and she slid down the incline. One of the volunteers went down with her. The rest went to assist her. Jerri walked over, pulling on the lead rope while another volunteer grabbed for the horse's tail. Two pulled on the halter and the other pulled her tail to get her to stand up. "Come on girl get up, hey up." The scrawny horse struggled to regain her footing. Sliding down again, they helped her up and she strained to get off the ramp. Four of the volunteers walked her to the medical barn where she went down again, only this time they could see that she was in labor. The foal was being born. The ladies started to scream for Jerri. "Doc help us. She having a baby, Doc, Jerri get in..." Their voices escalated with every call. The air rattled with their panicked voices. Jerri flew into the barn and reached inside the mare to help remove the foal. The foal was born. The mare reached over to lick her newborn. Jerri finished with the mare and foal. Instructed the volunteers to keep an eye on them. But let Mother Nature do the rest. She went back to examine the rest of the horses. The five other mares seemed to be doing better. The next few days would be touch and go for all of them. All the volunteers quietly went into the barn to see the new mommy and baby. Both were resting and baby started to try to nurse. Jerri told everyone she didn't know if the mother would be able to nurse, yet again the strength and will of a mother could over take any weakness.

First notice on the board was the naming contest. For all seven horses with the new baby. Eventually all the mares became stronger except one. April, never could keep food in her. She continued to lose weight and she never recovered. One day in the pasture she lay down and died. Her beaten and feeble body was too badly damaged. As with any death the entire population of the barn grieved, especially the women who had rescued them. They all were more angry then grieving, they wanted revenge for her death. A few thought of ways to settle the score with Russ the owner and a few other often gossip about what they had overheard of his troubles with his vehicle. One time all of his door locks were super glued. Another time his back window just simply fell out. His tires were deflated and another time he found his gas tank crammed full of bananas and horse urine. The police chalked it up to kids being vandals. Then it stopped as quickly as it started. The cost of repair to his truck was expensive. He knew who was doing the damage but he couldn't prove it. Overall around the facility he received more ridicule and zero sympathy. They would giggle and say karma got him with a sharp pair of spurs. Eventually Russ became a piece of history and gladly forgot

# Chapter 10

The mares were all eventually adopted healthy to good forever homes. As part of the contract when a mare is adopted the owners may not breed her. The stallions were under the same rule. Except when they were on any property they had to be kept secured with higher fencing and kept away from all mares.

A few of the volunteers joined a special interest group to stop the nightmare of using mares for urine. They wrote letters to their congressman, used their knowledge to inform the public. The crusade to stop the use of the product became a part of fundraisers educating the public. They were able to set up a table to inform them about the pharmaceutical companies which were still using the chemicals. The whole incident left a huge impression on the ladies who were involved with the rescue of the mares. Debbie felt that this was what helped the service of rescuing horses. It was all part of it what they did primarily to inform the public of everything that was happening to horses.

The next few months they were able to foster a few horses and a few more were adopted. Sadly, one of the first and oldest residents Oliver passed away. They speculated that he had to been around thirty-five years old or older. He was the first rescue they had found when the foundation was established. He had been left to die in a grassless pasture. One of the board members saw him and she brought him in herself. She took apart the strap from her purse and she walked him five miles to the shelter. Leaving him with the workers, she walked back to get her car. Oliver was a Quarter horse and it was easy to see that in his younger days he was a striking horse. For some reason he never was adopted and eventually as he got older they considered him un-adoptable. He was the mascot and spoiled. Hank had become attached to Oliver. The two would walk around to get exercise. Hank would bring in his small TV and the two would watch the football games on Sunday afternoons. Oliver seemed to be as interested in the games as Hank. It was just a couple of old guys hanging out.

The day he passed away he knew something was wrong. Oliver didn't eat his dinner and he had been sleeping more that day. Hank went into his stall and sat down next to him. He talked to Oliver about the football game he had watched. Oliver was attentive to him as if he knew every word Hank was saying. The two sat together for about an hour. Hank picked up Oliver's head and set it in his lap. Hank looked down at Oliver, stroked his neck and said "Good night, best buddy". Oliver closed his eyes and he passed away about fifteen minutes later. Hank held his best friend for awhile then got up and covered him to the shoulders with his winter blanket. No one knows for sure how long the two stayed together before Hank called Debbie with the news. She came out to sit with Hank and could see his eyes were red from crying. The day they buried him Hank sat at his grave for hours. Debbie and the others would occasionally look out the window to check on him. Hank went home that day but he looked like he had made peace with it.

The memorial for Oliver brought all the Executive Board members and volunteers from the past came to show their respect. It was said that Oliver had more people attend his memorial then most humans. Someone donated a real headstone for him and it read "Respect him who endured and survived". The headstone was made of granite and the engraving was classic. Just about everyone had a funny story to tell about Oliver. At some point everyone who came to the barn got involved with Oliver. One of the funniest stories was told was by Hank. It was the time Oliver figured out how to let himself out of his stall and he could unlatch the door and went to all the stalls and one by one he opened all the stall doors releasing all the horses. Hank had fallen asleep but was shocked awake by having one of the horses nudging him. He knew who the culprit was because Oliver was the only horse innocently standing in a stall. The only problem was Oliver was in the wrong stall. Hank laughed and put everyone back in their proper place and when it came to breakfast he made Oliver wait until last. Another volunteer recalled a time when Oliver refused to come out of his stall. The volunteer fought with him to move to his pasture. Oliver refused to leave. Nobody could figure it out until another volunteer walked in and found three bottles of Vodka stuffed in a corner under dirt and shavings. The man hid his bottles in Oliver's stall so he could drink while he was at the barn. Many of the volunteers suspected he was drinking but they could never find the booze. It was Oliver who busted the guy. Once they removed the bottles Oliver went out to the pasture. Another round of laughter and more tears. The stories continued for a awhile then everyone walked out to the memorial garden and many placed small items on his grave. The party broke up and with all people attending it was totally silent.

Debbie was the only person who showed up the next morning to feed and take care of the horses. Kate came in three hours later apologizing for not helping. Debbie told her that it was ok. "I needed to work off my sadness." All the stalls were cleaned except for Oliver's. They left it as he did. Debbie thought that someone would strip it but she didn't have the heart just yet. Debbie and Kate lounged in the office, neither one felt much like working. They had the TV on watching reruns of Mr. Ed. All the horses were all fed their midday hay and everyone was just hanging out.

Debbie got up to grab a drink out of the refrigerator. "Wow, it's never this quiet Kate. Can't ever remember when the last time this happened."

"Shut up, shut up, shut up," Kate threw a paper plate across the room. "You just cursed us. When are you going learn to..."Both women looked at each other, hearing a loud noise coming up the driveway. It sounded like a semi-truck dragging a rattling trailer. Walking outside they saw a rough looking young man jumped out of the truck. He looked back at the ladies starring at him with their mouths open in shock.

"So where do you want them? Come on ladies, I don't have all day." Kate looked at the guy and said. "What the hell is in there?"

"You are the proud owners of fifteen donkeys, ladies. I was told to drop them off here and if you won't take them to just shoot them and leave them on the side of the road. Now one more time, where do you want them or do I shoot them". He pulled a gun from a holster on his hip.

Both said in unison "No we'll take them."

Debbie finally overcame her disbelief. "Can I ask how you got them and why are you bringing them here?"

Without turning her head. Debbie said "Oh great another donkey deal."

Unlocking the trailer door, he turned to them. "Some guy owned a small carnival, like the kind at the local churches. He said the guy who owned the donkeys robbed him and left the animals behind. He told me he found you on the Internet and I was to drop them off here." Opening the trailer door, the donkeys started to file out as if they knew exactly what they were supposed to do. They all wandered over to the green area and started to calmly graze.

Both ladies started to laugh. Kate looked at the group and turned to Debbie. "I told you your statement cursed us."

Debbie walked over to the burly driver. "Do you have any paperwork on these guys? Can you or someone tell me if they have been vaccinated? Medical history? Can you give me anything?"

The driver walked to the cab of the truck and pulled out a large yellow envelope and handed it to Debbie. "This is all I got. Don't know what's in it. Good luck, I got to go. Any by-the-way. The gun thing works every time."They both gave a half of a wave and turned to look at fifteen donkeys happily grazing on their front lawn.

Debbie opened the envelope and pulled out papers which she could read had information on the donkeys. Their health records, diets and each one had a name. "Kate how do you tell the difference? Who is who? You won't believe this but seven of them are named after the Seven Dwarfs. This is going to be fun trying to figure out which is which. Any suggestions? "Kate stood facing Debbie then faced the donkeys? "You have seven names what are the rest?" Kate walked over to the group and started to call them. "Sleepy? Anyone? Sleepy? Ok no Sleepy. How about Doc? Which one of you guys is Doc?" None of them responded to their name. "Dopey? Where is Dopey? Who is Dopey?" One donkey raised his head and walked over to Kate and just stood next to her as if he answering her. "Quick Debbie get me a permanent marker and put his name on it. This is Dopey weather he knows it or not. Doc, do I have a Doc, nobody wants to be Doc, and Bashful which one of you guys is Bashful?" They heard a sneeze coming from the group. Kate grabbed another halter picked out the one who sneezed and so he became Sneezy. One stepped on Kate's foot, so she named him Grumpy. Talking to group as if they were a bunch of kids in a school play, "Now who wants to be Happy and Sleepy? Oh hell." With this the last four she wrote their names on the halters. "You are Happy and you are Sleepy and you are Doc. Last but not least you are Bashful. Now go stand by the rest of your buddies."

Debbie had tears rolling down her face from of laughing. "Let me get the rest of the papers, Kate. We have eight more names to figure out." Skimming through the papers she laughed again. "Kate you are not going to believe this but we have more names here. We have three papers, with information the names are Peter, Paul & Mary. Look for Mary. She should be easy to find in this group."

Doti drove up, jumping out of the car squealing. "Wow, can we keep them. I love them. Can I have one? Where did they come from?"

Kate popped her head up from the crowd of donkeys. "Doti come help me. I'm looking for a Mary."

Doti dropped to her knees crawling around the donkeys looking under them for the one named Mary. She yelled out, "I found her, oopsy, Bashful is really Mary. You better change that." All three women were hysterical with laughter. Eventually, Peter and Paul came forward. They answered to their names. Kate took the papers from Debbie, looking at the other papers to see if they had some sort of description of each donkey. They had names for just about all of them. Separating the ones who had names from the nameless. Five remained. A wind picked up and all the papers went flying. The three dove for the papers, chasing them around the front lawn. Still giddy from the confusion they gathered the papers putting them under a rock to stop them from flying around.

Debbie handed Kate and Doti a name form. She kept one for herself. "Let's see who we have left. This leaves John, Paul, George and Ringo. What was this guy thinking with these names?"

Kate hollered "I found Ringo. Check out the ring around his neck, gimme a halter."

Doti threw a halter to Kate, and then went back to calling for John, Paul and George. The last donkeys didn't respond all except one lone donkey standing all by himself, looking lost. Debbie said "I think this is Bashful. He is so sweet." Walking up to him she put the halter on him and gave him a hug. With her arm around him she looked him in the face "OK little Bashful, you have a name." He followed Debbie all over after she hugged him.

Kate and Doti threw halters on the three guessing their names. Debbie turned in circles, looking around. "What do we have left? This should leave one more. Which one of you ladies have the papers, what is the last name?" She pointed to one donkey without a halter.

Kate flipped the paper over. "Well this shouldn't surprise you, his name is Elvis".

Walking over to the Donkey she wrote Elvis on the halter. "Come on Elvis, get the gang and let's get you all into the pasture." One by one they followed her to the only open pasture, calmly walking in line until they all found an area of grass to graze.

Other volunteers started to arrive, surprised at the sight of fifteen donkeys. They all gathered around the fence to watch the new arrivals.

Everyone was full of questions and the talk of the events of what had happened.

One question that came up more than once, "Can we keep them or one?"

Debbie thought it would be a good idea to keep a few donkeys on the property. It would keep the coyotes away. They were great burglar alarms also. She had to talk to the Board Members to see how many they could keep. She had hoped for three or four but she would accept whatever the outcome. She had already fallen in love with Elvis, he was her first choice. She enjoyed watching the volunteers play with the donkeys, and the donkeys appreciated the attention they were getting. Everyone came in with a favorite.

Debbie told the volunteers that they could have first choice if any of them wanted to adopt a donkey. Looking over the group she could tell she had a few interested.

That afternoon she called a few of the Board members to let them know what had just happened. They all got a big laugh out of it and they promised to be out to the barn to see this for themselves. Hank arrived for his evening shift. Standing at his car he stood gapping at the sight of the pasture full of grazing grey animals. Walking into the office, he saw Debbie and Kate sitting at the table. "What in the hell did I miss? Are we keeping any of them?"

Shrugging her shoulders, Kate said, "We hope we will be able to keep a few, but not all of them. Debbie is going to the courthouse to claim them tomorrow morning. Some of the Board members are coming out this evening. Hopefully they will let us keep a few. Do you know anyone who would be a good home for them?"

With his arms across his shoulder. Hank reached up and rubbed his jaw. "Ya know, I do know of someone who would take a few of them. Let me make a call. Do you remember the young couple I told you about who adopted the four boys with Down's Syndrome? They have a nice piece of property west of Orlando. I wonder if they would be interested in a few. "The Board approved of Elvis to stay." Debbie chuckled.

Over the next few weeks the donkeys were adopted. One family took three of the Seven Dwarfs. Another family adopted the Beatles. Peter, Paul and Mary went to a neighbor who had a few cows. He wanted to have a few donkeys around because he had lost a few calves to coyotes. The family with the boys took the other four of the Seven Dwarfs. Everyone was happy that they were able to keep most of the group together. They hated the idea that they all would be split up after being together as a group for so long. This left Elvis to be the rescue's mascot. He made friends with the other donkey. He loved the horses and the horses loved his company. If a stranger pulled up onto the property he would sound his boisterous alarm.

# Chapter 11

It had been business as usual around the barn. Doti finally took her horse home now that she could afford it. Kate adopted one of the horses, a mustang, Cody, who had arrived blind in one eye. He had some serious issues but Kate was able to work it through with him. Debbie would laugh because she would overhear Kate arguing with him as if he was a child. The two became a close duo. The loss of sight never became a disadvantage for him. When the opportunity arrived they would take the horses out for a trail ride and sneak a flask full of wine. The topic of discussion was always about the barn and how to get more money. They brainstormed a few more fundraisers. Then tried to find a company sponsor who could help. For the first time in years they were able to reduce the amount of horses to the barn. This kept the expenses of it lower. Debbie admitted to Kate that she was getting tired. It's been going on ten years and she could use a vacation or something. That's when she begged Kate to keep a secret. Kate feared the unknown of what she was going to hear. "Tell me what's going on."

"My back is really bad, the disk is totally worn down. I'm having a problem with my thigh going numb. Sometimes I can't feel my leg under me. Yet other times I can sling manure and do everything and it doesn't bother me. I need your help. I hate to add more to your schedule. I did ask Judy to call all of the folks who will help us with an evacuation in case we have a hurricane. Amy said she would work with the volunteers to review getting the horses into trailers and who would be involved with an evacuation. Then there is the hay and feed room. We have another inspection coming up from the insurance people. They have warned us about the hay being stacked too high. The feed is on pallets but they are unstable. They fear someone will get hurt. That whole area needs to be reinvented. Can you organize this for me?"

"Debbie, why didn't you tell me what's going on with you? Do you think I can't handle some of these things or is it that you think you have to do it all superwoman? Kate threw out the last of her wine and turned her horse around.

"Kate, wait it's not that. I just can't delegate well. I'm sorry, I know you are perfectly capable of running this place single-handed. Even better than me at times. I get so overwhelmed I'm afraid to say something. My biggest fear is that if I make a mistake I will damage a horse. Or even worse let everyone down. Tell me what I should do? Please, you've been a friend too long.

"Would you even take my advice? Kate hissed. "I'm supposed to help and this goes to show you can't do it all. I'm taking over some of the decisions around here or I'm gone. You make me feel bad that you're hurt. I feel like it's my fault that I didn't do more. I'll meet you back at the office. Think about it or find out if you can get yourself a wheelchair to muck stalls."Kate walked off leaving Debbie.

Leaning over her saddle horn, she talked to her horse. "Well, that went well don't you think? She's right you know. Hate that when I'm wrong. Hate it even more when someone points it out." The horse snorted and continued to search for something to chew. Debbie lightly patted the horse on his neck. "Thanks for your opinion buddy." Debbie turned the horse around and walked the long way back to the barn. Thinking the longer it took her to come back that Kate would be calmer. Although she knew better.

The next week Debbie turned over a few of her duties to Kate. As it turned out it gave Debbie more time to follow up on the adopted horses. Spend more time with the horses. Being prepared for the Executive Board members when they came or had a meeting. Over time Debbie made time to go to physical therapy and she felt it starting to help. Judy came in for the whole day to work on her Public Relations work. Amy became the volunteer trainer. Kate took more control of the barn. It was a relief for Debbie to give up on some of her responsibilities.

Judy came out of the office and called to anyone. "Someone found a hurt horse, they need help right away."

Kate, Debbie, Amy, and Doti took off running. They drove for what felt like forever. Finally they saw two boys waving them down.

"He's in the swamp, awful skinny. I know who owns him. The crazy bitch with the trailer about a mile down the road."

Jerri showed up right behind them. They all got out of the truck and followed the boys. The mosquitoes were awful. They sank in the stinky muck and the deeper they went the flies were attacking them. They all could feel the bites on their arms and face.

Debbie asked. "How much farther?"

The boy turned and said. "Just a little bit but the mud gets worse. Oh, and there are snake and I spotted a gator when I came out to meet you. Watch yourself." Rolling their eyes the five looked at each other. Jerri lost her shoe in the muck. "You have any idea how expensive they were, It is just plain gross having to walk barefoot."The boy pointed, "He's over there. He's stuck up to his chest."Amy pulled out her cell phone and talked to someone telling them the situation. "Do we have some sort of directions for someone to help us?"The shortest of the boys said, "I have my GPS. I think it has the latitude and other thing for directions. Debbie, Doti and Kate approached the horse. He struggled to release himself and he flung his body around. Debbie could barely move in the knee deep swamp muck. They all tried to calm the horse. The boys tried to dig around his legs, but every time the horse moved he got himself stuck deeper. Jerri gave the horse an injection to calm him. He dropped his head and heavily snorted. His breathing was labored. His own weight was starting to crush him. Everyone tried to dig deeper to get the horse out. They were making progress but the horse didn't have time to wait. The longer he was stuck the more his internal organs were being crushed by his own weight. Amy's phone rang,. "I can hear you, you sound close. Any chance you can get in here? Ok, drop the sling but we need help. Were not strong enough to wrap it around the horse."Suddenly the wind picked up, branches flew wildly around and the roar of a helicopter blades was churning everything up. Dropping down through the trees appeared a giant body attached with ropes. All the ladies looked at him and smiled at the good-looking firefighter. "Ladies, this is my cousin, Ronnie," said Amy, wrapping her arms around the handsome, tanned, and very muscled man. "We can admire him later, please." The firefighter called on his radio and another body just as good-looking, tanned, and muscular dropped down out of the sky. Doti yelled, "Thank you God! Could you keep dropping them for me. This one's mine."In unison they all said "You're too young."Both men went to work ignoring the women. They covered the horse's face with a cloth. One tried to roll the horse to get the sling under it. The other took a shovel and tried to push it through. The ladies pulled and pushed with the men. The horse had started to give up the struggle. After what seemed like hours, they finally got the material under front of the horse. One talked into the radio on his shoulder and they could see the rope tighten. The front of the sling started to raise the horse. The movement startled the horse and he slipped out of it. They all started over and this time they had more room to slide the sling under the horse. Orders called into the radio. "Lift, lift". The horse started to rise into the sky. It hung from the sling, and didn't move. KABOOM, everyone jumped. Looking around the group people were stunned. They saw one of boys lying on his back with the shotgun a few feet away. He sat up looking at everyone pointed his finger in another direction. The only thing that came out of his mouth was. "Gator". He fell backward. Everyone turned to see a ten foot gator about twenty -five feet away facing them. They could see him moving forward but he dropped his head. The boy had shot the gator in the head. Debbie looked at the group and said, "No one would ever believe me if I told them what we just did and add a gator to it. That only happens in the movies." Ronnie laughed and said, "You should write a book, maybe they would make it into a movie." Everyone chuckled. The group walked out of the swamp covered in mud and muck. They looked like they had been buried in it. Animal control had the horse in their trailer. They were taking it back to the owner. Jerri checked the horse's condition and considered that he was healthy. Didn't seem to have any serious injuries. They all talked for awhile and the fire department van showed up to pick up the two men. The boys took off in their mud machines. Everyone high-fived each other and Doti was still flirting with the other fireman. Jerri left in her truck and everyone else slowly crawled into the truck with Kate at the wheel. On the way back to the barn the conversation was about the gator and how close a call it was. They were going to be gator bait, as much as people joked about it. It was going to be a reality for them if the boy didn't shoot it. They had to somehow thank the boys for the call and the help. Debbie offered to call Ed to see what he could suggest. Doti offered to personally thank the fireman. Amy mentioned that she would tell the guys they appreciated the help. Back at the barn everyone saw the group almost fall out of the truck. Looking like mud zombies. They were exhausted. Narrating the story each one left to go home and get a hot shower. Kate stayed the longest to find out how the horse was doing and if the owner knew what had happened. Just as she about to leave a news truck pulled up. Kate, mud soaked went through with the interview. When she got home she laughed at seeing herself on TV. She hadn't realized how dirty she was. That night Carl, the Board President called Debbie commending her on a job well done. "I appreciate it Carl, but I didn't do it alone."His voice was light and you could hear his pride as he spoke. "I know and we made the news. I received a call, the big tire company in town, and they offered a large sum of money. The owner was impressed with your work and wanted to help.""Oh Carl, that is great. Can we put in a new shower?"They both laughed and said they would talk again in a few days. Debbie started to notice a drop in volunteer attendance. They were short on help. She asked a few of the longer term volunteers, "Has anyone heard from some of the volunteers? We seemed to have lost a few."Nobody answered her questions, which was strange because gossip is constant in the barn. Debbie didn't like what she was seeing or not seeing. That evening she made a few calls to a few of the ladies. She left messages for those who didn't answer the phone. The few who did answer appeared to be very evasive with their responses. Her inner alert feelings were going off like a fire alarm. Finally her phone rang. The caller ID read it was Lois, one of the volunteers calling her back."Hello. Lois, thank you for calling me back. I'm concerned because I have a few good volunteers who haven't been coming in. Is there a problem? Is this something I can help?"Lois had been a volunteer for well over six months. She had a regular schedule of every Monday, Wednesday, Friday morning and Sunday afternoon. It wasn't like her to quietly slip away without mentioning anything. Debbie had problems in the past and had high suspicions that there was a conflict going on among the volunteers. Lois opened up to Debbie what was going on and why she had to quit. "Debbie, I'm more upset that I left. I love being at the barn. I need to be at the barn". After losing her son to the war in Afghanistan over a year ago, it was good therapy for her. Debbie knew she was in a fragile state of mind. Debbie let her talk and Lois opened up to all the nonsense going on among the volunteers. There was a small group of ladies who let everyone know they were experts on horses. They were a loyal group but they were snobby and they not only knew it but didn't care. Lois explained how the horse she was assigned was never left for her. They took her from Lois. Every time she was with a horse one of the ladies criticized her, actually walking up to her making rude comments and taking the horse away. She recalled one time when she went into the pasture to walk the horse. They all followed her down the trail and continued to make comments on her ability to handle the horse. They told her that she had to walk the horse on the right instead of the left as she was taught. One of them took red food dye and saturated the top of the horses' tail, telling her she had hurt the horse. One of the ladies sat her down and told her how she prayed for Lois every day that she could be nicer. That she would see how it would be better for her to read more on horses because everyone would laugh at how she did her work. Another time they made fun of her clothes. Then Lois dropped the big bomb. The ladies were drinking alcohol in the stalls with the horses in with them.

After hearing the story, Debbie didn't need to call any one. She knew this same story would be repeated. She was angry and embarrassed. Debbie worked very hard to keep the drama out of the barn. The tension was not only bad for the humans but it affected the horses. They would easily pick up the strain in the atmosphere. Debbie thanked Lois for her honesty and said she would get back to her. Debbie knew what she had to do first thing in the morning. She made a call to Kate recapping her conversation with Lois. "They are all history, they are going, and I don't need that kind of sophomoric attitude. Poor Lois and all she had had to deal with losing her son. That is wrong."

Kate promised to be at the barn early the next morning. She didn't like most of the ladies in this group. They were rude to everyone except Debbie. They came to the facility as a social event, thinking everyone was stupid, however, that was all going to change in the morning.

Debbie and Kate drove in at the same time. They fed the horses and left the stall cleaning to the ladies when they came in. Both talked about the strategy they would take. "I'm so angry with this. Nobody has the right to hurt anyone. We have enough of that with the horses, we shouldn't be doing it to ourselves. What I don't understand is that this is a volunteer program. Who do they think they are ruining it for others who are no different than they are?" Debbie was getting more furious as the conversation continued.

Kate nodded her head. "Ya know I thought something was going on but I didn't think that grown adults would act like that."

Around nine o clock the ladies walked in together. Looking around one said with a huffy tone in her voice,. "Hey why aren't the stalls cleaned?"

The rest looked around and one said, "I'm not doing them. They have plenty of little volunteers to do the stalls. I'm taking my horse and going to the round pen."

Debbie and Kate walked out of the office with Carl, President of the Foundation.

"Ladies can we have a word with you?" Debbie opened the door to the office and motioned for them to walk in.

One by one they entered the office. Kate walked to the couch. "Sit down, we are going to have a talk." The room was silent.

Sliding over a folding chair facing Carl sat down facing the group. "Would any of you like a cup of coffee?" No response from the set. "I've been told and have verified a problem among a few volunteers. Can any of you verify this or bring any information to the front to discuss?"

One volunteer, Betty slowly raised her hand. "I pray every day for all of our horses and volunteers. I see problems with a few of the volunteers. They are not presenting themselves in a manner conducive to the clientele we would like to associate. The foundation needs to help sustain the financial bottom line. It is essential to preserve integrity and have an ideal situation to provide us with the prominent people we need."

Carl tilted his head looking questionably at Betty. "Let me ask all of you. Is this a mutual thought among all of you"? The group nodded their heads in unison.

With a loud sigh Carl said, "You're wrong, all wrong, dead wrong, completely wrong. Any questions?" Not allowing for any of them to answer. "I will not allow anyone to humiliate or demean any volunteer in this rescue. I also will not permit any person to decide who will stay and who is good enough to be associated with this facility. You are not in any position to make those pretentious statements. You deeply hurt a few of our volunteers who are here to help and make this establishment function with compassion. Go play golf at your country club." Pointing to Debbie and Kate he continued, "These ladies here work their asses off for this place and you are not going to destroy it with your pompous way of thinking. Your service are no longer needed. Please take whatever you came in with. No! Just get out, all of you. Good Bye."

The ladies rose from the couch and one by one walked out. The door quietly closed behind them. "Good job, Carl. I never could have done it as well." said Debbie.

The office door flung open, one of the ladies with tears streaming down her face walked in. "Please don't make me go. I didn't go along with them. I just kept my mouth shut, I should of said something. I was wrong. Please let me stay. I'll apologize for myself and them. I can't give this up." She stood in the open door crying. Carl looked at her and said, "Ok, but you're on probation, one slip up and your gone. You understand?"

She nodded her head. "Can I go clean the stalls now?" Not waiting for an answer she turned and walked out.

"Can I go now?" Carl asked the ladies.

Laughing at him, Debbie said "Yes, but you're on probation."

Carl saluted them and walked away.

# Chapter 12

The next few weeks at the barn were very quiet. Carl fulfilled his promise and had a shower installed. The security cameras were perfect. They had night vision and the best part was Debbie could save everything to her computer.

One of the volunteers walked into the Office. "Hey Debbie, a guy out here is interested in one of our horses."

Debbie got up and walked out extending her hand. She could see he was wearing an expensive suite. "Hi I'm Debbie how can I help you."

The gentleman responded with his hand to her. "I'm John Grady, I own Grady paper company. Heard of me?"

"No sir, I can't say I have, but how can I help you today? Debbie answered.

"Can we go outside. This office is very warm." Perspiration droplets growing on his forehead.

"Oh I'm sorry, I guess I don't feel it anymore. Can I offer you a bottle of water." Debbie reached inside the refrigerator.

"Yes, please." Taking the water bottle from her.

As they walked outside the temperature dropped by ten degrees and a cool breeze drifted through the barn.

Debbie watched the man looking out toward the pastures with the horses.

With a big smile on his face he turned to Debbie. "I'm looking for a lawn ornament".

Debbie gave him a puzzled look, "John, Mr. Grady. Hmmm, let me see". Looking around, she pointed to the small flower garden. "I don't know if I can see them but if you want to buy one ok, with me. Which one would you like? The garden fairy, smiling snail, flamingos'?"

He scowled his forehead and with a sarcastic tone in his voice. "NO, I'm looking for a LAWN OR NA MENT!"

Debbie responded to him with the same tone he spoke to her. "We don't have any LAWN OR NA MENTS HERE!" She could hear the ladies giggle at the conversation going on. "What are you looking for Mr. Grady?"

He raised both of his hands in the air. "A horse, my wife wants a horse for the property. She's not interested in riding one, she just wants a horse."

Debbie took his elbow. Come walk with me. He followed her to the barn.

"Mr. Grady, here are a few of our horses. They need forever homes. They come to us abused or neglected. It's our job at this place to give them back their lives. Give them dignity. They are breathing, feeling creatures. Lawn ornaments, as you call them, are made of cement, plastic, or metal. They don't hurt, bleed or starve to death. Horses feel pain, hurt, and they understand when they have been abandoned by someone they loved and were loyal to". "These horses look good. I don't see anything wrong with them." John said

Debbie kept staring at the horses. "You're right, you see them right now, but you haven't seen the work that has gone into them. The love and dedication. The people you saw sitting at the table. They are the lifeline for these horse's. They volunteer their time. They don't get paid, yet they come in and work hard in the heat, rain and whatever is required. They see each horses as a feeling being. I have some volunteers who work forty hour's at a job and still come in. They do the evening feed, they spend their free time on the weekends. Many of them use their own money to help with the horses needs. This isn't a play thing or whatever is fun. These volunteers give their heart and blood to help these horses survive. If I did an 'all call' which is a phone call to come help, they would all show up to help. These are hard working people with hearts larger than they are. Come here and look out into that pasture. You see just horses. Let's walk a little closer. You need a good hard look."

They approached the pasture and Debbie could see his face shocked with horror. He saw skeletal horses grazing. A few were lying down and with their ribs protruding. Another one with bandages wrapped up his leg. Another had half of its fur gone. The rest were scattered in the pasture. Debbie walked to the gate and opened it. Grady followed her. They entered the pasture. few of the horses started to walk toward them. They were curious about the new visitor. Debbie reached out to let them smell her hand. Taking the man's hand she guided it to a horses nose. She saw him smile for the first time. Giggling like a little boy. He raised his hand to every horse he could. "What happened to them?"

"Well John, like your plastic and cement lawn ornaments, this was all man-made damage. They don't deserve what happens to them. Horses are very loyal and they want to please their owners. However, in return we hurt them for being loyal. If I handed over one of these horses those ladies in that barn would never let it leave. They have their hearts invested in them. The volunteers realize these horses can feel pain, and loneliness. We, as humans are supposed to be the rational and thinking beings. Yet, we hurt and destroy horses because we don't feel the pain. It doesn't make any sense to me. I'll never understand how people can hurt any animal. If a horse is stung by a bee they will cry out. They feel the same pain as us."

They both walked away and a few of the horses followed them to the gate.

Turning to look at the horses, Grady asked, "Debbie why are they following us?"

Smiling at them and him. "They're curious about you."

Walking backwards looking into the pasture Grady said, "Debbie can we go back to your office? I would like some information on this place."

Debbie opened the door to her office. She went to the metal file cabinet as Grady sat down at her desk. She raised an eyebrow. "John make yourself comfortable" She noticed he pulled out his check book.

He handed the check to Debbie. "Here I hope this helps you and please help that horse get his/her coat back."

Debbie accepted the check and she saw that it was for the amount of one thousand dollars. "John, this is very generous. Thank you and I will go out and buy that horse a new coat." She chuckled.

Turning back to her desk he wrote another check. Tearing it out he handed it to Debbie. "Go out and get some gas gift cards for your volunteer's car. They are doing a wonderful job."Thank you, John, they will appreciate it. Bring your wife back and you can give her the tour."

John extended his hand to Debbie, but it was a completely different hand shake from the one they had when they met earlier. She reciprocated with the same. "Thank you again."

As John left the office he waved good bye to the volunteers.

Debbie came out of the office a few minutes later and told everyone what had happened. They all high-fived each other. Debbie sat down at the table with the other volunteers and they all just talked about nothing in particular. It was turning out to be a nice day. Lee was stopping by after work. They were going to have dinner at the barn. He enjoyed coming out. He said it was the best way to take away the stress of the day. But she knew different. Lee had grown very fond of one horse named Chance. He was an older guy. Most of the time you never knew he was even around. He just went along with everything, just very easy going. Lee was spending a lot of his time with Chance. The two would go for walks and Lee had bought him his own set of brushes. He had picked up at a barn rummage sale. He had also gotten a winter blanket and painted Chance's name on it. She had seen many times the two spending time together. She never let on she knew it, thinking he would mention it eventually. Debbie and the five volunteers were all sitting around the table relaxing. Suddenly someone said, "Do you hear someone yelling?" They sat real quiet listening for the sound again. Then the words drifted through the barn loud and clear. Two words everyone feared and dreaded,' Horse down'. All at the same time they jumped from their chairs running. They could see Apache on the ground. He refused to get up. The two volunteers were pulling on him. Yelling at him to get up. Everyone arrived at the horse at the same time. Two pulled on his tail and the others were pulling on his lead rope. The horse wouldn't budge. He kept putting his head down. Everyone knew he was colicing. It was the number one killer of horses. It didn't have a bred or age preference. When it struck it was never a sure thing. Colic could strike without warning. The horse was unable to defecate. Their intestines became blocked and many times twisted. It was extremely painful for the horse and other then being able to remedy the horse, sometimes surgery was an option, however, many times it proved to be fatal. The volunteers started to bark out orders to each other. Debbie grabbed her stethoscope and the medicine Banamine. She threw it at the girl in the front. They all quieted down so she could give him the medicine. Debbie added a large syringe of mineral oil. Handing it to her. They started to walk him. His gums were light and he wanted to lie down. They wouldn't let him at this point. Everyone walked Apache back to the barn. It was easier to work on him. Other volunteers came running with warm water and gently rinsed it over his back. Others were messaging him. Everyone went into survival mode for him. Genna was working with Apache. She had plans on adopting him. The application had been submitted and approved. She was waiting for an opening at a barn to board him until her barn was built. Everyone could see tears running down her face while she worked on him. If he started to go down she would yell at him. "No Apache. We have a place for you. Stand up please." Debbie putting her stethoscope to her ears she checked for gut sounds and she wasn't hearing anything. It was time to call Jerri. They needed a professional to save the horse. Debbie turned away from the group and called Jerri. Amy called her back and said that they were on their way. Debbie reassured everyone that Jerri would be there shortly. She watched them all walk him, a few comforted Genna. Apache went down again, they couldn't stop him. He was exhausted. Debbie told them "Let him lie down for a few minutes, as long as he doesn't roll."

One other lady brought a bucket of hot wheat bran to see if he would eat it. Genna sat on the ground putting her hand in the hot mash and tried to hand feed him. He sampled it but showed no interest. Within a few minutes Jerri and Amy showed up. Jerri examined Apache and didn't hear any gut sounds. The ladies tried to get him up. Jerri called to them to let him stay down. "I want to put an I.V. in him, he needs fluids." Amy handed the bag of medicated liquid. Jerri skillfully inserted the needle into the horses neck. Attached the bag and opened the valve for the fluid to flow. "Now get him up and walk him to the front pasture with the run-in shed. I have to hang this bag from someplace high." After a bit of coaxing, he got up. Amy held the bag of liquid above her head. Walking to the pasture they were able to guide him in the covered shelter. Amy found a nail hanging and she slid the bag onto it. It wasn't the first time they used this shelter for a horse with an I.V. The tube was long enough to stretch across the covered haven. Leading the group was Genna. She stayed at his head, everyone else stood next to the horse in case he started to go down. Two of them continued to give him a light massage and everyone else kept close. Amy checked the bag and said, "As long as he is in pain keep this attached. I have ten of them for you." Genna nodded but she didn't comprehend anything. She walked around to listen for any stomach sounds. She didn't really expect any at this time. They needed him to produce manure. The pain started to disappear and he didn't look stressed anymore.

Jerri walked in. She had a plastic sleeve encasing her arm to her shoulder. "Ladies, I need you to keep him quiet so I can do this without being kicked." Jerri inserted her arm into the horse's rectum. Apache wiggled to get away but he didn't have enough strength and everyone held him in place. Jerri pulled her arm out with a handful of manure. "I'm going in again." She produced more manure but that was all she could grab. "Ok ladies keep him up and relaxed." As Jerri and Debbie walked away they heard the ladies start to quietly sing. She could hear the softy tone and words "Wild Horses...." Jerri looked at Debbie. "I don't think this is going to end well. I think he's twisted. We could do surgery but that is still a 50/50 shot. It all depends on how bad he is. He is a young horse but with his history I think the damage to his internal organs is bad." Apache had arrived at the rescue about a year earlier. He and his brother were used to transport drugs. The drug smugglers put bags of cocaine into the horses anus for them to travel with the drugs. Both horses were abused and it became a regular thing for them to insert the drug and have the horses in a trailer taking them to meet the sellers. It wasn't until one day a Highway Patrol officer noticed the trailer traveling a few time up and down the highway seemed to be suspicious. He pulled them over and found out they didn't have any papers for the horses. Their story didn't make sense. The officer had a horse of his own and they didn't seem to know what they were talking about. He called for back-up and they searched for the drugs and failed. Refusing to release the truck with the horses he pulled both animals out and walked them around for a few minutes. When he saw nobody was watching he picked up the tails he could see they were being used for smuggling. Calling the other Officers over he explained his suspicions and they radioed for a vet to come and examine the pair. Easily, the vet confirmed the officers suspicions. He removed numerous bags of cocaine from the horses. The smugglers were arrested and charged with drug smuggling and animal cruelty. Both horses were turned over to the local animal shelter and then sent to a rescue. Apache's brother was adopted by the officer who found them. Apache went onto live at the Equine Rescue Me because it was at the time the only place with an opening. He adapted well, except he would kick and squeal if anyone tried to touch his back hips. Eventually he trusted Genna enough to let her brush his tail, but that was all she could do. It was an instant friendship that quickly turned into love between Genna and Apache. It took a year for him to understand she wasn't going to hurt him. She spoiled him to the point Debbie had to tell her she needed to stop because he could become a problem. They all knew she continued to spoil him but only more discreetly.

Throughout the day the group stayed with Apache. If he would start to go down they would hold him up. Other volunteers came to help. They worked in shifts except for Genna. She refused to leave him and argued the point. Debbie told everyone to leave her alone. That night a few stayed who were there from the beginning. They all talked and worked on Apache. They finished the I.V. bags and he started to look better. He was able to walk around the barn and the property. He actually started to nibble at the grass and drink some water. Genna sat down for the first time and slept for a few minutes. As the sun started to come up Apache was down again. Jerri showed up to check on him. The prognosis wasn't what they wanted to hear. His intestines had swollen from being twisted. It had gone too far, no turning back. Apache wouldn't make it. Jerri gave Genna time to say goodbye. Her husband and son pulled up and ran to her. They sat with him for a few minutes.

Jerri walked over looking at them. "Ready?"

Genna pleaded, "No, can we try again? Please help him Jerri, don't take him from me. He deserves a better life, a longer life. Please don't do this." Genna cried but she knew it had to be done. All the others left to give the family privacy. Jerri administered the lethal mixture. Apache slowed down his breathing as Genna, her husband, and son comforted him. He was gone in a few seconds and the trio sat with him. Genna was devastated, both her husband Rick and her son Tyler huddled together. Debbie could see out the window that they eventually left. The other volunteers went out to say their goodbyes. One cut his tail for Genna. They would make a memory bracelet for her. Tears didn't stop that day. Everyone came out to give their respects. Lee drove out to give his wife moral support. He never got used to it. He walked out to Apache and gave him a pat on the hoof as much to say go run, be free. Late that afternoon at dusk one of the male volunteers buried Apache in the Memorial Gardens. The officer who had Apache's brother heard the news and came out to give his sympathies. He offered to donate to help with the Memorial Garden. It was gladly accepted.

About two weeks later Sheriff Ed stopped by and he took Debbie into her office for a closed door meeting. "Let me ask you something. Did you hear about the dealer who owned the horse you had got his ass kicked and kicked really bad. Whoever did it literally broke the guys tail bone. He will be hurting for the rest of his life. You wouldn't have heard anything through the vines?

Debbie smiled and shook her head no. "You really think if I knew I would tell you anyway? I'd give them a medal if I knew. Besides, what do you care? Especially after what they did to those horses."

"I don't care Debbie, but I do worry that whoever did it could be in trouble. These guys have friends in really low places. I went over to Genna's place and had a talk with her son Tyler and his friend BJ. I know that kid was upset and that is putting it mildly for his mom. He doesn't seem to be the type to go and do something like that but when it comes to family, revenge can come."

"Ed, did he mention he saw someone?"

"No, he didn't even know how many, he said they never said a word. They came up behind him and beat him. He's lucky to be alive but I have a sneaking suspicion that whoever did it wanted him to suffer and not die. We're not pursuing it, but curious about who did it. Between you and me I think the scumbag deserved it."

"Funny Ed, how karma can come around calling and he got it with a strong cold steeled set of horse shoes."

Ed left and Debbie hugged herself. She wanted to know who did it and she had the same thought as Ed. Tyler and his buddy probably did it. Neither boy was a bad kid, never a problem for Genna and Rick. It was just the opposite. The boys were very quiet and both were more silly than anything else.

Debbie reached into her secret hiding spot, finding a cigarette and lighter. Walking out of the office she headed for the Memorial Gardens. Lighting the smoke she sat down on the ground.

She never felt it strange to talk to the horses who were lying in the memorial garden. She would come up and talk to everyone. It seemed to help the hurt go away for her. It was her mental medication coming to the gardens to relax and sometime blow off steam. The sadness seemed to build up and this peaceful place seemed to be the cure for her. Debbie sat and thought and every now and then she would talk. Ultimately she had to return to reality but until then she was in her good place.

"Hi everyone. Hey Apache did you hear? The guy who hurt you is in hurt city himself. He got his ass kicked literally. Hi Blu, how's my baby boy? How is everyone else up here? Well let me tell you all something, I hate to hurt, seems like it's getting harder and harder for me. But I can't let you guys down."

Feeling revived, Debbie was able to pull herself and her inner strength to face more strained hurdles for the day.

# Chapter 13

Kate walked into the office with Lauren. They had an idea for a fund raiser. A huge 50's party with costumes and a consignment sale. Lauren knew a group of guys who would come to play music. A giant movie for the kids. Put up an old fashioned soda fountain. They would dress up the horses in costumes, have kids come in costumes and sell some of the junk they had lying around. Debbie agreed and thought it was a great idea and told them to go with it. The heat hung in the air without any relief. They were bringing in the horses during the day and leaving them out at night. A few of the older horses didn't sweat and they couldn't cool themselves off. At least in the barn they had heavy fans over head. The hay bill increased because they wanted to give more hay to the horses to keep them busy. A few of them had already kicked the side boards on their stalls. They weren't used to the schedule change. Then with the heavy storms and lightning they all had to come inside more often. None were happy with this idea. But they really didn't have a choice. It was the same every summer. They were short on volunteers this time of the year. Some went on family vacations and others couldn't tolerate the heat and humidity. Yet there were the diehards who showed up and worked through it. Debbie always had something special for them because with being so short handed it made everything else more work. Hank had to limit his outdoor activity. Debbie and Kate showed up extra early to do stalls. Then there was the water issue. All buckets had to be cleaned and fresh water added all day. With being in the middle of hurricane season they had practice runs with the volunteers getting the horses in the trailers. Some of the volunteers didn't have the skills to do it. More important every volunteer should have specific training. They had a few horses who refused to go in and the older guys were a problem. Between the barometric pressure from the hurricanes and the stress a few of the older horses could stress colic. It could be possible to stay in the barn but if it was a serious category four, five the barn wouldn't stand. The best chance was the medical barn but that only help about held at the maximum five horses. If those guys even got along and didn't start to kick each other. If someone stressed they would be in bigger trouble. Even if the hurricane wasn't serious they had the concern for tornadoes taking the place down. It seemed to Debbie it was always something to worry about. She couldn't expect the volunteers to stay at the barn they had their homes and families to worry about. Until that happened she didn't want to think about it. Aside from hurricane season, she made a list of training sessions she wanted every volunteer to attend. She remembered how some didn't have a clue when they dealt with colic. Then she saw a few not understand how to take a horse's temperature or understand when they are in pain. The training of volunteers was falling apart. Lauren lost a few who had helped her with the fundraisers. She was on her own many times. New rules and procedures with updated policies were on the list to be worked on first. Kate was overwhelmed with her duties and everyone was getting burned out. Amy was with Jerri almost one-hundred percent of the time. Doti fell aside when she met a good looking boy who had a horse. Her reliable help was winding down. She needed to up the help. She and Kate were on their own except for the adoption committee. They had a waiting list to join. It was the easiest task and most fun. They were a good group but they didn't do much else. She slapped her desk with her hand and typed out a memo and tacked it to the bulletin board. "ALL VOLUNTEER MEETING ON SATURDAY AND SUNDAY," she sent out an email to every volunteer. Those on vacation would receive a copy and if they needed to have a second meeting they would schedule one. Debbie restructured the committees and she included Kate and Lauren to have their input. Plus, she eliminated the horseback riding unless they had worked the day before and unless they signed up for a committee. She made them earn points to ride. Those who had horses boarded must work at least ten hours or more a week or move their horse and pay to board. Changes had to be made and Debbie blamed herself for letting it happen. Kate and Lauren added some ideas. Lauren was promoted and became a paid employee. She quit her Public Relations job and used her experience to help and work at the barn. The Executive Board was pleased with the changes and promotion. They felt Kate and Debbie were putting too much on their shoulders. Lauren was a wonderful addition. She even started to learn about the horses and found one that she was secretly having fun with. Grace was a black and white Paint Quarter horse. She had come in six months ago because her owners lost their property. They didn't want to leave her behind. The family was heartbroken at the idea of losing her. They did the best for her, and at one point they thought about having her put down. Thankfully they didn't have the heart to do it. Lauren fell in love at first sight with Grace. The two clicked together. Both were pretty and quiet. Lauren wasn't sure what to do with a horse. She had never ridden one except for a few pony rides as a kid. Kate and some of the other volunteers taught her simple things to do with Grace. Brushing, halter, feet, and walking with her without having her step on Lauren's feet. Nothing was said but Debbie caught it and pretty much everyone could see the sweet attraction. Lauren acted as if she was just trying to help out but she mainly worked on Grace. They all knew it was just a matter of time before Lauren walked into the office with signed adoption papers.

The following weekend it was amazing how many of the volunteers showed up. Except for a few, everyone was on board and willing to do what was needed. Some of the volunteers changed committees and others added to the barn. It went better then Debbie thought. She considered herself lucky to have the group she did. They were good people. Just when she was about to lose faith they all came around and it was all for the horses.

Late one morning Patricia from the Executive Board drove up in a large van full of men and women. Debbie's first thought was that they were friends of her they would have to cater to and entertain. They had been through that with her before. However, she happened to know a few of the ladies climbing out of the van. Her heart went heavy. She knew why they were here. It was something she never wanted to get involved with.

She said hello and hugged a few. Maddie better known as Mad Max, Kit also known as Killer Kit. Two of the craziest ladies she had ever met. Then Louie and Dennis, the big bad leaders or co-leaders. Maddie and Kit let everyone know who ran the show. The others she had seen before but wasn't familiar with.

"What brings you guys to our humble home?" Debbie welcomed the group.

Maddie introduced the four others. Danny, Clem, Jordy and Julie. Patricia ushered the group into the barn with Dennis and Clem dragging a large cooler. It was stocked full of drinks.

The volunteers stood staring at the group, confused to what and who they were.

Debbie stepped up and said, "I would like to introduce you to the Anti-Slaughter folks. These are the craziest people you will ever experience. They are dedicated to putting the slaughter of horses out of business."

One young volunteer raised his hand. "Where do I sign up? I saw this stuff on the Internet and it's horrible."

Hold on, you going to abandon us?" Kate asked. He looked around the room, "Uh no, I just want to help.""I think that is the reason they are here, they want us to help." Debbie introduced the volunteers standing around. They all made small talk for a while. Kate showed a few of them around the place. Lauren introduced herself because, as usual, they forgot quiet Lauren. Maddie called everyone in. "Let's get this started." The group gathered around to hear what had had them all in suspense. We represent the Anti-Slaughter Organization. Horses are being stolen and purchased at auctions then sold for meat overseas. Slaughtering of horses is against the law. Family horses are being taken away and hearts are broken. The people, and I use that term loosely, they are not human. We have been working all over Florida but we need help. Debbie, Kate, and a few others from here have assisted us. It's important for everyone to understand for the first time in eight years, horse slaughter plants were poised to open in New Mexico, Iowa and Missouri. On January 17, 2014, they were stopped dead in their tracks when President Obama signed the Omnibus Spending Bill containing language to defund FDA inspections. Yet, we have Missouri and New Mexico pushing to open horse meat plants. We have the BLM which is the Bureau of Land Management using taxpayers' money to run down horses with helicopters. This process is cruel and it has been seen many times. A mare is ready to foal and she will drop the foal in fear she continues to run in a panic. The foal will get trampled by the other horses. They are in the same flight mode. Fear of the helicopters chasing them. Once they are rounded up, they are kept in holding pens without food and water. Then transported over the borders to be slaughtered. The Wild horse roundups have now become an economic burden and are costing tax payers up to $200 million dollars per year. This is a cost to the USA that is unnecessary if they are left to roam free on the taxpayers land. The argument the government has is that the horses are causing a heavy financial responsibility. That is stupid because they are on their own land. The government doesn't have to pay for feed. It's the battle with local ranchers who think they are entitled to use our tax dollar, and allow their cattle to graze freely. Those who are fighting this battle have taken pictures of wild horses in lush grass and water and they are being fenced off on land that the ranchers don't own. The horses who are corralled are starved and die from thirst in the area they are held. Ladies and Gentlemen, this is our government who tells us they are broke and shut down. The wild horses are to be protected and allowed to roam free under the wild Horse act of 1971."We as Americans don't eat our pets. There are legit businesses where animals are used for food. However, there are many who have illegal roadside stands selling goats, chickens and horse meat. This is not only dangerous to eat but the animals are not treated humanely. There are numerous organizations in place to stop this. We are one of them and we need your help. I can use a few examples and for those who are weak in the heart I will tell you right now, what I have to say is gross and brutal. I know, I have seen it for myself." Looking around the room Maddie turned to Debbie, "Are you sure of everyone sitting here? Debbie scanned the room, "If you're under the age of twenty-five you need to leave. I know your adults, but I know how much you love horses. I can tell you that when I first saw these pictures I couldn't close my eyes. I spent nights doing everything I could to not see the pictures of horror. A few of you really need to think about this before you jump in." A few of the younger girls refused to leave. One stood up and said "I know what the pictures show. I don't need to see them. I'm in." She walked away heading to the horses outside. Kate spoke up from in behind everyone. "She's going for a hug. She needs it. I can tell you from personal experience. If you make the decision to help with this cause it will change you." With a silly laugh. "You do hug horses more than you ever thought you would."  Maddie continued to speak to the crowd sitting around her. She pulled out her tablet and instantly gruesome pictures of dead horses appeared. "Well here goes my speech. Horses are usually stabbed in the heart with an everyday household instrument. Other times they are strangled with ropes and again stabbed in the jugular vein. I've read that the monsters will cut their vocal cords in their throat to stop them from screaming in unimaginable pain. They are often butchered while they are alive. I recently heard of a case where the family went to visit the horse, who was pasture board, and when they arrived they found the horse dead. Only a head, legs, and only scattered body parts. The horse was gutted and its meat stripped from it back. Another story, someone found horse parts on the side of a road. It was butchered not far from his home where he was taken. It's not only horses. It's dogs, cats, pigs, just every animal around. Many are used for religious sacrifices. Many times horses are pickup from ads on Craigslist. People think they are giving or selling their beloved animal to a loving family and little do they know the horse is doomed. Some people argue that horse slaughter helps the sick and reduces the population of unwanted horses. Well, folks, I hate to tell you but how many of you ever see a skinny cow. They want the young, fat, and healthy horses for slaughter. Don't buy that crap from anyone. It's a fight and we need help. The one happy thing about this is that all those hungry horse eaters are poisoning themselves. They are feeding themselves and their family pounds of cancer. Our horses are given vaccinations, fly sprayed and other things that don't hurt the horse but it can make humans sick. I don't wish cancer on anyone. My sympathies don't stretch to those who have been known to eat horse meat and they are sick. They are killing their kids and families. I say tough shit for them. This is the truth and we need help from anyone who can offer their assistance. But before you jump in, understand what is happening here. When we go places it's repulsive to see the atrocious condition of the horses. These people play for keeps. They have slashed our tires, shot at us, and we have been beaten up. I'm on my fourth vehicle in less than two years. The insurance company won't insure me with new cars. I buy junk cars and use them. There will be a time you might be asked to go to a place where we have found horses slaughtered. We are now trying to expose the kill buyers. These assholes go to horse auctions and bid on horses. They outbid the father who is trying to buy his kids a family horse. Kill buyers drive around with horse trailers looking to see if they can find horses left in fields. They scout an area for the thieves to come in. We have to expose them and send them away. Again, I want to remind everyone, it can get rough and these guys are not playing. We are dealing with criminals who carry guns, knives, and other weapons. I'm not afraid of them. I don't have to hide into the night with my life. Hide behind covered faces and do my dirty criminal work in far hidden places. If they are so proud and feel they are not doing anything wrong, I don't understand why they have to run and hide. That's my speech. If you're interested please complete our form. One important thing. Please do not take your time from this place. Debbie and Kate and all the horses count on your here. Don't abandon this rescue please. Thank you for listening."

Maddie looked at the mesmerized group, and a silent heavy blanket covered the group. They were all trying to digest the dreadful ideas they had witnessed.

Debbie walked up to Maddie and the group. "You could sell ice to an Eskimo. You know if you need me I'm there. Thank you for adding that they not leave me. So can I interest you in a horse? When do we start at the auctions? I haven't done one with you in a long time."

"Two weeks. Ya ready?" Maddie looked over Kate's shoulder and glanced at Lauren. "Who's the new lady?

Debbie motioned for Lauren to come over. "This is Lauren. She came aboard about six months ago. She does our fundraisers and she has come on to assist Kate."

Maddie extended her hand to Lauren. "That was pretty powerful speech. I have to give you credit. I would be a mess. I have to say that I'm not strong enough to witness the ghastly scenes you come onto. But if you need me I will gladly help behind the scenes."

Maddie thanked her and said she would call in a few weeks. We need someone to feed the news people to expose the creeps. Is that possible for you?"

Lauren nodded. "Call me. I'm glad to help where I can."

Patricia walked over with two of the ladies who had come with Maddie. "Debbie this is Jordy and Julie. They want to adopt. Both have their own property and are ready to be a forever home."

Patricia leaned over to whisper in Debbie's ear. "Maddie is also finally looking to adopt. That's great. She needs to have one."

"I'm always happy to meet someone who wants to adopt. Let me grab one of the volunteers and have them show you around. They will give you their history and you can see who you like."

Both ladies walked away and Debbie called Tracy over. "Can you take those two ladies around. They want to adopt. Which is perfect with you being on the adoption committee."

Tracy smiled. "Always glad to find a home for these guys." Tracy walked toward the ladies. And she lead them to the pastures.

Maddy stood looking out the barn door. Kate walked up to her. "Ya want a new kid?"

Smiling, she said, "Yes, it's time for me to give someone a home. My place has been standing alone too long. I think Cesar will understand."

Kate put her arm around Maddie. "It's been five years since he's been gone. I hate to see someone like you not take in a horse and give it a good home. Glad to hear you're ready." The two walked off to seek out a new kid for Maddie.

Maddie had found Cesar when she was in college. He was left behind by one of the equestrian students. She didn't think the horse could help her succeed. She had left him behind at the end of the school year. Maddie saw that he was in the pasture all by himself. She could see in his eyes that he was hurt she left him. Maddie called her parents and they helped her get him home. They knew too well that if they didn't she would get the horse home one way or another. The rest is history. He fell in love with her as much as she did with him. The famous story about Maddie and Cesar was the time they went out riding and Maddie jumped off him to relax, and when she jumped off she twisted her ankle and broke it. In the days without cell phones Maddie was in trouble. She couldn't get on him to go home. She tried to lean on him and walk but her leg wouldn't hold her up. They struggled and she fell. Finally she gave up and figured someone would come find her. Cesar instinctively knew that she was hurt. He pushed her with his nose, but she just sat on the ground. After prodding her he got down on his knees and she climbed onto his back. He carried her home. It was a remarkable event but they had a close relationship. The only time he ever got mad was when she met her husband. Cesar got jealous. It took him a long time to accept him. But they did because they had a mutual love for Maddie. As he got older they discovered that he had cancer and eventually he gave up the fight. Maddie was distraught and grieved for years over losing him. It was time for her to love a new horse that needed her.

# Chapter 14

 Later that afternoon, all the volunteers left for the day. Kate, Hank, and Debbie worked the evening feed and stalls. Hearing a car drive up, Kate walked to the barn and saw it was Ed. He was out of uniform. Kate waved. "Is this official business or pleasure?"

Ed walked past her, giving her a crocked smile. "Need to talk to you. Where is Debbie? Hank working tonight?

"This sounds serious Ed. Let me get them." Walking through the barn she called to Debbie and Hank to come in.

As the group came into the office it was obvious whatever Ed was there for was serious. Looking around the barn. "Are we the only ones here?"

Hank nodded to answer his question.

"I have a problem and I need your help." Ed explained why he was there on unofficial business. "I can't tell you that I received an anonymous tip. I also can't tell you what the call was about." With a big sigh he looked at the group. "It's not against the law in these parts to shoot your own horse. I don't understand it but if you want to kill your horse, you can put a bullet in its head. Here is the part I can't tell you. A guy is going to shoot his horse to get revenge on his wife. She kicked him out of the house. He was served with legal papers and he told a friend he was going to kill the horse as a payback. The friend called me and I told him I can't step in to stop him as long as the horse is in his name as the owner. This not the way to settle the score but divorces get messy. He plans on doing it the morning before he has to leave so the wife or ex-wife will come home and find the horse freshly killed. I can't tell you this because I can't step in to save the horse." Looking at the group he turned and walked away, dropping a piece of paper on the ground as he left.

Kate walked over and picked up the memo. Unfolding it she read an address written on it and it said that the rear fence behind the property was broken. She turned toward Hank and Debbie. "Hmmm, Ed dropped this. Just fell out of his pocket". She opened it and slid it on the table.

Debbie grasped the paper. "We've done this before. We're going to steal a horse. Tonight! Anyone want to see the sights of this special neighborhood? I'm thinking I might want to explore and find out if there are any properties for sale. Ya wanna take a ride?"

It was as if the three were on some sort of secret undercover foreign agent mission. They'd done this before. It had been a few years back but it was a similar plight, revenge on someone by killing the person's beloved horse. What they planned on doing was against the law and they could go to jail if they got caught. The threesome pulled it off the last time and saved a horse and owner from distress. Eventually the horse and owner were reunited and both were grateful and safe.

The trio made plans to become criminals, horse thieves to be exact. It could be dangerous. Driving out to the property they found the broken fence where they could make their entrance and quick escape. If the horse cooperated it would be fast and easy. If the horse didn't want to go with them and load into a trailer they could be in trouble. The last time it took them a few minutes to load the horse. But they got a clean getaway. They drove the horse to a private property well hidden in case someone came looking at the rescue facility.

They all met that evening in different vehicles with two different trailers. Sitting in the heavy tree-laden path, they watched the house for the lights to go off. Kate slinked closer to the house to see if she could see into the windows. Reporting back, she said that she could see a shirtless man in his mid-thirties drinking a beer.

Giving her a confused look, Debbie said "Kate how close did you get? Now we'll be arrested for being peeping toms or whatever they call people today for looking in other peoples windows."

Kate giggled. "They have oversized kitchen windows and he has all the lights on in the house. I got a look at the guy. He's a scrawny little weasel-looking ass. I could take him myself."

"Kate, you're turning weird on me." Debbie said.

Hank just chuckled at the two women. "I'm going back to the trucks. Give me the small flashlight. Be sure to signal me with yours when you are close."

All three nodded. They waited for the lights to go off in the house. The man inside was pacing the room. They could see he was not going to sleep early. As they crept around the barn to see if they could find the horse, Debbie fell over a bag of feed. To them it sounded like the barn was falling. Looking toward the house, they saw that he didn't come out. Kate whispered, "Watch where you're going."

Debbie whispered back, "Can you see where you're going? This place is total darkness." They shuffled their feet along the dirt aisle. They kept the small flashlight low to the ground to get a glimpse inside each stall. Debbie had her hand on Kate's back so she wouldn't trip over her. Kate came to a quick halt. "Oh my God. Debbie we have a monster here. Look at this." She held the small flashlight. Starting at the bottom of the dirt stall. The light glowed on a very large hoof, slowly skimming up the leg of the horse, to his chest, neck and finally his head. He was staring back at the two women. Both of them gasped and said "Look at the size of him." The horse snorted at them and stepped closer. They both looked up at the enormous animal. Kate and Debbie both slumped down, kneeling on the ground.

"Debbie, that's not a horse, that's an elephant." Both slowly rose to look over the stall again at the horse.

"Kate that's a draft horse. Don't know what kind, but how are we going to hid a horse that size. He has to be at least eighteen hands and weigh at the very least twelve hundred pounds. He won't fit in the trailer. Shit! what are we going to do?" Both started uncontrollably giggle. Both ladies couldn't stop laughing at the sight of the horse, and the predicament they were in. Barely able to breathe because of laughing. And with tears running down her face, Kate said. If we keep him, I'm going to call the beer people. He could be their poster horse for pulling small buildings. They both hysterically laughed at the situation they were in.

Debbie could hardly get the words out. "AND. We wonder why we get into trouble. This will go into the memory file forever."

Eventually calming down, Debbie walked to the front of the barn. She crouched down to see if the man inside was still up and walking around. Looking into the kitchen windows she could see him moving around. She stooped over and walked to Kate sitting on the ground in front of the stall.

"He's still up and moving around. I say let's try to go for it. He could be up all night and if he wants he could walk out here and get it over and done with. Debbie whispered. "Here is his halter and lead rope. Can you go in and try to put it on?"

Kate gave her a questionable look and asked, "How do you expect me to put this thing on him, you got a ladder?" Sliding into the stall the horse started to nervously move about. Kate tried to reach up to easily slide on the halter but he refused to lower his head. "Come big guy, shhhhh, we got to get you out of here." She slipped her hand into her pocket and pulled out a few forage treats. Putting them to his mouth, he gladly took them. She was able to reach up and shove the halter over his head. Buckling it, she reached over the stall door and flung the lead over the door hitting Debbie in the head. "Hey, what are you doing Kate?" Looking over the door Kate had her hand on the bottom of his jaw."Let's go with this monster." Debbie pulled the lead rope, and as the horse started to step out he came to a dead stop. He wasn't moving."Come on buddy, now is not the time. We could get shot." Debbie pulled on the rope again. The horse wouldn't budge. Kate walked around and she grabbed the rope along with Debbie and pulled. The horse pulled his head up and both ladies went to the ground. The horse backed into his safe stall. Sitting up on the ground Debbie said. "He doesn't want to come. Got any ideas?"Kate shook her head no. She fumbling in her pocket she pulled out a few of the forage treats. Putting them to the horse's mouth, she was able to coax him out and follow the treat. She gave him one and made him follow her to get her out of the barn. Debbie held onto the rope. She whispered, "Let's hope he doesn't take off flying when we get to the door. Kate grabs the other side of his halter." Quickly and quietly they made their escape with the monstrous horse. Both invariably turned to watch the house. Neither one would admit it but they were frightened. Moving as fast as they could without suggesting to the horse to start to trot, they would never be able to keep up with him. Half way across the path the horse stopped again. Refusing to move he flung the ladies into each other. Debbie rolled and grabbed the rope. Kate jumped up and tried to grasp at the halter. They pulled at him as hard as they could. The horse would not move a foot further. "Kate do you think you could get on him? Maybe with you on his back he would move with you giving him commands." Kate's patience was running low. "Debbie how in the hell do you expect me to get on him. Again, do you have a ladder? Oh wait, I'm sure there is a step. Should we walk up to the door and ask the guy inside, let's see what do we say? Oh how about, Sir, we're stealing your horse. Could you help us with our undetected getaway? Debbie get real. Normally I love your sarcasms, but, not when it's directed at me. It's only funny when it's someone else." she hissed. Debbie laughed at her friend. She knew when Kate had enough. Her sarcasm was loud and clear. "NO! I will get down and you can step on my back. Or put your leg in my hand." Just as they were about to try it, they saw the outside light on the house glow, illuminating the entire front of the property like the middle of the day. They could see the guy come out looking around. Stepping forward he started to walk around. The three froze in place. With the bright light they could see him. However, they were shielded by the dark. Neither one moved.

He yelled to the barn, "Tiny, enjoy your last few hours. You will be a mound in the back pasture. We'll see how she does without you." He turned and walked back into the house and turned off the brilliant light.

In unison both said, "Ohhh, Tiny."

Debbie stroked his strong neck. "That fits a horse the size if a Clydesdale named Tiny. That's about the same as naming a black horse Ivory. Now Tiny will you walk? Did you hear him? You may not understand it but we are trying to save your life. Now walk, dammit. Kate do you want to try getting on him?"

Debbie will you stop your stress babbling?

Kate shrugged her shoulders. "I guess so, I just don't know how. Neither one of us is tall enough."

Debbie cupped her hands. "Come on, put your foot in."

Kate grabbed onto his long mane. Putting her foot into Debbie's hand she attempted to pull herself up. At that very moment Tiny lowered him himself. His head bowed down and his front legs folded under him.

They were stunned with what they were seeing. He was trained to lower himself for his owner to get on him. Kate and Debbie got on his back. He rose up and they walked him to the open fence to make their getaway. Once they passed the heavy brush, they made it to the waiting trailer.

Hank stood there for a few seconds with his mouth open in awe of the horse. Once they reached the open trailer they slid off the giant horse. He easily walked into the trailer. Closing the door became a problem. His back end was too big, he was too long for the trailer. Debbie climbed in to try and turn his head to the side so he could move up. She laid hay on the floor. Tiny moved in just enough to get the trailer door closed.

Hank looked at the animal. "That's a big horse. He has to eat tons of food."I'll bet he fills a stall full of manure."

Debbie said. "Let's go!" We have to get this monster to the sanctuary before it gets light out." Driving down the back road slowly so as to not make any commotion to attract anyone's attention, they headed straight to the Sanctuary to hide him.

The Sanctuary was owned by two ladies. They had owned horses for many years but as they and the horses got older they just took in as foster people for horses. They also helped out the Sheriff's office hiding horses for cases like this. Debbie and a few people knew where the place was. From the road you would never know there were forty-five acres and a ten stall barn. It stayed well hidden for a reason. It was a sanctuary and would be a safe haven for any animal who was there for protection Tiny would be safe there.

Debbie took all the back roads to get there. She called when they were about fifteen minutes away. One or both, of the ladies would meet them at the gate. The two hour ride and being up all night was starting to wear on both Kate and Debbie. The adrenaline rush had worn off and both are fatigued. The call to announce their arrival was made and both ladies met them at the heavy gate.

Pulling the secret load into the property, they backed the trailer to the pasture gate as they were directed. There was hay waiting for the horse. Once they opened the trailer door, without problems backed himself out. He looked lost, confused. He didn't have any idea why this was happening to him. Kate walked him to the water bucket and he drank from it. He walked over to the hay on the ground. The other horses grouped around at the edge of the fence in their neighbor pasture. They were curious about the new arrival.

Hugs as greetings for the exhausted ladies, in addition two oversized mugs of hot coffee. With a wide smile on her face, Suzie, the older of the two ladies, said, "If this is the only way I can get the two of you to visit I will find more horses to rescue."

Kate looked around as she took a large gulp of the hot coffee. "The place looks great. You made nice changes. Love the new fencing."

Peggy, the other lady was smaller and much more petite with white hair. "Kate, wait until you see the new room we built. Now we have a place to sleep when we have to spend nights out here. Come on, I'm proud of it. We did most of it ourselves except for the plumbing and electric." She laughed. "Yup, we thought we were smart enough in the beginning to try it ourselves and found out we are not plumbers or electricians. Damn near drowned and fried ourselves. Best to leave some things up to the pros. "Kate put her arm around Peggy. "Come on, show me the new addition. I need a bathroom and to get out of the heat." All four ladies walked into the barn and as they entered they faced a full wall mural of running horses. The place looked like an old time saloon. With a bar stool resembling a horse saddle sitting at the edge of the kitchen area, the sink was an old copper tub, old distressed leather chairs and a sleeper sofa scattered around the room. The woodwork surrounding the room was from old barn board. The floor even creaked as they walked across. The refrigerator looked like it came from the nineteen-forties. The walls were covered with painted horse pictures. Old refurbished lanterns replaced modern lamps. It was a room where people could kick off their boots and relax. The only modern item in the room was the fifty-two inch television.

Debbie looked around the room in awe. "Suzie, Peggy, the room is beautiful. You both did a great job. Can I move in?" Everyone laughed.

They all relaxed in the comfortable chairs and discussed the story about the night before. It seemed funny now while they relived the event.

"The owner will be picking up the horse tomorrow. I gave her your number for you to meet with them." Debbie said. "I didn't tell anyone where you are. I know how important it is to keep your place a secret. Peggy offered another drink to the ladies. "We know you're always good for that. It's never a worry."They all sat and talked for the next few hours. Debbie and Kate said their good-byes. They had a two hour drive home.

# Chapter 15

A few weeks later the heavy afternoon rains continued. The pastures were flooded. The property was covered with mud and water saturated the ground. Many of the horses were getting edgy staying in their stalls for any length of time. Debbie mentioned to the volunteers that the barn needed to be re-organized, if anyone was interested. Opening up the heavy sliding door to the tack room, with her hands on her hips she let out a heavy sigh. "Where do I start?" She walked up to the tallest plastic grey shelves pulling junk off the shelves. Like an avalanche the items all fell to the floor. A few of the ladies walked in to help.

Laughing at the mess, everyone started to join in to help. Someone turned on the radio and everyone was either dancing to the music or going along with the rhythm. The tack room was loaded with junk and had a musty smell lingering. Separating useful items from junk, the mounds grew. Lined up on the floor were saddles, English and Western. A few had the horns broken off, leather splitting at the seams. The underside of the saddle, where there should have been soft cushioning to protect the horses back were shredded and in parts missing. A few saddles were in perfect shape, they needed to be cleaned, and nonetheless they were useable. The next step was separating items to be cleaned from the ones to be repaired or tossed into the garbage. Everyone in the room started to sneeze from the dust swirling in the air. The musty air transformed into a sweet fragrance of flowers while the cleaning continued. Someone would reach to the top shelves pulling off a heavy box and once it was opened the person would say. "Oh wow, look at this". Everyone would stop to rummage around the contents. One box in particular stopped everyone in their tracks. Instead of the "oh wow", they heard a light voice say, "You should see this". All the workers stopped to examine the contents. It was a memory box of horses and volunteers who were the original people and animals before it was taken over by the foundation. As they pulled out old pictures they were all passed around. Photos were taken of every horse brought in. Pictures of volunteers with the horses and the old barn. Memories kept in a cardboard box shoved in a corner. Debbie picked up the box and moved it toward the door. She said with a sigh," That's sad that wonderful memories are shoved in a corner and forgotten."

The volunteer who pulled the box off the shelf offered a suggestion. "Why don't we have a wall of fame? I have an old shelf stuck in my garage. I will clean it up, paint it, and we can put this out for everyone to see." Debbie, along with everyone in the room, agreed, and another one offered to help. Debbie made a suggestion that she would like to have every horse, donkey, whatever brought in to have their picture taken with their story. Jean, one of the ladies cleaning the room, raised her hand in the air. "Oh, oh I have an idea. Listen to this. Let me take the pictures, make a memory book to have on the shelf and add them to our web site. I can do that, is it ok?" Laughing at the grown woman with her hand in the air Debbie said, "Jean we're not in class. You can lower your hand and you can do whatever you want. I think a memory cove just outside this room would be a perfect place." The next few hours flew by with everyone soaked from the heavy humidity hanging in the air. Shelves were cleaned, all the saddles hung up with halters, bridles, blankets and saddle pads. Plastic bags were filled with winter blankets to be washed. Other plastic bags had saddle pads which were going to the laundry with the blankets. The leather halters and bridles were bundled together to be cleaned. In the wheelbarrow were items to be thrown away or taken apart and used as bits and pieces to repair other tack. A few of the ladies were given objects if they thought they could be used. Much of the double tack would be given to another rescue or if it was nice enough it would be sold at the yearly rummage sale. It took them four hours to clean the one tack room. Walls were brushed down, floors scrubbed and everything organized.  With her hands on her hips, Debbie grinned. "This is the cleanest this room has ever been. If anyone can use some of this stuff, please take it home or put it in your lockers. I will ask if anyone would be willing to clean some of the tack. But as for today, we are done. Thank you everyone." A few of the volunteers left and the rest stayed to feed. The following days were busy with horses leaving and it gave them a chance to lighten the load. A few of the horses needed their annual and semi-annual shots. The hay bin was cleaned out, tack room scrubbed. The barn was having a nice make-over.  Debbie and Kate walked around the barn admiring the work they had accomplished.

"Kate, what do you think about rearranging some of the barn, with older horse's together, younger ones across the aisle, all mares on the other end of the barn. In the center we can put all new ones as a way to keep an eye on them until they adjust to their new surroundings. Kate agreed to the idea. "As long as some of the mares don't start kicking at each other and the younger ones don't bother the older horses. I have a suggestion. Why not put the mares across from the older ones. They will keep them quiet. Let the younger ones have the whole other end."Debbie agreed that it made sense to her. She loved to change things up. It kept things new and fresh for her. They both started to clean the empty stalls and move the horses around. It was all trial to see if it would work. Debbie and Kate left for the evening. Hank was watching TV and had his flashlight in his hand. After he watched the news he would take the manure spreader out and it was his way of checking on the property before he was in for the night.It was the calm before the storm. Debbie arrived in the morning and found four horses wandering the front property. She saw Hank standing away from the horses with his arms across his chest. As Debbie got out of her car looking at Hank, he raised his arms as if saying "I have no idea where they came from." "Let's get some hay and see if we can round them up. Pasture five is good. Can you get the cart, Hank, and I will try from the left if you come around from the rear. Let me make a trail of hay." Hank nodded and jumped into the motorized cart. Debbie had a few flakes of hay to entice them. Dropping bits of hay as she walked, one horse started to follow the hay trail. Another one wandered away. Hank drove up and Debbie yelled, "Yea, come on, go on". Excitedly waving her arms at the other three they calmly just looked at her like she was crazy. They continued to graze and nibble at the grass around them. Hank circled the horses, however, they didn't move for him and his loud cart. Debbie shook her head and laughed. "Well, I guess we can't move them. Let's see if we can get halters around them to lead them in." In the barn Debbie mumbled to herself, "Thankfully we cleaned this up, I can find stuff now." She walked back out toward Hank and the horses. As they both cautiously approached the small herd, Debbie, with a reassuring voice, attempted to approach the horses."Shhh, shhh, its ok, kids." As soon as she raised her arm to position the halter over one of the horses head it kicked up dirt, both legs kicking wildly and ran off. Hank let the one horse go and he tried the small horse close to him. That horse did the same thing. He side-stepped back and away from it. He was so close to the irrational horse that he could feel the breeze from the kick. Debbie yelled to Hank. "Watch yourself." He nodded but said nothing. The rest of the horses mimicked the action of the kicking horses and running off to follow them. Watching the horses graze they knew they couldn't leave them out. The other horses would be walking in the area to their pastures and they didn't have information on the new ones. "Let's leave them until more help arrives I think if they get hungry enough they might come in." She looked at Hank with a question in her voice. "Let's hope?" Hank walked into the barn and started to feed. Debbie followed him in and helped. Eventually a few of the volunteers arrived. The group walked out to the grazing horses. Hank led the group and in unison they all started to wave their arms over their heads, running and yelling at the horses to round them up. Slowly they were able to herd the horses into the back pasture to keep them in one area. All the horses walked around and contentedly grazed on the tall wet grass. A few of the volunteers returned to the new herd to see if they could get close to them. One small white mare allowed Lucy, one of the volunteers, to approach her. She accepted a few treats and permitted her to touch her neck. The other horses watched the interaction of the two. Lucy was wary of the horse and it was obvious the horse felt the same for her. Keeping her hands behind her back, Lucy stood in silence next to the mare. Both tested each other to see how close they could get. Lucy stepped back and the mare followed her. As the mare moved in closer Lucy raised her hand in the air and set it there. This confused the mare and yet she found this intriguing. As Lucy lowered her hand the horse stepped back away. She raised her hand again in the air and let it sit. This encounter continued for almost an hour. Slowly the horse would go to her hand and inhale her scent. The trust was installed with both Lucy and the horse. She permitted her to set the halter around her and the two walked to the quarantine barn. Just as they entered the barn Lucy turned to the group and hollered while pointing to the white mare. "Get me the adoption papers. This one is mine and her name is Mara that's Polish for ghost." Everyone laughed and the rest imitated Lucy's hand in the air process with the other horses. It didn't work for them. Using their own initiative they each found a way to capture the horses. Later that afternoon Jerri came out to exam each of the horses. Later she told Debbie that they all appeared healthy. She would know more after the blood tests came back. The ladies said good-bye and both went in different directions. With the commotion of the day settling down, Debbie strolled out to visit one of the older horses. Ellie, a small bay mare, was a permanent and oldest resident of the rescue. She had come in with a woman whose husband was breeding her too much. The mare was a baby maker. The wife felt sorry for the horse. When she wasn't being bred, he used her for kids to ride on. He was a hard man and mean to his horses. They argued about his callous treatment of the horses. Finally, she couldn't take it anymore and turned the horses into the rescue and called the Animal Control office. She reported him and served him with divorce papers the same day. He had four horses and he mistreated them as much as he mistreated his wife. In the end she won and he lost the farm, wife, kids, and all of his money. Debbie spent extra special time with Ellie because she wasn't pretty anymore. Her bones were weak and she couldn't be ridden and was at times cranky. Debbie always paid special attention to Ellie nobody seemed to want her because of her frail condition. They were good friends, Debbie would walk her out and down the road for exercise, groom her, and they seemed to understand each other. Ellie would never allow Debbie to show any unhappy emotion. The Mare could read Debbie's emotions. She was like an old best friend who knew a person better then they knew themselves. Debbie would walk Ellie down the road to get her off the property and they would walk and talk about everything. Many people knew Ellie. She had become the rescue staple. That day they were walking the dirt road Debbie could hear the grunting sounds of a group of wild hogs. As the two walked Debbie saw the hoof impression from the hogs. They must have been just ahead of them on the road. Debbie could feel her fear of the hogs coming to the surface. She knew they could overtake her and Ellie if they felt threatened. Their strong and destructive tusks could pierce them both. Ellie brought her head to the ground, sniffing the scent of the hogs. Unexpectedly Ellie dropped to the ground, rolling and rubbing her back on the hogs' scents. This surprised Debbie and she understood what the horse was doing. She wanted to take the fear away and unpleasant reminder of the hogs away. Leaving her sweet scent on the road in their place. She watched the horse roll and slowly get up from the ground. "Ellie, you're gonna hurt yourself acting like a conqueror of all that smells evil. Come on, let's go back home. You can save the day at the barn, not here on the road."

The pair turned around to walk back. Debbie loved walking the shadowy road with the canopied trees. The road always seemed a bit ominous at times. The fragrance of the foliage and muffled sounds as they walked were comforting. They both casually walked the road back to the barn. Sharing more secrets with Ellie and the mare enjoying in the special attention from Debbie. Once they reached the barn Debbie took Ellie to the wash rack to scrub her down. She used a special shampoo for the horse's sore muscles. Debbie massaged her back and legs until her arms ached. Nevertheless, Debbie knew that Ellie's sore and older body throbbed with pain due to her age and over-worked life. The discomfort in Debbie's arms were nothing compared to Ellie's. The sting in her arms would recover. But Ellie's pain remained a daily reminder of her life as a beast of burden. After the bath and massage she walked Ellie to her pasture and not thirty seconds later she turned to watch Ellie roll in the dirt. Debbie groaned at her and all the hard work she had put into the horse's bath. When the rolling horse returned to her feet she shook her body shedding the sand and dust from her back. Resting her arms on the top rail of the fence Debbie laughed as she hollered back to the horse, "You can be a dirty ol' girl, if you want." Debbie returned to the tack room and replaced the shampoo and washing items. Walking into the office to check her email she suddenly realized how much work it was washing Ellie and she was wet, dirty, and tired. Kate and Lauren walked into the office. They laughed at Debbie soaking wet. Katie asked, "Who got the bath? You or Ellie? "Sure does look like me doesn't it? Debbie answered. "So what do you ladies have up your sleeves? With the look on your faces you have something to say?"Lauren opened a folder and pulled out papers. "We have the costume party planned. We want to go over a few things with you before we put this on our website and announce it to the world." Debbie acknowledged both and said, "Let me dry off and grab a sandwich out of the refrigerator. Let's sit down and see what's planned." The two ladies walked out to the patio and opened the folder, spreading papers all over the top of the table. They anchored down the plans with horseshoes to stop the wind from carrying them away. Debbie came out with a drink and sandwich in her hand. "Ok, let's hear the plans. I can see you're both excited. I have a funny feeling the horses are not going to be happy with your ideas."Lauren handed Debbie the first page. "We are going to have a costume party, with a tropical theme. We all wear

Hawaiian clothes and dress the horses up with grass skirts and floral shirts. Coconuts, flamingos, the whole tropical island theme." Debbie just sat and nodded. Katie handed out the second page, "We are having the usual food, drinks, and treats. We are going to have an area dedicated to re-sale items, we are able to add more vendors to sell stuff and they will donate a portion or rent a table. Now, with the next idea. I really need for you to keep an open mind."Debbie rolled her eyes, looking at the two ladies. "I hope you are not going to have some idiot put on demonstrations again. Remember the guy who showed up looking like the electric horseman? Lauren you weren't here but this guy shows up, he's a scrawny guy who is all dressed up. Like I said dressed in sequins and fringe. He takes one of our horses, climbs on its back, stands up on the horse's back and pulls out a gun. KABOOM! He shoots the gun. It scares the living crap out of everyone. Kids start to cry, people duck and drop to the ground. Next thing we see he pulls out a bullwhip and cracks it over his head. The poor horse stood frozen in fear. As he stands on the horse he tries to get it to walk and the poor horse refused to move. He swings the whips again just as you hear the crack the horse rears up, dropping the cowboy to the ground. One of the volunteers runs toward the horse and takes the horse away. To make matters worse the idiot is still on the ground and as he starts to get up he tries talking to the crowd how he can teach any horse to stand still and be bomb proof. He then has the nerve to yell out his phone number to all the single ladies. By this time Lee had had enough of this moron. He walks up to him, grabs him by his huge girly bling belt buckles and throws him off the property. As Lee is dragging him off three cans of beer fall out of his shirt. Then Jack runs up and grabs the guy with Lee and they threw him over the front fence. The next week our website was full of comments about how stupid the guy was and the best part of the show was when the horse threw him. We were lucky we didn't have any problems with the crowds with this guy." Kate added to the conversation. "The funniest thing he parked his truck on the side of the barn and he left food in the front seat. The barn cats got into the truck and they ate his food and made a mess of the thing. The same horse he was using kicked the side door in. Then to add insult to injury for the guy, Ed had his vehicle towed off the property. Then about two weeks later he shows up here and asks to volunteer. He then offers to clean the private parts of our horses for a fee. The two ladies standing and listening to him picked up handfuls

of manure and threw it at him. Screaming at him, calling him a pervert. He was covered with manure. After that Ed paid him a visit and issued him a restraining order to stay away from us. Lauren, do you remember the older ladies who come here during the winter? Willie and Audrey, they spend their winters in Florida. They mainly take care of our gardens. They are the lady manure throwers."
Lauren nodded, "I know who they are, they are both really funny."
Debbie raised her hand saying, "Oh wait, the story gets better. Mr. Electric cowboy goes to another rescue in Palm Beach County and tries the same thing with one of their horses. He stands on the back of the horse and as he shoots his gun, the horse takes off. He flies through the air and lands on the ground. The horse comes around and stomps him. He breaks three ribs, a shoulder and fractures his leg. He was lucky he didn't get killed. All three ladies laughed at the story. Debbie said, "Ok now what else? We have costumes and horse parade, re-sale, silent auction, music group and vendors. Did we get a water slide for the kids? Who is doing the music?"
Lauren said "I did find someone who will donate the water slide and Kate found a country western group who are really good will come and entertain for the day."
Debbie shrugged her shoulders, "If that's it? I think you've got it all. Good job ladies. What is the date for this party? "
"The second Saturday in October", Lauren answered.

# Chapter 16

Debbie spent the better part of the first week of the month checking on the adopted horses. As part of the adoption process the rescue had the legal right to check on any of the horses' welfare. The new owners had certain responsibilities or they would have to return the horse to the rescue. Debbie always arrived without notice and she would freely come onto the person's property. Over the years Debbie had found the horses in poor condition and had to take them back. All mares were not to be bred. She found a few over the years who had foals and they were removed also. Only once did they lose a horse. They never heard from the owner again. It was times like that when Debbie would worry for days and many sleepless nights. For the most part the owners were all very good and she found happy horses. The first horse she checked on was a min. The family had a mini already, but when theirs died they wanted another one for company. They greeted Debbie with hugs and proudly showed her how well the mini was doing. It was evident that the horse loved his new home and pasture mate. Both were playing with a large ball, chasing it around the pasture. The owners told stories how they both went into the pond and rolled in the water. They asked if the rescue had another mini they would like to have the first chance at adopting it. She was satisfied with what she found. She spent the day visiting with families who had adopted the horses. Pulling up to a property she could see the horse from her vehicle. The horse had lost a lot of weight. It was standing with his head in the corner of the fence. Debbie's worry radar sirens went off. She didn't stop at the door like she usually had. She walked straight to the horse. It was an older Arabian gelding that was rescued from a family who claimed the horse was mean and bit people. That was their excuse for beating the horse. They were glad to see the horse go. The new folks seemed to be perfect for the little gelding. Debbie examined the horse, worried about the weight loses. He had what looked like dog bites around his coronary bands. The wounds were treated but the rear leg was swollen and infected. As she approached the door a women came out and asked her who she was. Debbie identified herself and wanted to know what happened to the horse. The older woman was tall with white hair. She stood with her arms folded across her chest is a defensive manner.

Looking down at Debbie she said, "What you want? The horse is fine. He ran into a few of the wild dogs in the area. He's fine."

Debbie stepped onto the porch the wood creaked under her weight. She faced the defiant woman. "He's not fine. I'm Debbie and I represent Equine Rescue Me. I do house calls and check up on the adopted horses. Who are you? You're not the lady who adopted him from us. I need to speak to her."

The lady glared down at Debbie. "My name is Robin and the folks left the horse here when they moved out. We got stuck with it and it's mine now, so you can't tell me what do with it."

Debbie moved closer to Robin's face. "No the horse is mine now. I can tell you what to do. Consider yourself unstuck with the horse. I'm taking it with me, is there a problem?"

From behind the door a man appeared. He was shorter than the women with a shaggy over growth of a beard. He walked over the door threshold and stood in Debbie's face. He had a half smile and said, "I heard her tell you the horse stays and it's her horse. Get the hell off my property or I'll help you off."

With a deep breath Debbie looked the man straight in the eyes. Her face was within inches of his face. Her arms tight against her body, "Listen here Mr. Robin, the horse leaves with me. I'll be off your property in minutes. Get back from my face, little man. I run the show here with my horse. We can do this only one way. From what I see the horse is neglected and that will bring legal charges against the two of you. I can take the horse and be gone. How do you want to do this?"

The man stepped even closer to Debbie. Looking down at him she had an urge to start laughing.. She could feel the giggle start to rise inside her. Refusing to move back from him, she looked up at the women and kept her defiant stance at the door.

Looking down at him, without laughing she had to keep herself firm with this. "Listen, by the way what's your name Mr. Robin?"

He scowled at her. "My name is Paul. Robin is my wife's name. You sure are stupid calling a guy his wife's name."

"Paul, the horse is going with me. We can pretend you won the fight and gave me the horse, ok? Or I can call the police and they will have you both in court on animal cruelty charges. I'm getting tired of this and I'm going to walk away." Debbie couldn't help but start to laugh.

The woman at the door moved onto the porch. "Hey, can I keep the horse, he's not a bad thing. We just can't afford much food for him."

Debbie started to soften and said, "I saw the amount of beer in the refrigerator in the barn. If you can afford that much beer you can afford feed for him. I can see you chose the beer over feeding him. Sorry, he comes with me." She looked back at the man defiantly standing with a smirk on his face. "By the way, you really do drink some shit beer, but then the beer fits the person." He mumbled under his breath. Debbie returned with a smirk. "I'm a bitch when it comes to these horses. You will never win with me," and walked away. She loaded the horse into the small trailer and left the property. Once she was down the road she pulled over and started to laugh. She couldn't help but laugh at the two of them. Recalling the event she couldn't wait to get the barn and tell everyone what happened. For now the small gelding was safe and would be taken care of. No more beer baths or whatever they did. She drove back to the barn with her new guest.

As the two pulled around to the back to unload a few of the volunteers wandered over to help. Debbie opened the trailer door and the horse backed himself out as if he knew he was in a happy place. Everyone turned around when they heard a voice yell, "Chance, Chance! Let me see him".

 A volunteer named Edie ran up to the horse. She put her arms around his neck and hugged him. He knew her, and he responded to her like an old friend. Little did anyone know they were old friends. Debbie looked at the horse again and said, "Chance? I never would have recognized him. He is so thin and his mane is cut. His coat is dark grey from the dirt.  This isn't the name they had for him. They called him Kimball or something like that?"

Debbie handed the lead rope to Edie and let her walk Chance to the medical barn. She unhooked the trailer and parked her truck. She wanted to tell everyone what happened with the former owners of Kimball who was really Chance. She knew Chance would be fat and happy again. Her day was done and she felt that she had made a difference in one horse's life today.

One her ride home Debbie was thinking about a nice glass of wine and a refreshing soak in the pool. Her phone rang and interrupted her wine and pool plans.

Debbie didn't answer with a friendly hello, the caller ID told her who was calling. "Hey Maddie, I know why you're calling. I read in the newspaper we have our first horse auction on Thursday night. I will round up the crew and meet at your place." She hung up as she reached her driveway. Debbie had one thing on her mind and that was to float in the pool with a glass of wine. Lee came home at the same time and the first thing out of his mouth was, "I see we have our first action tomorrow night. You ready? I found four young guys who work for me. They want to help. They are built like football linebackers. Jack and I are getting old and we need more muscle."Debbie heard him and this was nothing new for either one of them. The horse auction brought kill-buyers. These sleazy guys bought horses at the auction. They sold them to a group who slaughtered horses for their meat. This group will sell the horse meat on the side of the road. The Anti-Slaughter group went to the auctions to stop the kill-buyers from making any purchases. Everyone had a job to do. Debbie followed the kill-buyer, and when he sat down she pulled out a sign with an arrow that read: KILL-BUYER. She sat behind or near him and pointed him out to the auctioneer and everyone in the auction. Once he was found someone else took his picture. They followed him around and kept him busy. The buyers got nervous when the anti-slaughter group showed up. The group understood that they ran a high risk of getting hurt. Kate hung around the horse pens. After the buyer made his purchase she removed the horses and met with another person in the group.  They took the horse and put them in a trailer hidden somewhere. While the kill buyer was in the auction Lee and Jack unhooked the buyers trailer, flattened his tires and disabled his vehicle. The young guys who were the muscle for the group took care of the entourage the buyer brought for his protection. The buyers were referred to as KB's. Pictures of the buyers were posted on the Internet. Animal Control and other Anti-Slaughter groups kept the pictures to identify the men. In the past it had gotten messy and dangerous. The buyers wanted to make money and the anti-slaughter group works hard to make them lose money. Last year one the buyers got away from them. He had four horses in his trailer. The group lost him at the auction. As luck would have it, the truck and trailer had broken down. He ran out of gas and the gas cap was super glued shut. Jack, Lee, and a few of the guys found him broke down on the side of the road. They pulled over to offer him help. Lee opened the guy's hood and removed the battery cables. The others unloaded the horses from his trailer and transferred them into theirs trailer. The buyer pulled a gun on the men, but they took the gun away from him as they all had their own weapons. Lee and Jack told him, "KB you brought a knife to a gun fight. You lose." His gun ended up in the swamp. A few of the KB's bring their own muscle and the group had in the past been shot at, windows blown out and tires slashed. The Anti-Slaughter group had their own tactics. They purchased used, old vehicles, such as pickup trucks, vans and a SUV. The tags on the vehicles were old expired tags from different States. They had one from Nebraska, Kansas, and Wisconsin. This prevented the kill- buyers from being able to track the group down through their license plates. They attached the license plates to their vehicles after they get to the auction. Everyone was dressed in disguise to avoid being recognized and having their picture plastered somewhere. It was a serious game without rules. Thursday night everyone met at the Anti-Slaughter office. The women changed their clothes. Some looked foolish, they had pants that didn't match the shirt or shoes. They all wore wigs and were heavy with the makeup. It was like Halloween. Everyone got into a vehicle to the auction. The back entrance was always closed, but they knew how to get through the gate. Everyone scattered in different directions. When someone found the KB they notified everyone on their cell phones. The women worked the auction and the men stood guard. The younger guys Lee brought stayed close to the ladies. Jack and a few other men went to hunt for the KB's trailer. Usually someone saw them come in. The call for the auction to begin sounded and the horses were being escorted to the center ring. Debbie found her man right away. She crawled over the bleachers. She pulled out her sign with the arrow. She stood directly behind him with the sign reading KILL BUYER - HORSES TO SLAUGHTER. People in the arena started to point at him, take pictures of him and started yelling to kick him out. He figured it out right away. He turned around to see Debbie holding the sign. He tried to get up and leave but on each side of him was one of Lee's big boys. This gave Debbie time to get out. The KB got up after the boys left. He moved to another area. They let him make a buy. He paid three-hundred dollars for a good looking warm blood. The horse was stocky and had nice muscle. It was only about five years old. The group waited for him to pay for the horse, and lead him to the kill pen. When he walked away Kate took the horse. She led it to the back door where another person took the horse and loaded it on a waiting trailer. They let the buyer make another purchase and then took that horse. When he came back and found another horse gone he knew that they were around somewhere. He knew that he had to get out with the one horse. People pointed at him and made comments about him being a horse killer. Just as he was about to load the horse into the trailer a couple of younger men approached him. The younger of the two wanted the horse he had for his little girl. The buyer outbid him. The three men started to argue and the man with the horse turned to get out when he could. The horse was loaded in the trailer and the truck wouldn't start. Sounded like battery problems for those standing around. One of the young linebackers opened his hood to offer his services. Looking around the hood he said, "Yup, sir you have a battery problem. Let me see if I can help."

The man refused his help. He knew what was going on, he'd been this route before. He didn't want to lose the horse he had. This one would bring in a nice amount of money. The butchers paid per pound for the horse. The one younger man stood at the truck door leaning on it. He was trying to have a nice conversation with the nervous buyer trapped in his. Maxi came around opened the trailer door, climbed into the trailer and backed the horse out. She handed the horse to the man who wanted him for her daughter. She told him to get going. Her buddies would follow him out and get the horse home safe.

The man was stunned. He didn't know what to say except, "Thank you, thank you. What do I owe you?"

Maddie returned a smile. "If you want to help take care of the horse, and we can always use people to help with this."

The two men left with their horse. Maddie walked up to the truck window. She tapped on it for him to lower the window. His window wouldn't go down. He didn't have any power to open it. He opened the door and looked at her.

She smiled. "Listen you lost over a thousand dollars tonight. We are going to continue screwing you until you and your buddies stop killing horses."

He looked at her with a grin on his face. "Fuck you and when I get home, I'm going to fry myself up a nice horse burger, bitch."

Maddie just smiled at him and walked away. While he was stuck in his truck the boys took his tires off the truck, pulled the wiring from under the hood. They took his trailer too. Everyone got back into the vehicles, high-five all around. The wigs came off, the honest license tags replaced. It was a good successful night for the organization. Back at the office everyone cleaned up, shared a beer and laughed that for once they had achieved a victory. They all knew too many times they had lost. While they saved these horses that night, there were many who traveled to their final destination to spend their last hours in terror as they watched other horses being slaughtered. Maddie had been with the anti-horse slaughter group for many years. Each time she attended an auction memories of her worst attempted recovery of a horse in central Florida returned. The kill-buyer named Norman purchased a horse. She followed him in her truck attempting to single-handedly stop him. He knew he was being followed. And he pulled into a deserted road. He stopped, jumped out of his truck. Fearlessly she jumped out of her truck facing him. He had his gun pointed at her. He told her to stop following him. Maddie told him that she was taking the horse. As he pointed the gun at her he said, "Bitch, I'm going to teach you a lesson. Don't fuck with me." Just as he said those words he pointed the gun and shot the horse in the head. The horse made a groan and there was a heavy thud as its body dropped, shaking the trailer. Maddie was stunned, and froze from shock from what she had just witnessed. Her stomach churned, she tried to scream but nothing came out. As she started to fall to the ground Norman raised his other arm and knocked her down. As she picked up her head she faced the glazed eyes of the dead horse. Blood streamed out of the side of the trailer. Her hand touched the blood and she griped her fist with the bloodied hand. Norman walked to open the trailer door to try and pull the horse out. He wrapped a heavy chain around its back legs. Unhooking the trailer he pulled the truck to the back of the open trailer door. Taking the chain and attaching it to the front bumper Norman got back into his truck dragging the dead horse onto the dirt road. He walked up to the crumpled women, and with a hard yank on her arm he pulled her to where the horse lay. He tossed her like a rag doll on top of the horse's body. With his hand he pushed her face into the horse and said. "Next time, bitch, you're going to be dead, understand me?" She nodded her head. Exhausted, and powerless to fight back she laid her head down on top of the dead horse, sobbing.

Blood from the horse covered her.

Meanwhile, Norman attached his trailer to the truck and drove off. Totally drained she could barely stand to go to her car to call for help. While waiting on the pitch dark road she stroked the dead horse's neck. Heavy uncontrollable sobs echoed into the desolate sky. She begged for forgiveness from the horse. "I failed you, I'm sorry, I can't fix this. I'm so sorry, sorry, sorry." She wasn't sure how long she knelt next to the horse. She could see a set of headlights racing toward her with police lights trailing the lead vehicle. Her husband Mark ran up to her, saw her covered with blood and assumed that she was hurt. She nodded her head no, pointing to the dead horse. The police officer ran to assist the couple and investigate the mess. Helping her up they could see more vehicles racing down the road in a cloud of dust. The group helped remove the horse from the road. Maddie sat in her van and answered the officer's questions. She never identified Norman, knowing full well she would retaliate; this wasn't over for her. Mark drove her to the hospital to make sure she wasn't hurt. The emotional damage overpowered the physical. Knowing his wife, Norman would see her again and he knew who would be on the losing end next time. He had always worried about her and these dirt bags mixing it up and it had finally happened. He vowed she would never do this alone. Concerned the next time she would be found dead on the side of the road. He loved his wife and she would never face another creep alone again. The following week he purchased hand guns and they received concealed weapon permits.

All too soon Maddie was able to get her revenge on Norman. She spotted him at a bar. He had on his cowboy hat, fancy boots, expensive jeans, and was liquored up. Poor Norman never saw her coming. He walked outside to have a smoke and she put her gun in his back and told him to walk away. She directed him to a heavily treed area. A full moon peeked through the trees, just enough light for them to look each other in the eyes. Norman knew who he was facing. While they walked she said to him, "Revenge is a bitch Norman. It's not what you did to me, this is for the horse you killed." Pulling out her pink taser, she ordered him to turn around. The last thing he felt was the zzzapp touching his groin. Norman fell backward unable to move. She zapped him again in the same area. He groaned and begged her to stop.

"No, sorry Norman, this will hurt you more than me and after this, the war will stop between us. You murdered a horse and in my heart that is justification for revenge. But it will stop now or the next time I will use my gun".

As she looked down at the ground she saw a small fire ant mound. She quickly grabbed a handful of fire ants and pulled open his jeans and threw them down the front of his pants. He screamed in pain as the ants fiercely bit him. He struggled to take his pants off but he was still having horrific spasms from the taser She gave him another zap from her taser. Looking down at him she said "That one was for good measure. Yup, we are done!" Walking away from him she knew it wasn't over between them. She thought to herself that she might have gone too far with the ants. No, thinking about it, all's fair. A few years later she read in the newspaper that Norman was shot in the back, hip and shoulder trying to steal a family's thoroughbred. He would forever remain in a wheelchair in prison.

# Chapter 17

The horse auctions slowed down. The kill buyers understood that they were not welcome. Word travels fast in the equine world. All of their pictures went viral and they went underground to let things cool off for a while. It never lasted long, someone would sooner or later surface. Debbie and Kate walked the barn looking at all the new horses. Some were in better shape than others. One horse didn't have any teeth. The owner had pulled them to punish the horse. He went to jail for animal cruelty. They read in the newspaper that an inmate at the jail knocked out his teeth while he waited to go to court. The horse had to have specially prepared soaked feed and forage. He recovered and enjoyed his safe life at the facility. The tropical-themed fund raiser party was upon them. All the volunteers helped with the horses' costumes. They all did a wonderful job. A group of women prided themselves in being able to sew. They reconstructed old Hawaiian shirts to fit the horses. It was ingenious how they made the shirts to fit the horses. The mares had coconut bras and grass skirts, the geldings wore their bright-flowered shirts. None of the horses objected, they enjoyed the special attention and the atmosphere was fun. The volunteers all wore Hawaiian clothing and a few matched their horses. Vendors arrived to set up the tables, items for the silent auction flowed in. The giant water slide was being set up. Various food vendors and grills were fired up. The day was going smoothly and everyone wanted it kept that way. People started to arrive and a few joined in the costume fun wearing Hawaiian clothing. Cars started to stream in. Kids jumped out running to see the horses, goats, donkeys, and the mamma pig and her babies. Debbie watched as people placed items in the donation box. Shampoo, cream rinse, bandages, fly spray, feed, it just continued to fill up the boxes. One family donated a month's worth of hay. Shaking hands, thanking everyone for coming, Debbie was happy to see it all come together. The Television trucks arrived to share the event with the community. Debbie directed the reporter to the members of the Executive Board. Television cameras panned the party. A few of the volunteers were interviewed, it was great publicity for them.  One family in particular decorated the Memorial Garden, beautiful flower blankets, bright and cheerful wreaths. The wooden crosses all had small red buds woven around them. Red hearts hung from the small fence encircling the garden. Debbie did the honors of taking visitors up to pay their respects. One rule was that no children under the age of sixteen were permitted in the area. Debbie had felt it wasn't a place to discuss death and what was buried on the land. A few placed their own keepsakes with painted horseshoes, decorated halters and stirrups encased with flowers. To see the beauty of it was overwhelming. When anyone would walk in they would whisper as if in religious reverence. These horses didn't die in vain and most important they were remembered. Lee had a wreath with bright blue flowers, small baby's breath and yellow carnations along with a small statue of a horse attached to Blu's final resting spot. One grave was still fresh, grass hadn't grown over. However, it had a full colorful flower blanket covering it. Many visitors were former horse owners or volunteers. Other visitors were very touched by the garden and strolled over to pay their respects. Those who had never visited the sacred grounds asked questions and she often watched tears roll down their cheeks as she spoke of the victims who were buried. Very few who made the silent march to the forever garden walked away without a show of emotion. Some cried openly for the souls beneath them. It was always silent, a cool breeze lightly drifted as if being respectful to not disturb anyone. It was a special peaceful place surrounded by love and admiration. After the group's visit to the garden Debbie always felt emotionally exhausted. Feeling as if her heart had been given a good thrashing. She walked to the shower area and she had to collect herself before joining the event. Lee always knew how it drained her every time they had an event and she escorted visitors to what she often referred to as God's acres. He was always ready to be the soft shoulder she needed to vent her sadness.

 Shortly after Debbie regrouped herself and joined in with the festivities. Her children arrived along with other friends. The horse parade was about to begin. Each volunteer escorted a horse though the barn doors as Ed would read the name of volunteer and horse. He would mention something about why the horse was there. Spectators applauded lightly as horse and volunteer swaggered past. As the horses paraded past the visitors many giggled at the site of the decorated horses. The television cameras documented the parade and the clicking of the photographers would show the best side of the rescue facility. The media were always generous to show the hard work done at the rescue and understood it would help.

Debbie moved to the entertainment area. She clapped and tapped her feet to the music. The silent auction continued and the vendors were doing well with the huge crowd in attendance. She went to join in the auction and check out what was for sale with the vendors. Colorful tents lined the pastures with vendors selling horse items. Decorative items for the barn and home. One sold funny fly mask, with cute faces painted on them. Another sold bright colored halters, blankets, and cute t-shits. Further down an equine dentist was giving a talk. Next to him was woman who made cute wall decoration out of horse shoes. Debbie loved her beautiful work. She made a mental note to go over to visit with her. She donated most of the money she made and added her decorated horseshoes to the silent auction or raffle.

he air was filled with the sweet smell of deep fried pastries, cotton candy, homemade fudge. The breaded hot dogs stand was busy. A new vendor made fancy non-alcohol drinks with twelve in plastic glasses. All of the containers had a horse printed on the outside and when the drink was finished the bottom of the glass revealed a small picture of a horse.

She could hear the children's voices as they ran around and climbed the water slide. Searching for the sky to see if any rain clouds were forming to drench on the bash and dissolve the fun, so far all she saw were blue skies with light fluffy clouds.

The day continued as crowds came and went. She took two more groups to the shrine and closed the door on that for the day. She couldn't emotionally do it anymore. Her heart couldn't take the pain. As the late afternoon turned into early evening the party was going strong. She knew it was going to be a late night. Watching the volunteers move through the mass of bodies impressed her. They all knew that without them none of this could function. All looked as if they were having a good time. None showed any signs of retreating, their stamina proved to be endless. Debbie joined her family for dinner and she danced with her grandchildren. Kate joined her with a secret glass of beer.

Wrinkling her nose she stated. "This is going to be a mess to clean up tomorrow. I love the parties, hate the clean up. Did you hear that we have six offers to adopt? Six more are serious considering the idea. That is awesome for one day."

Debbie raised her hand and gave Kate a hard slap of hard high-five. Drinking the cold beer felt good and she started to finally relax. "Have you checked or anyone checked on the horses lately? I will if it hasn't been done."Kate crossed her eyes as she answered Debbie. Being silly she said, "Yup boss, they have been tucked in for the night and are all safe and sound. I swear I heard a few snoring. They all were tuckered out from the excitement of the day."

Debbie returned a cross-eyed look. "Good now why are we looking at each other crossed eyed? Belly laughing, Kate motioned that she had no idea.

The bash continued well into the night with the volunteers being the last to leave. They formed their own after-party. The music had ended, which led them to bring out their own musical entertainment. One volunteer dragged a cooler over to the group. Opening it she reached in and handed everyone a beer. She raised her bottle of beer to toast everyone. "To success. We made it a success and to more successful events. Let's keep the love going at this place." The others joined in raising their bottles of beer, and clinking them to each other they all retorted with a "here, here." Each one had a story to rehash the day of what went on, what they saw and did. They were all hyped up, they wanted to plan another party. Lauren and Kate just gave each other a look and laughed. They were in no hurry to plan another affair even though this one was a wonderful success. Everyone needed time to recuperate.

Somewhere around two in the morning the last of the group left. Hugs were plentiful and it would start all over again in the morning. These types of events always brought the group closer, new friendships formed and volunteers would become more active and join in new committees. Times like this did good things for the organization as well as those who worked there. The last die-hards packed up and left. Debbie went to check on Kate, who, had crashed on the couch in the office after her second beer. Jack said he would stay the night with her.

Debbie crawled into Lee's truck, leaving her vehicle parked until tomorrow. He would drop her off in the morning. Her eyes closed during the drive home. She didn't fall asleep, but the motion of the vehicle relaxed her. Once they arrived home she jumped into her sleeping clothes and fell asleep as quickly as she put her head on the pillow.

Waking up around noon, Debbie felt like she had a hangover without the alcohol. Her feet were sore, her back ached, and she was worn out through and though. She wandered through the house with a cup of coffee finding Lee in the computer room. She barked at him, "Why didn't you wake me? I have to get to the barn to relieve Kate."

Lee turned around to face Debbie with sarcasm in his voice. "How 'bout you're tired and you needed the sleep, Jack stayed to help Kate and she had three more hours sleep than you did. You're not super woman and other people can take care of that place. I'll take you back when you can stop acting tired and cranky to prove my point you needed the sleep." Lee returned to face his computer. Debbie spun around and walked away. Pulling out a chair on the patio she thought how she shouldn't have jumped down Lee's throat like that. She owned him an apology but right now she was too lazy to get up. Admitting to herself she was tired, too drained to move at that split second. She would apologize later he would forgive her, he always did.

As the day wore on Debbie sat on the patio, and she didn't move much. She realized that she was not going anywhere that day. If there was a problem at the barn they would call her. She was assured of that. She also was positive that she had quality people who could take over for her for one day. Debbie moved from the patio chair to the lounge chair in the pool. There she floated as the water pump drifted the floating lounge.

After dinner, which consisted of box of readymade chicken, Debbie moved to the computer room to check her email. On her way she found Lee in the garage working on their old lawn mower which would be taken to the rescue.

She tapped him on the back. "Hey, I'm sorry about being a bitch earlier. Didn't mean it."

Lee learned down and kissed her. "I know you're tired and I worry about you getting burned out or sick. You need to learn to slow down, you're useless to anyone if you get sick."

Smiling back at him she said. "I know, you're right. I'm on my way to check my email. You need anything?" Lee shook his head no. "Goodnight, honey."

Opening her email she discovered nothing exciting to read. She grabbed her half-read book and went to bed.

# Chapter 18

Thinking she was dreaming, Debbie heard her phone ringing. Her ringer sounded like an old-time phone. She rolled over to answer, but before she could say hello she heard a hysterical female voice. "Debbie, she beat Pepper, it's on a social media site. A trainer was videotaped whipping the horse. Debbie, we need to save Pepper... " With authority in her tone and talking over the hysterical voice. Debbie said, "Who is this? Who is Pepper? What the hell is going on? Calm down, I can't understand a word you're saying."The voice on the phone calmed down enough to talk. Her sobs continued. "This is Lana. I watched on a media site a women beat a horse. I recognized it as Pepper, you remember him?" Putting her arm on her knee as she sat up in bed, Debbie nodded. She interrupted the weeping voice. "Ok Lana, did you recognize the trainer and where this happened? Did you get a name? Can you meet me at the barn?" With a surprised look she heard her say that she was at the barn. Debbie jumped out of bed. Grabbed a pair of dirty jeans and t-shirt lying on the floor, she struggled to dress and run out the door. Lee followed immediately behind her. He was going to drive. She couldn't be trusted driving with her state of mind. Both layered their clothes over their pajama's. Barefooted and with groggy heads they were in the truck and heading to the barn. Debbie told Lee what she had heard over the phone. It might have been the fog from sleep but she couldn't remember who Lana was. Throughout the trip Debbie repeated over and over to Lee to drive faster. He ignored her commands and sped down the road. Eventually they reached the barn. Before he could stop the vehicle she jumped out and Lana flew out of the barn. Both women ran into each other almost knocking the other to the ground. Lee calmly walked behind them. Seeing Lana he said, "You need to calm down. This situation will be taken care of." He knew that his words were not being heard. Lana was still upset, her face was wet from tears, and her red flaming cheeks glowed. Once she saw Lana she knew who she was. She reached for her hands. "Lana calm down show me what you saw. Come on, let's calm down, we will get Pepper away from this bitch." Dragging Debbie into the office she saw her computer running on a social network. Lana slid her hand over the computer mouse and clicked it. The blank screen opened to a video showing exactly what she said had happened. Debbie started to fill with anger. They helplessly watched this female trainer as she took a whip to the horse and backed the confused animal into a wire fence. His head waved in the air, his eyes bulged. He fought to stay on his feet as she continued to whip the horse. His hind legs gave way and buckled. Falling to the ground it was painful to look at the computer screen. The horse thrashed about to get away from the beating. The trainer held on tight to corner the horse between the fence and her whip. He couldn't escape her. Debbie cried along with Lana. She remembered Pepper, he was young when he came in. His owner didn't want him because he couldn't barrel race. He had permanent injury to his tendons. They dropped him off as if he was a useless and broken appliance which was no longer of any use. The video focused on the trainer, giving Debbie a look at her. She didn't know this particular trainer and the camera panned to the horse's back and it showed two deep welts. He leaned against the fence to regain his footing. The horse couldn't move because it was hurt. Lana turned to Debbie sobbing "Do you know her? Where is Pepper?"All Debbie could do was drop her head and shake her head no. She clenched her fists as she turned to walk out the back door of the office. The screen door slammed behind her. Standing as if she was put in a corner for being a bad girl, Debbie lighted a cigarette. Letting the smoke roll from her lips she was helpless to do anything at that moment. She heard Lana crying and showing the video to anyone who walked in, begging them to identify the women. Jerri drove up. She was meeting with Debbie about new treatment for a few of the horses. Lana took her arm and escorted her into the office. She clicked the computer replaying the video. Debbie stood at the door. She couldn't watch it again. Jerri straightened up looking at the computer for a second. Tilting her head, she spoke slowly. "I know her. She is a bitch and has been in trouble before. I think she lives a few counties to the west of us. I remember something about her being in trouble before and rumors flew around that she sold horses to a kill buyer. She would buy them cheap and sell them for top dollar after she fattened up the horses. She's about an hour ride from here. Someone call Sheriff Ed. I think I know where she lives." Turning to the office full of volunteers she announced, "Who wants to go for a ride?" Hands went up with a cheer from the crowd.

Lauren walked in hearing the end of the story. Looking at Debbie she said, "I'll call Ed and stay here."

Lee waved his hand telling them, "I'll stay here to... Aw hell they didn't hear a word I said" Walking down the barn aisle talking to the horses. "Do any of you feel my pain when it comes to these women? Come on guys can I get a 'hell yeah, from any of you?" The horses peered over their stall doors at him, looking interested but not sure what he was saying. A few even shook their heads at him. Turning around, Lee casually walked back to the feed room.

The group of women ran to their cars turning up the dirt on the driveway. Jerri led the caravan of cars through the back roads. They all kept up with each other without leaving a gap between cars. Jerri could see behind her in the distance red lights flashing. "Uh oh. Debbie we have company behind us, we need to step on it and speed up. Pass the word to everyone to keep going. Debbie and Lana pulled their phones out and made calls to the vehicles behind them. Jerri increased her speed passing from one county to another. Entering the third county the red lights from the police slowed down. They couldn't enter into a jurisdiction, where they had no power. With a loud sigh she turned to Lana, who was glaring out the side window. "Hey Lana, we'll get him and take him home and get that bitch at the same time." Lana acknowledged with a slight smile. "Jerri that poor horse is never going to trust another human being. She ruined him." Jerri could see Lana through her rear view mirror. "I don't think so Lana. I believe if you give him enough love he will come around and be a good horse. It will take time but I know you can help him and fix him." Lana bit her thumbnail as she returned to staring out the window.

Jerri couldn't remember which dirt road led to the small ranch. All she knew was that it had three fir trees right on the corner which were surrounded by bamboo trees. They looked strange sitting on the corner of an empty lot. Jerri drove right past the street before realizing that she had missed the turn. She maneuvered the car to make a u-turn and everyone followed her.

Debbie's phone rang. As she answered it she looked into her side mirror and saw five police cars trailing the caravan. Laughing she said "Jerri, look behind us we have company again." Jerri could see the police cars behind the group. They turned left into a property that was old and run down with empty pastures and an old barn looking like it was ready to fall over. The trailer sitting next to the barn was in just as similar condition.

Walking down the metal steps from the trailer was the woman. The tall, heavy blonde with a barrel waist raised her hand into the air to tell the group of cars to stop. All the vehicles grouped around her and everyone got out of their vehicles. The angry group of women surrounded her. She could see she that had lost the war before it started and was alone in her world. She knew why they were there. As soon as the video was posted she received death threats. Her large shoulders shook as the outraged women encircled her. She had nowhere to go, and she was relieved to see the police officers walking toward them. One officer looked around at the women and said, "All of you move back to your cars." None of the women moved they wanted a piece of the lady they came to see. He could see that they were going to be stubborn and not follow his orders. Another officer stepped into the circle and addressed the group. "Ladies, I know why you're here and I don't blame you. I can tell you she is going to jail and will be charged by the courts. I can also tell by looking at your faces that you had other plans for her and I don't blame you. Let us do our job and arrest her. I talked to Ed and he told us to turn any horses on the property over to you. I agree, so please round all the horses up." The group separated except for Jerri, Debbie, and Lana. Standing in front of the abuser Jerri was the first to speak up. "Lady, I will spend my last dollar putting you away and renting billboard signs with your picture and name on them once you're convicted. Or if you don't like that idea we can go behind the barn with dueling whips and see who comes out better." Jerri gave her a sarcastic smile and remarked to her, "Bet I win. Ya want to, come on bitch your real tough with a whip. Try it out on me see how far you get." Lana stepped up to her face almost touching her chin with her forehead. "Bitch, you're better off in jail. I'm only sorry the police showed up when they did. I'm going to sue you on behalf of Pepper, the horse you beat. Not for money but for justice. Hang on, bitch, you're not getting away from any of us."The three ladies stepped back as the officer placed handcuffs on the woman. She never said a word. She was escorted to the open police car and appeared relieved once they closed the door. Lana walked toward the pasture. She saw Pepper standing behind a palm tree. As she crept toward the injured horse, he shied away. He could barely walk. The welts on his back crisscrossed like a road map. It was painful for him to take a step. His fear made him move. Lana called to him. "Pepper boy, come on, were going home. Steady boy." The horse slowly crept backwards away from her. Lana continued to gently talk to the frightened horse. She caressed him with her words like a mother soothing a hurt child. "You don't remember me, do you? Its ok we were salt and Pepper, do you remember that? Salt and Pepper we were a team. Salt and Pepper, you and me, sweet boy. "The horse stopped backing. He stared into her eyes as he tried to remember the time and place he had known her before. Lana stepped closer, and, he allowed her to move in toward him. She reached for his neck giving him a hug. His head went down draping over her shoulders as if it was two old friends uniting after many years. He knew her and she had saved him. He didn't know it at that moment but he was going to be hers alone. Lana slowly lead her horse to the trailer, slow and guarded he walked in he knew he was saved.

A small pony in poor condition with healed over deep welts joined Pepper in the trailer. Lana joined the two ladies talking to the police officer. Turning to the car she motioned to the woman sitting in the back seat with her hand to her ear as if she was making a gesture of a phone. Bending down at the window Lana silently motioned with her mouth. "Call me bitch" and winked. The woman starring out the window sunk back in the seat rolling her head back against the seat. The officer saw Lana at the window. With imposing authority in his voice he instructed her. "Hey, hey lady, get away from the car. Don't start trouble or you'll join her."

Lana raised both of her hands and said, "OK, OK!"

Jerri directly ordered her to get into the truck. Lana followed the orders.

Returning to the barn and unloading the two horses, Jerri examined them while Debbie completed the legal forms to take custody of the horses.

Lana stood with Jerri while she examined Pepper, listening to every word. "Jerri, I want to adopt Pepper. I lost him before and I won't do it again."

Jerri smiled. "I thought you would do that, but what about your husband? Wasn't he against you having a horse?"

Lana enormous grim covered her face. "Yup, he said it was the horses or him. I guess we know who won that one." She wrinkled her face and gave Jerri a thumb up.

Evening closed in around the barn and Lana requested permission to spend the night. And permission was happily granted.

Jerri slapped her hand on the wooded door. She laughed. "Lana, I was just thinking about this afternoon. I can't believe that we are a bunch of tough and fouled mouth women. We all think we are tough as nails. It has to be funny to watch us in action."

Lana gave her a smirk. "We are an over-confident group, next thing you'll see us giving gang signs."

# Chapter 19

The next morning Debbie was awake and refreshed to face her new day. The air was crisp and clean. A light low fog hung over the road. Drinking her hot coffee while she drove the back roads. Punching the gate code to enter the property Debbie heard nothing, saw nothing. It felt strange. Her inner feelings told her something was wrong. She thought to herself she needs to put back into working order her paranoid feelings. If something was wrong she would have received a call. Scanning the pastures she didn't see anything out of place or out of the normal. Arriving at the barn it was all too quiet. Walking into the barn all the horses were fed. She could hear them chewing on their hay. Turning around in circle she knew something was missing. With a gasp she called out "Hank? You here?" Turning to the back of the barn she heard a groan. "Hank? where are you?" "I'm here in Ellie's stall." His voice cracked and sounded weak. Debbie rushed in finding Ellie lying down on her side with her head on Hanks lap. She could see Ellie had passed away. Her eyes were glazed and fixed as if looking to the sky. Looking down at Hank, she saw a crumpled mourning man. Debbie sat down on the dirt stall floor next to him. She reached over to stroke her head and mane. She put her arm around Hank's shoulders and gave him a reassuring squeeze. She could see that the man's heart was broken. "Hank, are you ok?" His response was a shrug of his shoulders. Tears ran down the front of his tee-shirt. Looking lovingly down at the horse. He tried to talk. All he could do is caress Ellie's neck and mane. Debbie remained quiet and waited for him. Hank continued to look down at the horse. "Isn't she beautiful? I looked in on her around three a.m. I told her we would do breakfast as usual. I fell asleep on the chair and when I woke up, I fed all the other horses. I walked to her stall and found her. Thinking she was just sleeping, some mornings she enjoyed sleeping in. I called her name; princess Ellie. She didn't poke her head around like she usually does. I had her buckets ready for her breakfast. I found her down, I tried to wake her." Grievously he said "I couldn't. I wasn't there for her when she died. She died alone with nobody to help her go in peace. I left her. Friends don't leave good friends."Debbie hugged her old, dear friend. "Hank she might have wanted it this way. It could have been too hard for her to say good-bye. She couldn't leave knowing you were hurting. She had to do it her way. She knew it was her time." She cried for losing her dear friend Ellie and to watch her old trusted friend broken and grief stricken. She loved Ellie, yet it couldn't be compared to the hours Hank and Ellie had spent together. The two were a great couple. They enjoyed their meals together. Hank would sit in her stall while he tried to teach himself to use his new laptop. She kept him good company every night that he worked. Ellie was the horse everyone would divulge their deepest secrets or problems.

They heard Kate calling, "Where is everyone?"

Debbie gloomily called out, "We're down here with Ellie."Kate's rapid footsteps echoed through the silent barn. All the horses were overly silent out of respect for one of their own or it was their way to grieve for their long-time friend. Silence hung over the barn like an empty church. Entering the stall, Kate saw her friends on the ground. Dropping to her knees she reached over to Ellie. Crawling on her knees, she dropped her head on Ellie's back. "Oh Ellie, sweet, sweet Ellie," she cried. Without looking up, "Hank, I'm so sorry. We know she was your best girl." Kate sobbed into the soft fur of the horse. Lauren stood at the stall door watching the sadness. Clearing her throat she motioned with her lips that she would make the call. Debbie acknowledged with a silent "yes" gesture. Lauren tiptoed to the office. Looking down she bumped into one of the volunteers. Lauren explained what was happening and asked the volunteer to leave for the day until they could get Ellie buried. She handed the volunteer a sign to put on the front gate reading "No volunteers today, email will be sent. Thank you"

Lauren's next chore was to call the man down the road who helped when a horse died. He would bury them. He never asked for any money. He felt it was his obligation to help with the foundation. It would be hard to move Ellie in the stall. He would remove part of the stall wall. Debbie had seen it a few times and it was not a nice scene to watch the horses being taken out. It always seemed so disrespectful. Lauren walked down to join the others with Ellie. Being the first to speak Lauren said, "I remember the first time I met Ellie. I was at the computer in the office I looked up and this was this giant face in the window staring at me. I jumped out of the chair thinking she was coming directly through the window. I stared back at her." She giggled. "We had a stare down contest. She won. I blinked first. Many times while I worked at the computer I would feel like I was being watched and sure enough I would look up and standing in the window was Ms. Ellie."

Everyone smiled at her thoughtful memory.

Kate spoke up next. "I remember how Ellie was the first horse I ever work withed. She taught me. Poor thing, one day I put her fly mask on upside down. She looked so silly and I think she knew I did it wrong. I would see her watching me all day. When I finally realized it she made me chase her in the rain. She got her revenge on me." Debbie spoke up. "I just went for a walk with her the other day and for some reason when I walk with her I open up and dump all my feelings on her and it's like she takes them away. But I remember the day she arrived. Skin and bones, her long legs looked like string spaghetti. With the amount of weight she had lost we didn't want to feed her too fast or too much. At the time we didn't have the medical barn. I walked to this same stall. She kicked the door down. Sticking her head out of the stall she stepped over the door and walked out like nothing happened. We learned how she had been stuck in a stall for almost two years. Manure and urine soaked her legs to her belly. Flies and a skin infection made her lose her fur. She refused to be confined to a stall. We left the door open for months until she allowed us to close her in. What great memories she made for all of us." An email was sent to all volunteers and foundation members. A small memorial service was scheduled for the next evening. The memorial services always presented a sober atmosphere, but this time Debbie wanted a comforting service for Ellie. Tables were set down the aisles with light drinks and snacks. Pictures of Ellie were scattered on each table, carrots were draped over the frames, later they would be offered to the other horses. The first to speak was Hank. "Ladies and Gentlemen, can I have your attention please? I would like to raise a glass to Ellie, the icon who was a remarkable survivor and special lady." His weak voice cracked. "To Ellie. A beautiful horse and now even more beautiful soul. May the stars shine brighter with her gracing the heavens." Raising his glass everyone attending followed his signal. A few quiet voices sounded in an "Amen".

Stepping forward Kate spoke of her memories of Ellie and many others joined in to commemorate about the beloved regal mare. Tears flowed freely among the crowd, the happy memories were bitter sweet. The evening closed in silence while everyone hugged goodbye.

Hank, Debbie, Lee, Kate, Jack, and Lauren stayed behind to clean up. Lee offered to stay the night with Hank. Secretly, Lee smuggled in a six pack of Hank's favorite beer. They could guy talk and help Hank through his grief.

# Chapter 20

The weeks that followed felt grim and empty. Someone hung a gold-painted horse shoe above Ellie's stall. Out of respect it would remain empty for a long time. Fresh shavings were neatly placed and plastic carrots hung on the hay rack.

While working Debbie received an email about horses being stolen in the area and around the big lake. As the days grew shorter darkness came quickly, and the thieves could slink around undetected. This was the first time in many years horses were stolen in the area a little close to home. Debbie posted the notice on the bulletin board. Lee and Jack hung brighter lights at the entrance of the driveway. More cameras were added and a few hidden in the trees, giving the road a better view of who or what was coming down the road. They prepared the best they could to avoid being a victim.

Maddie came over to give the description of the stolen horses and a police sketch of a man seen in the area, along with the make and models of the truck and trailer he was driving. The situation had become epidemic. The police kept a close eye on the areas but with the budget cuts they had limited manpower. A few farm owners took matters into their own hands as they heavily-armed patrolled their own area.

Debbie knew in her that heart this was not going to end well. The seasonal horses were brought down to avoid the harsh northern winters. They were prime and fit for the criminal elements.

Everyone was on high alert and Debbie waited for the devastating outcome. It was only a matter of time before the news of the casualty came down. Word of the thefts passed like an out of control wildfire around the equine community. The Federal Bureau of Investigation was involved because a few of the stolen horses were very expensive show and race horses. Weeks passed and the news was never good. More horses were being stolen. The numbers were adding up quickly. Despite the vigilant watch the thieves were winning the battle. There had been over forty horses stolen. Panic swept every corner of the areas. Guns were purchased and these folks were out to catch someone. The men and older boys took their all terrain vehicles into areas they normally would not go. The swamp was full of gators and poisonous snakes. If a person didn't know the area well enough they could get lost and more likely never found.

Most nights at the rescue the men stayed over to patrol the property and surrounding areas. They took shifts safeguarding the barn and they would make the rounds with neighboring property owners. While some slept in shifts the others kept alert. With the number of horses on the property who would easily follow anyone, they had to be on their toes even more.

Jack and Lee had just relaxed in front of the TV when they heard gunshots. Both men jumped up running to their vehicle. The others started to yell. "Heard the shots, don't know what direction." Another shot exploded in the air. The younger of the group pointed to the north and yelled, "Come on over that way."

The four men raced toward the sound, over the steep ground and splashed through the swampy ground. As they came around the back of the dirt road, a heavy-set older man stood out on the road. "They took off. I saw three of them. I couldn't get a clear shot without hitting my horse. My wife called the police. They didn't get the horse, he ran back to his stall. I wanted to shoot that son-of-a bitch. Coward hid behind my horse. Thanks for coming, name is Jim."

Leaning over his mud bike, Jack shook his hand, "I wish you would of shot him. We could put him up for public display for other thieves to see what we do around here." Jim, their new friend, nodded in agreement.

The air filled with the sounds of police sirens and more terrain vehicles wildly headed in their direction. The dark road was bright as daylight with headlights. Police light flashed an array of color. Everyone talking at the same time. All the officers were taking notes from the statement the property owner gave. Now they had a better description of the truck and trailer. The driver wasn't as easy to describe except that he was short, skinny and wore a cowboy hat. Two more police cars arrived. They tried to chase the truck but it left the highway and they lost him.

Lee talked to one of the officers explaining they had a video camera on the road. The thief might have driven past the rescue. He offered to review the video and see if he could find anything suspicious. Little by little the police left and a few of the other guys patrolling the area started to leave one by one, yelling back to keep in touch.

Jack and Lee with the others they had with them returned to the barn. They all knew that the rest of the night would be quiet. They didn't need to worry about horse thieves tonight. Lee turned on the television to watch until his adrenaline slowed down. Jack took a shower and found himself something to eat. While standing with the refrigerator open, his head inside the door. He called to Lee. "How come there is more food in this thing than in my own house where I live full time?"

Lee smirked. "Because the ladies who volunteer do more shopping then our own wives. By the way, it's going on four A.M. you better get a few hours sleep if you're going to work."

Both Lee and Jack fell asleep and the next thing they knew Hank walked into the office. He looked at the crumpled mess. "Rise and shine boys. It's seven o'clock. Time to get up and go to work."

Both men threw their pillows at Hank and missed him by ten feet. He stood laughing at the chaos in the office. Hank knew perfectly well that the ladies were going to have a hissy fit when they saw the chaotic mess. He was smart to stay out of their way and visit the horses. He had always made the short journey to visit with Ellie before he started his day.

Within the hour both Debbie and Kate arrived, with Lauren a few minutes behind them. Walking into the office they gasped at the mess. Debbie climbed over to make coffee and Kate opened a bag of donuts and egg sandwiches. Debbie rambled through the full brown bag of goodies, "Wow, you brought enough to feed a troop of Marines. I'm taking the chocolate donut and bagel and egg sandwich before the guys devour the bag full of food. I can't believe they are sleeping through us talking. Wonder what happened last night?"Kate walked over to Jack patting him lightly on the shoulder. "Hey get up. What happened you guys are so tired? Jack? Are you waking up? Coffee is almost done."

Lee and Jack woke up smelling the coffee. Sitting on the couch and pull out bed the men looked like they had been in a battle.

Kate handed Jack his cup of coffee. Debbie walked over to change the channel on the TV. Lee pointed to the television, "Look, they're interviewing Jimmy, the guy who was the one they tried to steal the horse from." The four were glued to the morning program.

Lee stood up. "I know that guy would have shot the slimy thief if he had the opportunity. I don't think he is the kind of guy you want to mess with."

The ladies started to clean up the office and both men left to go to work. Almost all of the volunteers showed that morning. The talk was all about the excitement of the events of the night before. Lauren peeked her head into the office. "Safe to come in?" Moving to the desk, she began organizing it. "Let's hope this is the last of the horse stealing."

Debbie shook her head. "Don't think so. They will lie low for a while thinking that we scared them off and they'll be back. Let everyone know to still keep an eye open."

Everyone went about their own business for the day. Debbie had a nagging feeling that she couldn't shake. It was starting to bother her more. She couldn't figure it out. As much as she tried she kept feeding the feeling of something wrong.

Later that afternoon Maddie and her crew paid them a visit. Tension started to brew between Debbie and Maddie. A few volunteers had left to go to help with Maddie's cause. She could afford to give her volunteers better rates on boarding horses and she had horses that could be ridden more than the rescue.

Debbie was working with one of the horses when Maddie walked up. Debbie turned to her, "So your here to interview for more of my volunteers?"

Maddie rolled her eyes. "Come on Deb. I'm sorry I didn't intentionally go out and steal your volunteers. They wandered over to my place. Remember you took a few of mine a few years back."

Debbie put her hand on her hip. "Maddie, I didn't take them. You got mad and kicked them out and you know as well as I do. I didn't want them either. They turned out to be a bunch of snotty bitches. It's not like I got your cream of the crop friend."

Maddie put her hand up in the air. "OK, I'm sorry, can we come to some sort of peaceful agreement? What if I ask them to step in when you need the help? I can't help if you charge more for board. I understand that you need the money more and the pricing is not something you have any control over."

Debbie groaned. "Fine, now what do you want from me."

"Can we go somewhere to talk, or walk away from here, please?" Maddie asked.

Debbie clipped the lead rope to the horse and both walked out of the round pen. "This sounds serious. What's wrong?"

We've been kicked off the property. The owner sold it out from under us. I don't know where to go. I have thirty-five thoroughbred horses, five are pregnant, and four donkeys. The foundation for our organization won't help us with enough money to buy our own place. I was wondering if you could go to your foundation and ask them to talk to mine."Raising her eyebrow, Debbie responded."Let me see what I can do for you" She squeezed Maddie's shoulder. "I don't know if they even know each other. That can be good or bad? "Taking Debbie's hand.'"Thank you and I'm sorry about the volunteers. I promise if any more come over I will talk to you first I promise. It's just that you have some terrific people and it seems like I don't get that. But again with fighting the kill buyers, it does get down and dirty."

Debbie shook her head. "That's what we do for horses. I have three horses to exercise either you can help or go home." Debbie reached out to hand her a lead rope.

"Oh no you don't, I have plenty to work with myself, and by the way, I did adopt one of our horses. She is a mustang and beautiful black and white paint, a little wild still, But she loves to run. I named her Crystal Blue because of her blue eyes. She's about four years old. Still a silly kid."

"Oh my congratulations!, It's about time, you needed one. I'm happy for you and love the name."

Both ladies hugged and said good-bye. Debbie returned to the barn to work her next horse.

# Chapter 21

The winter drought was playing havoc on the pastures as much as they tried to rotate the horses to prevent more damage. Sprinklers ran continually and the newly laid seed was eaten by the birds more than sinking into the dirt. Volunteers worked harder on the pastures then the horses. With so many horses and the lack of good grass it was a battle for all of them. A company came in to add more sprinklers and donated forage grass seed. It took forever for the grass to grow. Nothing could fix this problem but a few days of rain.

Debbie was pulling out of the gate when four dark-colored cars blocked her way. Two men in suits came out of their car. She could read the words on their shirts. FBI. Debbie sighed. "Oh shit! It finally happened. This is my worst nightmare. This is what had been gnawing at me." Behind the men Maddie got out of the car.

Rolling down her window, Debbie spoke first to the men. "I know why you're here. You found a slaughter house. Let me turn around and get my book." The FBI Agent turned away without saying a word. Maddie jumped into Debbie's car.

"They came to my house to pick me up, I had my book with me. I hate this Debbie, I hate, hate this."

Debbie remained silent all the way to the barn. Her stomach churned like she was on a roller coaster. Her mouth went dry and she could feel her heart beating in the pit of her chest. The cars followed and everyone got out and walked into the barn office. Volunteers stood staring at the scene. Most had a questioning look on their faces, wondering what was going on.

Lauren walked out of the office with Kate. Looking at the group, Lauren asked everyone to meet in the back of the barn.

Kate had tears in her eyes. "Ladies and gentlemen, the FBI discovered a slaughter house with about one hundred dead horses. This is what we have discussed with many of you. You always hope something like this never happens but it has. Those who are prepared to help we ask you to follow us to the property. If you can't do it we all understand. It is not a pretty sight."

Lauren started to hand haz-mat suits to those who came forward to help. Silently and mechanically they dressed themselves, holding the face masks.

Debbie walked out with the agents, her book of all the horses they had saved with their pictures and markings. This book could help them identify any of the horses.

Debbie, Kate, Lauren and Ronald drove in Debbie's SUV. They followed the agent's car with Maddie in the backseat. The drive was in total silence, they were mentally preparing themselves for the horrors they were walking into. Debbie felt a chill run down her spine and tears were already welling up. After the last one she was involved with she swore she would never do it again. She couldn't eat or sleep for months and she ended up being sick for three weeks. Mentally she was in worse shape than her body. Nothing prepares you for the sight she was about to walk into.

All the vehicles pulled off to the side of the road and stopped. They all got out and the agents walked to the group and finally spoke. The tall thin agent spoke first. "I'm Agent West. We received a tip this morning and were able to arrest all seven men. A court order was issued to confiscate the property and the owner has been arrested in another state. We need you to see if you can identify any of the horses so we can notify their owners. Agent Cannon, Meeker, and Patrick will work with you taking notes and I will be taking photos of the scene. Let me warn all of you this is the worst I have seen in my career."

As they all walked in Debbie could feel her legs weaken and her stomach shake. Kate walked like a windup doll and Lauren was as pale as the clouds. Ron just looked forward. Not a word was spoken. The closer they got they could hear the deafening buzz of millions of flies. The smell of death met them. Lauren was the first to stop, dropping to her knees to vomit. Ron took her head and helped her. Debbie could hear him comfort her. They trailed behind. Kate took Debbie's hand to hold. Her fingers were ice cold. Animal control officers were waiting for the agents to allow them in. Debbie could feel her heart beating uncontrollably. Kate continued to squeeze her hand and wouldn't let go. As they reached the gate Agent West turned to the group. "Please don't anyone be a hero. If you have to leave, go now. This isn't what you see in the movies. It's repugnant. I had grown men who had seen this before. Even with all their training. I saw a them cry like babies and get sick. I'm just preparing you. Don't say you hadn't been warned."

Debbie reached into her pocket, pulling out a jar of eucalyptus. She opened the jar and dipping her finger in brought up a small amount and rubbed the outside of her face mask. Passing it around she said, "It will help some with the smell". The small jar was passed around and returned empty.

Agent West slid open the heavy wire gate. It was hard to think over the sound of the flies. They started swarm the group as they walked in. Everyone swatted at the flies and animal control brought in a smoke machine to help eliminate them. They stopped to see the carnage all over the grounds, blood soaked dirt. It was impossible to take it all in. Horse body parts were scattered all over. Some were piled on top of each other. Lauren gasped, "This is horse holocaust" She immediately made the sign of the cross. Ron stood next to her. Not looking at the gruesome mess, Maddie moved to a secure place in her head. Opening her book to note any numbers of the horses who might be tattooed. The property resembled a war-torn third world country. The sickening odor was inescapable. It didn't matter where they looked, horses legs, heads, blood soaked fur scalped from the bodies littered the area. Body parts they couldn't identify that had been grounded up. Blood pooled into the ground. The group continued to finish their work. A disposal company came in to remove the carcasses. Silence remained as if speaking would be irreverent to the lost souls. Eventually the crime scene of investigators left. Walking through the gate to leave Debbie, Kate, Maddie, and the rest returned to their vehicles. The other cars drove off leaving Debbie and Maddie behind. Sitting on the side of road leading to the entrance of the property they watched as the sun set and nothing but two silhouettes remained. Both walked back into the property and returned shortly with the glow of red and orange flames behind them. The buildings fell as they burned, the crackling of burning wood, and glowing embers floating in the darkness signaled an end of the destruction. In the darkness the profiles of the two women clinking bottles of beer. The ground was cleansed and the souls of the horses released. Silently they returned to the car and drove away. Moments later passing a fire truck racing toward the blaze. The firefighter driving the engine truck looked down into the car slowed down to allow them to pass. He gave a thumb up to Maddie knowing why they were going to the fire. They would not put out the fire, only control it to not spread to neighboring properties. Maddie nodded in return returning to the road.

# Chapter 22

Days passed and the slaughter of the horses became a bad memory. Life returned to normal as much as it could. Debbie and the crew that worked on the investigation took time off from the barn. Volunteers stepped up to help those who needed time to recuperate from the ghastly scene. A huge show of support for those who testified at the court appearance of the property owner to see him get jail time. It was a mob attitude sitting behind him. Everyone attended the trials of those caught at the property who slaughtered the horses.

Debbie, Maddie, and a few others were asked to testify in court to what they found. Each person being questioned received a hard cold stare from the criminals, never removing their eyes from them. They showed them they were not afraid of who they were putting in jail, as if to defy them to say or do something. None of them did anything except lower their eyes to the ground. The defending attorney questioned Debbie and Maddie about the fire on the property. He wanted to know who the arson was. Both women gave him a sly smirk and said innocently, "What fire?" The verdict came back with guilty charges and the defendants all went to prison. The crowd of people attending the trial stood up cheered and applauded. The judge had them all removed from the courtroom. Leaving, they all gave handshakes with pats and hugs. The property was seized and would be sold. The settlement money from the sale would be divided among the rescues in the area. Debbie reported to the volunteers the final outcome of the trial. Cheers echoed the barn. Even a few of the horses gave a loud neigh as if they knew it was time to celebrate. Debbie, Kate, Lauren didn't talk about the details of the day, they did speak of having nightmares and sleepless nights. Lauren complained of stomach pains. Kate silently surrounded herself with her family and the horses. Debbie went to her favorite spot to talk to Blu, he was her therapists. She could cry, cuss and breath when she had her private heart to heart talks with him. All three ladies took on special projects around the barn to occupy themselves. Debbie started a special training project with a few of the horses. This would prepare them to be therapy horses for kids and adults with disabilities. Kate reinvented a few of the volunteer programs and Lauren redecorated the barn, office, and landscape. The three never stopped moving once they entered the barn. It was their way of healing from the traumatic scene they had witnessed.

In addition to their problems, three horses that were rescued from a kill buyer came in. It was just another reminder of the dreadful world they were dealing with. Ironically Debbie, Kate and Lauren took a special interest in these particular horses. More therapy for the three ladies. The horses were placed in the private barn where the volunteers boarded their horses.

A bright light for the ladies was another fund raiser which kept them busy and their minds occupied with other things. This fund raiser had a musical theme. Local singing artists came to perform. It drew a large crowd every year which helped in funding the barn. The Executive Board and Debbie both had these special funds spoken for. They wanted a hydro-therapy system for horses with muscle injuries and more.

Kate made it her obsession to have a famous musician finally come to this event. The bands and singers who came were wonderful. They all had followers and put on a great show. Kate wanted it bigger. She went hunting for a big name singer.

She wanted to name the new hydro- therapy system "Toujours Rappler," which was French for "Forever Remembered".

Her mission in life at that moment was to find someone famous and important for the fund raiser. Debbie and the fund raising committee didn't stand in her way and they understood that if they tried they would lose. Secretly they wanted her to find someone to make this fund raiser the best.

Over the next few weeks everyone lost sight of Kate. The flyers were kept a secret, under lock and key. She threw herself into the production and everyone started to see her smile again. She had a secret and a special sparkle in her eye. A few volunteers questioned Debbie if she knew what was going on with Kate, but for the first time in their friendship Kate kept her secret. Kate would come in to the barn and select a few volunteers for work she needed done. Mostly she did it all herself.

Six weeks before the show the announcement and posters were brought out to be placed around. One single line on the posters was "SPECIAL MUSICAL PERFORMANCE". The radio, newspapers, and TV companies were sent the announcement. Excitement grew with everyone speculating who Kate had found to perform. It had everyone wondering, including Debbie. Kate didn't tell Jack for fear he would tell Lee and the secret would be out because Lee would tell Debbie.

As the event date drew closer Kate was not the same person. She was like a giddy little girl. She dictated how the event would be set up, where the vendors would be, and all the horses would be placed in the riding arena. Decorations were all in green and gold.

Debbie stopped her in the office and asked why the color, green and gold. "You have the Green Bay Packers as special guests?"

Kate shook her head. "The colors are for gold bars and green for money." Debbie didn't answer. She gave Kate a bewildered look and made a promise that she would not ask another question. Closer to the date Kate started to calm down and looked confident. She still barked orders to everyone and by this time everyone ignored her barking. Kate approached Debbie to have a giant fireworks show after the band finished to complete the evening. Debbie had to discourage this idea due to the lack of rain. The ground was dry and foliage brittle. "The last thing we need is for this place to go up in flames". It was the only time Debbie had to rain on Kate's parade.

Two days before the event volunteers and event people started to set up the stage, tents, and signs posted for directions. The property was being prepped with the pastures grass cut. Fence boards were painted and replaced. The barn was decorated with small lights. The stall doors each had the horse's name with its history hung in a special plastic covering. Every inch of the barn was pressure cleaned. Tables were set out for admission and food. A wine bar was set up in front of the office for wine tasting. Generators were brought in for the sound stage, and bright lights wrapped around the scaffolding. A mysterious black tent was assembled behind the stage. Tables, chairs and a small refrigerator were placed in the secret tent. Huge fans were set up in front of the stage. Kate flowed across the property as if her feet never hit the ground. She talked to a few reporters who did everything they could to find out who will be the unidentified celebrity. Kate wouldn't even give hints if it was a male or female. Her only words were to "come and see".

The day of the event Kate sat in the office watching out the back window as the vendors started to set up the food tents. Beer and soda tents set up next to the food area. Merchants selling everything from horse decorations, saddles, and tack equipment to flowers and riding clothes. The silent auction area was managed by the Executive Board. They had a few high dollar items along with special artist painting and jewelry. The big item was a five thousand dollar western saddle donated anonymously.

The afternoon flew by and soon it was time for the gates to open. Cars streamed in, volunteers directed traffic with the help of off-duty police officers who volunteered their time. Word was out in over four counties. A huge barn party was going on with a special secret guest performer.

Kate sold raffle tickets for the winner to have their picture taken with the secret celebrity. She ran out of tickets before she ran out of buyers.

The music started. The aroma of food and beer engulfed the scene. Everyone in attendance was enjoying themselves. The party was in full steam and it was a success.

Two performers left, and Kate disappeared into the darkness. Debbie went looking for her. She couldn't stand the suspense any longer, she had to know who the mystery singer was. The finale performer was singing and he had the crowd jumping. He was a local boy who had made it big in Nashville. He adopted one of the rescue horses a few years back. His horse had a beautiful life on his farm in Tennessee. In the moment Debbie reached the bottom of the stag all the lights in the entire property went out. Everyone froze in place, a few of the audience started to yell, "Hey, put the lights on."

Debbie heard Kate's voice in the darkness, she couldn't see her hand in front of her face and Kate on the stage was totally swallowed by the darkness.

"Ladies and Gentlemen here is the surprise you all have been waiting for. The lights went on with an explosion, everyone for a second was blinded. The music blasted and everyone in the audience cheered, fists pounding the air. They went wild and began dancing to the excitement of the music. Tray Jones belted out his new song, "Green and Golden". People cheered and whistled as the music rang out.

Kate came down the stage steps right into Debbie's arms. Both ladies hugged each other while jumping up and down.

"Oh Kate, I love him, I love him, I love you!" Debbie bellowed over the music. They both continued to jump and hug. A sudden thud knocked them both down, Jerri jumped on them. "I love him Tray Jones, love him. Do you understand I love him?"

Debbie was on the ground under Kate and Jerry. She yelled, "Jerri get off of me. I love him more then you!" The three got up off the ground dancing to the music like a bunch of crazy teens.

Tray Jones performed for over an hour. Everyone had their cell phones pointed at the stage.

Kate pulled off the wildest surprise, successful fund raiser the rescue had ever had.

Tray performed an extra song after the screams from the crowd begged for more. He jumped down the stage steps heading straight to his tent. He took Kate's hand to follow him, she grabbed Debbie's hand, who grabbed Jerri's hand. Tray's security opened the tent flap for him and stood in front of the door. The security guard the size of an oak tree smiled at Jerri. She responded with her best flirt smile and added a wink. Tray dropped into a soft chair with his entire body covered in sweat. A young man opened a bottle of water handing it to Tray as the rest of the band poured into the tent.

The silence in the tent was awkward. Kate spoke first. "Tray, thank you so much for coming tonight. You helped the rescue with this event to put us over the top for our new hydro system."

Tray stood up and walked over to the refrigerator grabbing another bottle of water. Looking at his crew he said, "Hey, can one of you guys run over to the funnel cake tent and get me a couple and while you're at it, pick up a few of those deep-fried cakes."

One young man jumped up and was out the tent in seconds. Tray faced the three ladies. "You have a beautiful organization here and from what I've been told by Ms. Kate you work hard at saving these horses. I'm happy to help here and I understand you're raising money to put in a hydro system for the horses. That is what this is all about. I would like to donate the system. I'll have my assistant contact you to make the arrangements."

Debbie couldn't control herself. She lunged at Tray and hugged him around the waist. "Thank you, Thank you, thank you!. You sure do sweat a sweet smell." Tray hugged her back, laughing and said,

"You're very welcome and that is the first time anyone told me that. It really is an honor to have you ask me to come here. I have a few buddies in Nashville who could lend a hand here also."

Kate extended her hand. "Mr. Jones, I can't thank you enough for what you've done and for all of your generosity. It is more than beyond kindness."

"Again, you're welcome, and after what you showed my folks in the office with that horrific slaughter deal you all deserve more then what you're getting. I should be the one thanking you."

They all sat down to make small talk with him for a few minutes. He signed autographs and had pictures taken. Jerri was the raffle winner to have her picture taken with him. As they stood next to each other Tray leaned over to whisper in Jerri's ear. "My security guard wants your phone number. He's a good guy and he doesn't mess around." Jerri giggled as she walked over to hand him her business card. Talking for a few seconds, Tray Jones barked out orders to get packed up to leave. He was exhausted from his performance and he had to catch the plane for another concert.

It was after two in the morning before the party wound down. Volunteers dragged their sore feet to their cars. The tents had been taken down, tables removed. It started to look like pastures again. Debbie and Kate walked through the barn discussing the successful event. It had been the best one they'd ever had.

The proceeds would cover the construction of the hydro barn and more. Debbie sighed with relief thinking she wouldn't have to go to the Executive Board for the money. Her face shadowed by the moon in the dark barn turned to Kate. "You single-handedly pulled this entire show off all by yourself. Have you ever thought about doing this as a professional? You are good at it."

Kate shrugged her shoulders. "No, Debbie, I enjoy what I do here. At times I wake up in the middle of the night and think about the same thing you do. It's always about money and keeping this place running. What if we lost the board members and the whole organization that helps to financially back us? I have the constant fear we won't be able to save the horses. For example, we have six really sick horses. A few others are on expensive medication and we never know when we will have a horse that needs tens of thousands of dollars for surgery. We live off the generosity of others but we just don't seem to get ahead. The hydro barn is a big expense to maintain. What then?

Debbie shuffled the toe of her boot on the dirt. "Kate, I thought about that tonight after the show. The money we received from this could go a lot further if we didn't build the barn. Yet, we have so many horses who could benefit from it. I put in endless hours of thinking how to make this place run smooth. I think that running a rescue doesn't ever run smooth. We don't have deep pockets to make heavy purchases. I think I might have too high of expectations for this facility. It's a tough call. Will you help me with it?

A tired smile across Kate's face reassured Debbie that she would stand by her with whatever decision was made. Both ladies walked into the office to pick up their keys to go home.

Hank was sitting on the couch with the TV glowing and an infomercial chatting on. As they tried to tiptoe out of the office Hank lifted his head.

"You can forget about being quiet, ladies. I hear everything and by the way, Debbie, sometimes a decision can be made for you if you let it. Don't think so hard. Goodnight, ladies. You're intruding on my territory being here so late."

Both turned to leave. "Goodnight, Hank." See you in a few hours.

# Chapter 23

The profit totals from the event were sent by email to Debbie with an invitation for her and Kate to come to the next Board meeting luncheon on Friday.

"Oh, great," she thought. "I have to wear something nice and I don't own or want to dress up." Her thought was interrupted by a few volunteers calling her name.

Debbie sprinted out of the office. She knew the sound of panic. Something was wrong.

Ruth, a long time volunteer, slammed open the rear horse trailer door. A lady who appeared to be covered in mud and blood followed Ruth. Other volunteers ran for the medical barn to find first aid supplies.

Debbie and Kate reached the trailer at the same time. Both ladies opened their mouths, however, no sound escaped. Blood streamed onto the floor of the trailer. A beautiful chocolate- colored horse lay on its side with an arrow protruding from its shoulder.

Debbie spewed orders to call Jerri, Ed, and the F.B.I. Volunteers came running with bandages in their arms. The horse struggled to move its head but the pain was too great. Debbie heard the familiar sound of pain as the injured horse would grind it's teeth.

Ruth knelt down next to the horse, and covered the wound with heavy bandages. She stroked its mane and attempted to soothe the frightened horse with her soft voice.

Debbie shriek, "Who brought this horse in? What happened?"

A small voice standing outside the trailer spoke. "I did."

Responding to the small voice "Who is I did?"

"Debbie it's me June Callows."

"Oh hi, June. What happened, how did you find this? It's not one of yours, is it?"

With a shaky voice June said "No, I, was driving north on Carney Road and I saw this horse walking down the dirt road by the county park entrance. I knew it was hurt by the way he was walking and as I got closer I saw the arrow and the blood. You're the first person I thought of and the only place to get help."

The sound of sirens could be heard echoing in the distance.

"That must be Ed and where in the hell is Jerri?" Frustration exploded from Debbie.

Ed's car slid on the gravel road discharging loose stones. Leaping out of the car he yelled. "Who got shot? Did Debbie finally shoot someone?"

From inside the trailer Debbie called out. "Ed I didn't shoot anyone, yet! Come see this mess that just came in." Ed climbed in the trailer, stepping over bodies, and knelt next to the horse.

Seeing the blood-soaked horse and the arrow sticking out of the horses shoulder. "Oh for the love of God, what happened?"

Debbie was getting more aggravated. "I don't know Ed, you know just as much as I do. Ask June over there. Debbie shook her head to the side of the trailer where June was peering in.

Ed climbed over the same bodies getting out of the trailer. "June, come over to my car and fill me in." Both walked away as Jerri arrived. Ed pointed to the trailer. Jerri leaped inside, climbing over more bodies."Get out of the way" she ordered. Opening her bag she pulled out a hypodermic needle. Holding it up in front of her face tapping the bulb of the syringe and pushing up on the stem to allow the liquid to squirt out. Jerri poked the needle into the horse's neck. She continued to examine the horse with the arrow, unwrapping the blood soaked bandages. "I need whoever brought this horse in to driver him/her to my place. I can't remove this arrow here."

Debbie knelt across from Jerri. "June brought him in. She found him walking down the dirt road at the entrance of Carney Park."

"June who in the hell is June?" she barked.

"Jerri, June Callow, your cousin, you idiot" Debbie spat back. "What is your problem?"

Jerri's voice resonated in the metal trailer. 'This is the third horse in twelve hours that has an arrow in its body, plus one horse was injected with gasoline and it didn't make it. That's my problem Debbie."

"Oh Jerri, I'm sorry. We have some asshole or assholes running around killing horses or at least trying to." Debbie called for Ed to come over.

"Ed, did you know about the three horses Jerri is talking about?"

Ed leaned on the edge of the trailer, sweat running down the sides of his face. "Yeah, I was aware of two horses. This is number three. I'm afraid we might have more if we don't catch the perps doing this."

Jerri wrapped more bandages on the arrow to stabilize it. She called out "June, can you follow me to my place? Everyone get out" she bellowed.

June nodded her head as she ran toward her pickup truck. Debbie and the all the volunteers crammed inside the trailer slowly backed out, trying not to disturb the frightened horse. Jerri slowly closed the trailer door and raced to her truck. Sticking her head out of the vehicle window. "Ed, will you follow me home? Debbie, I'll call you when I get a chance."Debbie slightly waved her arm. The volunteers moved back from the trailer as it moved away. Ruth climbed into the front seat of June's truck without saying a word. As the convoy drove away everyone stood together watching them leave. They turned to Debbie as if they all needed directions."Ok, we have a serious situation. I need everyone to be on their toes for more victims. Use whatever resources you have to find the bastard's who are doing this. AND don't anyone tell me who they are until Ed has them in a jail cell. I will gladly go to jail for shoving an arrow up their asses." It wasn't very often the volunteers witnessed Debbie's anger, nonetheless she was entitled to her feelings. The crowd dispersed in silence, everyone deep in thought. A few volunteers had not experienced anything like this before. It would leave a lasting mark on their hearts for a long time. Debbie walked to the Memorial Garden to release her frustration and anxiety. Kate returned to the office, meanwhile Lauren slipped away to see if she could help Jerri. Over the next few weeks a few more horses were found with either an arrow in them or shot with BB pellets. All survived the experience. The television news continued to cover the situation. A few extra donations were flowing in to help with the medical expenses. Ed kept Debbie informed about the investigation. He knew that she would pester him for any piece of information. Little by little small tidbits of gossip flowed around the area. Yet, they didn't have any credible witnesses or call in tips. It's like the person or persons doing this had instilled some sort of fear in people. Nobody was talking which was strange for the area, especially when it came to the horse community. Over the next few weeks a few more horses were hurt and yet they had no idea of who was pinpointed the timeline they were all done, early morning. Like someone was doing it on their way to work or coming home from work. With a large map of the county he meticulously places red stick pins where each of the horses was found or the owners. All were within a few miles of one large property. Bevo Shuggy owned about one hundred acres in the center of the county. His great- great-grandparents were the first to live in the area. They staked the land around their homestead. Bevo had always been a thorn in Ed's side. As kids Bevo, beat him up after school. The family history was that they all were a bunch of bullies. He remembered as a kid Bevo's uncle Jeremiah was charged with raping and killing a girl. The family hired the best lawyers and the kid walked away from all the charges. Unfortunately for Jeremiah, the girl's family took him to the swamp and only a few body parts were ever recovered.

The Shuggy family had continual run ins with the law and Bevo was following in his family's footsteps. Ed busted him when he was first hired onto the police department. Bevo was charged with beating a horse with a whip until it died from infections from the sores. Every animal Bevo owned was abused until Ed took him to court. The Shuggy family was court ordered to never own an animal.

On his way home Ed took a ride over to pay Bevo a visit. Pulling into the heavy fenced and barricaded property he spotted one of Bevo's four sons. Smitty, the oldest and the meanest, turned toward Ed's car. Taking a stance and setting both hands on his hips, Smitty stared while Ed pulled in.

"Hey Ed, what brings you here?" Smitty reached into his back pocket pulling out a dirty rag. He extended his hand to Ed.

Responding to Smitty the men shook hands. "Listen Smitty, I was wondering where your Dad and brothers are. I'd love to talk to them for a minute."

Squinting his eyes, Smitty asked, "Why?"

"No particular reason, just stopping to say hi Smitty, you worried about something? Ed smirked.

The door to a small shed creaked open. Bevo, the size of an outhouse, walked out. The wooden steps groaned as Bevo stepped down. "Watchya want, Ed? Get off my property or I'll beat your ass like I did in grade school. No crime committed here."

Ed raised both hands. "Bevo, I just stopped by to see what was going on and no crime yet, it's early in the day. The reason I'm here is because we've had a series of horses getting hurt. You know anything about that?"

The giant man walked up to Ed with a mean scowl looking down. Ed refused to back away, both men stood close to each other refusing to yield. Ed was shorter then Bevo. But, his eyes were equal to his opponent's Adam's apple. Putting his hand on his hip Ed rested on this gun.

"Bevo, back up. I'm not playing your tough guy game. I can whip your ass any day, any time. You're too fat to fight. You can't catch your breath, which by the way stinks.

Ed could see the other Shuggy boys standing on the porch. Looking around Bevo he asked them, "You boys know anything about the horses in the area being hurt?"

All four boys just stood and stared back at the Sheriff. "OK, you don't mind if I have a look around? Just checking your following the court order about you not having any animals on the property. Tenny, Smitty, you want to show me around? How 'bout Woody or Tombo? You guys want to back up and let me take a look? You don't have a problem with that?"

Not one of them moved. Ed surveyed the property. The old wooden two story house looked like it had when the Great Grandparents built it. All the out buildings were covered in old brown worn wood. It amazed Ed how they all still stood without collapsing to the ground. Overgrown wild pepper trees and heavy bamboo growing wild everywhere. Tall grass in the old unused pastures. Dirt surrounded everything else.

Ed slowly crept past each one of the four out buildings, looking in through the windows or opening the doors. He noticed one building that he had never seen before. It looked as old as the others but he didn't recall ever seeing it. Walking around the front of the new building Ed carefully opened the door. His eyes widened and he gave a huge gasp. Snakes. Everywhere he looked stacked to the ceiling, cages of snakes. Ed slammed the door shut.

Bevo and his boys stood at the base of the steps behind Ed. They all started laughing at Ed's reaction. The first to speak up was the youngest of the boys, Woody. "Ed, you afraid of snakes?"

"Sorry to burst your balloon but no. I'm not afraid of snakes. It just took me by surprise." He stepped down the stairs except the last one making Ed face to face with Bevo.

Ed and Bevo were inched apart face to face. Ed smiled "Busted!" Bevo looked around. The boys were gone. They had left their daddy to handle the mess.

"Looks like they left you in the dust, Bevo. You know the snakes have to go. You don't have a license to have them. AND, you broke your court order with animals on the property. I'm calling it in and we'll remove them all from the property. You have a problem with it?"

With no sign of emotion Bevo just stared into Ed's face.

Ed pulled out his cell phone and let the office know that they had snakes to confiscate. Meanwhile, other officers started to arrive to assist. The cages were removed and two officers took inventory before they were loaded into the truck.

One young officer waved to Ed. He walked over and the young man pointed to a high- powered bow and a box of arrows hidden behind red cans of gasoline. Ed stood at the door with his phone in his hand motioning as if he was making a call. Within seconds every officer's phone rang. It sounded like a choir of strange bells, sounds and animated voices. Everyone looked down and read the message on their phones. In unison the click of their guns all pointed at the Shuggys.

Bevo and his boys all raised their hands to give up. They were placed in handcuffs and driven off in different vehicles. Ed called in the detectives to investigate. The next call he made was to Bevo's cousin, Zac. The only one in the family to graduate high school, college and land a good job as a chef. Ed explained the situation to him. Zac said he would come by and keep an eye on the property.

Later that evening Ed drove over to tell Debbie what had happened. Pulling up to the house he saw Debbie sitting on the front patio. He gave her the lowdown of the afternoon.

"Finally, it's over. We can breathe again with the Shuggys in jail," Debbie smiled. "I have to call the girls and let them know."

Ed said, "I'm going to call the families of those who were involved and let them know, they can come to the office and sign complaints to press charges."

As he left his phone rang. Ed hurriedly ran to his car and sped off. Debbie found out later the next day that Bevo died of a massive heart attack while in jail. Shrugging her shoulders she said to herself, "One less trial for the public to pay".

# Chapter 24

The summer heat continued to be miserable. The temperatures never dropped below 90 degrees, except for a few hours between four and six am. The horses were kept inside the barn during the day and let out at night after the sun went down.

Fans were scattered throughout the barn and frozen jugs of water were rotated for the water to stay cool in the horse buckets.

Volunteers hosed down the horses to cool them off. It looked like a wet production line. A few of the younger horses that stayed outside stood under the shade trees, barely moving.

The pastures were drying up and pasture grass was dying or eaten by the horses. It was the worst drought in history. In the evening the skies lit up like the fourth of July with the heat lightning.

Many of the volunteers hung Native American rain prayers on each of the stall doors.

Debbie laughed at the sight, yet her biggest fear was wild fires. Most of the state was under a severe fire watch and fires flared up. The national forest was burned down to the point where there were no more trees. The scorched land went for miles and the small area that survived was swamp land. No place for the animals to go except for human backyards. Life for humans and animals started to become a war in some counties. A few families woke up to find alligators cooling in the family pool. Larger animals were raiding garbage cans and even raccoons surprised folks by sneaking in though the doggie door.

To add misery it was becoming peak hurricane season. They desperately needed rain, yet, with the fires the land had no trees to catch the rainfall. It was looking to be a bad weather season no matter how it ended.

All the volunteers attended the yearly training meeting in the event of a hurricane or an emergency evacuation. Everyone had a particular job when the all-call went out. They organized drivers to pull trailers with the horses. Some would be a second seat with the drivers. Others were assigned tasks to transport feed to the evacuation facility. Others would stay behind to secure the buildings. Yet there were others who would do whatever needed to be done.

Debbie knew that she would be the one person to stay behind in the event there were any horses who couldn't be moved. They could spend the time in the medical barn that had been renovated to be a hurricane shelter and withstand heavy wind.

Lauren, Kate and Jerri would lead the evacuation and remain with the horses in the different areas.

Once all the plans were in place Debbie's final words were always the same. "Pray we don't need to implement the plans and we are all safe."

Everyone nodded their head, or said they agreed.

Over the weekend Kate with a few volunteers rescued two horses. The call for help came in when one horse fell into an old well and couldn't get out. The fire department was able to get the horse released. Once they saw the condition of the horse they called the rescue. The owners were elderly and couldn't pay for the amount of feed they needed. They could barely live on their meager Social Security funds themselves.

Kate offered to bring the owners to visit whenever they wanted. It was easy to see the loyalty and bond between the horses and their owners.

As they drove away Kate watched the couple holding each while they both cried as their beloved friends left. Kate felt the tears in her eyes watching them. She saw the hurt and felt their hearts break.

Lauren went to the house every three days to see if they wanted to visit. They accepted every offer. They would bring carrots and apples for the horses and they packed a lunch for the two of them. Lauren never rushed them. They could stay as long as they wanted. If she couldn't drive them one of the other volunteers would.

Both horses were always happy to see their owners, June and Paul. They would neigh and call to them as they came into the barn.

One afternoon the volunteers surprised the couple with a special lunch and made them honorary members of the team. They received a plaque with their names on it along with a picture of them sitting with their horses, ribbons, and a golden horseshoe decorated with small flowers. Everyone made a big deal out of them and it was easy to see how happy they both were. In spite of both being in their eighties they acted like cute newlyweds half their age.

Debbie had the couple read to the younger visitors teaching them all about the horses and telling them all the stories of each horse and how they came to the rescue. This gave Christine, a volunteer and idea. She had a great-grandfather in a nursing home. She arranged with the owners of the nursing home to bring horses to visit and they were thrilled with her idea. She would trailer a few of the horses to visit some of the residents. Caregivers pushing wheelchairs and gurneys took them to touch, pet, and give love to the horses. It made everyone happy and it became a special time for them.

The newspaper and television station appeared one afternoon to take pictures and video the special occasion. That helped draw in a few extra donations for them.

Days later Debbie spotted a horse lying down in the pasture. She walked out to make sure it was taking a nap and not down for any other reason. With a halter and lead rope in hand she went to take the horse into the barn. The heat and humidity were wretched and she was soaked with sweat by the time she reached the horse.

Once she got there she knew it was the Quarter horse, Jasmine, a rescue brought in a few months back. She was abandoned by her owners who didn't want her because she couldn't be ridden. She was lame from all the barrel racing and they left her in a pasture to die. The grey and brown mare was soaked with sweat and Debbie could see that she was having a hard time breathing. Reaching for her phone which she left on the desk Debbie turned and ran back to the barn. Yelling at the top of her lungs. "Horse down! horse down! Jasmine is down!" Volunteers came from every corner. Grabbing water, medicine, towels, and anything they thought would help. Debbie ran back to the mare, dropping to her knees she tried to soothe her, talking at a whisper to let her know help was coming. Lightly stroking the horse, Debbie asked her to get up, begged her to be ok. A few of the other horses in the pasture gathered around their pasture mate.

Debbie pleaded, "Jasmine you need to get up. Come on, sweet girl, can you see your friends are here they want you to get up?"

Wrapping her arms across the horse's neck hugging her. Debbie could feel the heat roll off the horse. Both were completely wet from sweat.

The help arrived and they immediately administered pain medication and made attempts to get her to drink. Wet towels draped the horse and they continued to apply new cool ones.

One volunteer yelled that Jerri was on her way.

Debbie saw the horse start to relax and hoped it was an opportunity to get her up.

"Come on, girl, get up, let's go," she demanded. Another volunteer pulled on her tail as Jasmine struggled to get to her feet. Her legs pawed at the ground, her head was up and reaching for the sky. Finally she pulled herself up to half-standing. She couldn't get her back legs to straighten out and fell back to the ground. They all tried again to get her up. One lady held her on her side to brace the horse. Jasmine got up and weaved as if she was drunk. Her legs shook under her. Debbie pulled on the lead rope asking, "Jasmine, come on, you gotta walk." She fought to walk and as hard as she tried she went down again with a hard thump. Jerri arrived spewing commands and questions. She didn't know the history on the mare. Debbie and Kate gave as much information as they knew. With her stethoscope on the horses stomach, heart and neck, Jerri reported she didn't hear any gut sounds and her pulse was weak. Looking at the group standing around, "I think she's colic and we are too late to save her." The horse laid quietly as if she knew it was her time to go. Jerri administered a light sedative to help the horse rest. "It's time to cross the rainbow bridge sweet lady." She spoke softly as if she caressed Jasmine with her words. Within a few minutes Jasmine was gone. Her eyes held a blank stare and her breathing slowly stopped. Jerri walked away. It was how she handled every case when she lost a horse. Debbie and Kate sat on the ground with the other horses surrounding them. A few would give soft quiet nicker, while the others stood quietly. They knew their friend had moved over the rainbow. Both ladies laid their heads down on top of the horse and cried. It was their way of dealing with the loss. A good hard cry helped. Each and every time it was hard to deal with the sorrow. As many times as they had lost a horse it never got any easier. Lauren walked up to the two handing them each a cold bottle of water and cold towel. Their arms, legs and clothes were caked with sweat and dirt. She could see the exhaustion, mentally and physically in both of them, and the heavy burden of the loss they carried in their hearts. At times like this Lauren was the strong one among the trio. "Come on, ladies, you both need to get up. She's gone to a special horse heaven. You've done everything you could. I called for the tractor to come and bury her. Come on girls it's time. Say you're goodbye. No, better yet, tell her welcome to heaven."

Silently they all got up and walked to the barn.

Dave, the barn maintenance man, quietly walked past the three women with a tarp under his arm. He wanted to cover Jasmine until the guy with the tractor could come to bury her. He knew it would be early in the morning the next day. He was concerned with her being a feeding frenzy for the turkey vultures and coyotes. The other horses stepped aside as he covered her. Only one horse, a gelding named JoJo, refused to move. He stood next to her as if he was an honor guard. Dave worked around him. Before he tucked the last corner of the tarp he placed his hand on her and whispered "Rest sweet girl. Find happiness and no more pain."

Lauren told the volunteers to leave JoJo but bring in the other horses for the evening. She walked up to where he was still standing and left his feed and hay on the ground. JoJo lowered his head to sniff at the food but he wasn't interested. Lifting his head, he remained on guard with Jasmine.

Patting his neck Lauren said. "You can keep an eye on her but you have to eat, too, buddy." JoJo stood at attention not acknowledging her. She knew he would eat when he got hungry. She tenderly her placed hand on his jaw. "You're a special horse, never quit who you are brave boy."

Lauren returned to the barn. Walking into the office she saw Debbie and Kate cleaning up. "Anyone need a glass of wine?" Without waiting for a response she poured three tall glasses of wine. She walked across the room and handed them each a glass.

The first to speak was Kate, slowly shaking her head. "It doesn't ever get easy. No matter how hard I try to reason it out, I just can't help but hurt."

Debbie agreed. "No, it never gets any better and it's even harder when it comes as a surprise like this. It always amazes me how quickly things can take a turn around here."

Debbie and Kate didn't leave the barn that night. They sat in the field for a few hours with JoJo. The felt they owed him the same respect he was giving Jasmine. Eventually they returned to the barn and fell asleep in the chairs.

As the sun rose they awoke, hearing the tractor off in the distance. Lauren arrived and sent them home to heal.

# Chapter 25

As the summer heat continued the drought turned into monsoon season. Pastures flooded, the barren land was unable to hold the water. Days and days of heavy storms battered the rescue. Horses once again had to stay inside to prevent problems with their feet and it kept them from stomping the ground. The lush pastures were mud and drenched with water sitting everywhere. One evening Kate called Debbie telling her that a tornado had hit the back pasture, trees uprooted, fence boards scattered, and two horses were cut with flying branches. Lee drove along with Debbie to help Kate. He had not been able to spend time with her lately. Her schedule kept her away from home. They seemed to pass in the night, morning, and afternoon. They hadn't had a quiet dinner together in weeks. It was either horses, volunteers or money problems that kept her away. Another thing, Lee had suspicions. His wife was a terrible liar. If it had been another man he could go out and beat the guy, but if it was a horse, he knew he would be on the losing end. They talked often about another horse, however, Debbie never wanted to replace Blu. Many times he wanted to discourage her getting another horse. He knew if she owned a horse he would never see her. The horse came first with everything, Blu ate before her, he also had his medical, feet, and complete care before him. It was hard for him to admit, but he had a tinge of jealousy with Blu. Debbie knew how Lee felt about Blu. Playing second fiddle to a horse just didn't sit well. At times the kids complained about the amount of time she spent with him. Being late for birthdays or leaving a party because she had to care for him. Even worse not showing up at all. Yet, they all understood her passion for horses. Lee waited for his window of opportunity to get Debbie to talk. Hopefully the middle of the night drive to the barn was the opportunity he needed. Watching her drive he could see her face in the dark. Worry was written in bold letters. Without turning his head he asked, "How is it going with the problem you had with those volunteers? Did you get that straightened out?"Carefully watching the road, she answered, "A little". Some people just don't understand it's about the horses, not their egos. Ya know every now and then we get a few who think they can run the show. At times I want to throw my hands up and tell them to go ahead. Do my job, see how well you can do.""I understand that, it's like that at work for me too. Except I do run the show and you have employees who always know everything better, until something goes wrong then it falls back in my lap. Anything else going on? Any new horses? You mentioned a few were adopted." Lee continued to carefully drill Debbie without raising suspicion.

"Yea, we did get in a few new ones. Two came in together from the auction. They literally stole them from the kill buyer. A new group is doing spectacular with attempts to put the kill buyers out of business. The two were both geldings. We think they are brothers. One is brown on white and the other is white on brown. They look like a couple of book ends. Real sweethearts."

Lee released a loud sigh, thinking to himself, "Great it's not just a horse it's two horses." Wonder when she is going to tell me?"

They arrived at the barn and it didn't look too bad at first but when they got to the parking area it was obvious with the mess in the pastures that there'd had been a tornado. Walking in the barn the horses were all restless, shuffling in their stalls a few circling. Looking at Lee she said, "Can you grab some hay and see if that might help to calm them down?"

Lee walked into the hay room, grabbed the wheelbarrow with hay inside and tossed it into the stalls. It did immediately quiet them, however, he wasn't sure for how long.

Debbie found Kate mending the two horses cut by the tree limbs. Picking up the first-aid box she said. "Not too bad. They will be ok. One has a bad cut, but we don't need stitches. I will start them on antibiotics in the morning."

Lee saw Debbie casually walk by two horses on the end and reach into her pocket handing them both treats. He could see they had developed a close friendship. Thinking to himself, "So there's my competition, I have to check them out."

They all met in the office and wanted to survey the property. The three hopped in the golf cart to check out the damage. What they saw was not good. With the spotlight they could see the damage. Fifty feet of fence was totally ripped apart, two large oak trees had fallen and one was split down the middle. This was going to take heavy power to repair.

Kate was the first to voice her opinion. "This pasture is out of commission for a few weeks. Do we have the funds to repair the fence?"

Debbie continued to scan the damage with the light. "Not really." Her voice was telling a story of being stressed more then she already was.

Lee offered, "I can get some of the guys from work to come out and clear this away tomorrow. We can try to salvage parts of the fence." They drove back in silence. Debbie and Lee left Kate to go in and try to relax for what was left of her shift. While driving home Lee wanted to make another try at getting her to admit about the horses. "Debbie, is something bothering you. You seem really preoccupied lately. Need to talk?"No why?" He knew his wife. When she answered a question with a question he knew she was up to something. He thought, I'll he would give up for now. She'll confess sooner or later. The next morning Debbie was greeted by a few volunteers, and thinking "Now what?" Casey, the newest volunteer, blurted, "Have you seen the weather? We have a hurricane coming toward us." Debbie had heard. She watched the weather this time of the year. "Yes, I saw it and we have an evacuation plan just in case. Casey, will you be the one to update us on the weather? Send emails to everyone with every updates." Debbie knew this would keep her busy to not continually pester her. She turned around with her finger pointing toward the sky. "Oh and could you send emails out to the committee leaders? We need to have a meeting with the storm brewing." Casey took off for the office to send the emails. The rest of the volunteers separated and went to do their work. Lee and his men arrived with plenty of equipment to start clearing the pastures and make an attempt at repairing the fences. Debbie took off to have a breakfast meeting with the Executive Board members. They wanted to purchase the back five acres for another barn. With another barn they would qualify for some government financial assistant. Debbie didn't agree with the idea. Opening a new barn would be a financial burden and she would need to consider having a few more paying positions. They were stretching the limits with the volunteers they already had. She always felt like the only one other then Kate who understood the process. The Board appeared clueless at times. They needed to put on a pair of work clothes. And come out to work instead of sitting in their ivory tower coming up with stupid ideas. She liked all the members, it was just at times they frustrated her. Arriving at the Executive Board's office building she was greeted with fresh donuts and hot coffee. She knew that she would have her sugar fix for a few days while in the meeting. After three hours they broke up the meeting and the purchase to buy the acres was still not agreed upon. As soon as Debbie brought up the idea of having to pay people to help run it they backed off of the idea. All she needed was three more members to place thumbs down on the idea and it would be all a bad pain-in-the-butt memory. She knew the others could be persuaded eventfully by those who were against the whole idea. She liked the idea of trying to get one more person on the payroll. Lauren needed some help and it would take pressure off of a few of the volunteers who worked hard daily. They could relax and enjoy the horses. Debbie had a few errands to run, stop by the feed/ tack store to order feed, hay and other supplies. She later treated herself to a hot cup of coffee and a walk on the beach. Finally it was time to return to reality. While she drove her music blasted the air. Driving right past the barn she went home to fix a nice dinner for Lee. It was time to confess that they were the owners of two horses. She knew that he suspected something was up. Working on how she was going to tell him, she thought that she would give him one of the horses as a birthday gift. No, that wouldn't work. What about having two horses for the grandkids? That still wouldn't work. They would still be two horses and more work. Thinking that she needed to make a desperate move, she would get him drunk. Again, not a good idea. She laughed to herself that just being honest would be a new concept and he just might buy it. Settling on the honest route being the best, she fixed his favorite dinner of baked Salmon and cheese potatoes with a nice cherry pie for desert. Just as she finished setting the table Lee walked in the door. Seeing the table, he could smell fish baking and he saw the cherry pie ready to go in the oven.

He crossed his arms on his chest. "Ok Debbie, what have you done? What are you going to do? Who are you going to do it with? When are you going to do this, whatever it is? How are you going to do whatever you have done? Come on confess. You need a full or half glass of wine?" She turned around to face Lee, holding a glass of wine. "No, I have one. You wanna drink? Raising one eyebrow. "Do I need one?" She giggled, "Yeah, it wouldn't hurt." Lee poured himself a brandy and soda. "Ok, now talk!" With a sly smirk on her face she blurted every word going a mile-a-minute. "I adopted two horses. You can have one? I couldn't help myself. They are wonderful. You need a horse of your own. We can ride together off into the sunset. Have romantic evening rides. They are brothers, I couldn't separate them. I don't know what came over me. They had some sort magical power. I really didn't want to do this but I thought I would do it for the rescue. You understand don't you?"

Lee bent over laughing, spilling some of his drink. He looked across the room at his frantic wife. "You had me up until the magical power excuse. No, actually knowing you, I do believe the magical powers they held over you. Why didn't you come to me? Let me meet them. I knew you were starting to think about getting another horse. You will never replace Blu, I knew one day we would have another horse in the family. Truthfully I didn't expect two. They are the two paints in the back, right?"

She smiled at him.

As much as he didn't like the idea, he was coming around to having a horse to ride with her. Might be fun and as they say, 'if you can't beat them join them'.

They enjoyed the nice dinner together and talked about the horses. She wanted to change their names from Sticky and Dickey to Cole for the black and white, Chip for the brown and white. Lee actually liked the names and he enjoyed being a part of the changing of the names.

After dinner they took a ride to the barn and had a small welcome to the family party.

Both horses were presented with new halters and fed apples and carrots.

Lee thought he would like Chip for his horse. He liked the name and they seemed to click together well. What Lee didn't know was that Chip would nuzzle up to anyone. Debbie knew that he would pick him and that was perfect. Cole was a little more to handle, she discovered. They were a two horse family now. It would be harder to tell the kids then it was Lee. She knew they would say that they didn't need another horse or two. She had Lee on her side to back her. When they did tell them they all looked at their father as if he had lost his mind.

# Chapter 26

Hurricane season was well under way. Weeks ago, both North and South Carolina had been battered with a category three storm. The Atlantic Ocean was brewing with two storms churning at the same time. Everyone was on edge as the storms continued to fly off the African coast. It was only a matter of time before they would were hit. They could only hope that they would be spared for another year. Everyone was glued to their televisions. It was a yearly event living in Florida. Hurricanes were as much a part of them as Disney was with tourists. Each year they somehow managed to escape but the odds were closing in on them.

One storm heading directly toward the coastline seemed to do a complete turnaround. The emergency evacuation team calmed down and everyone went back to normal, breathing a sigh of relief.

Three days later the same storm did another complete turnaround and headed straight for them. Debbie thought this couldn't be happening, storms didn't do things like this, and this storm had a mind of its own. It was determined to hit land. They were directly in line of the storm. The storm team gathered to discuss the plans again. They had enough trailers to move the horses. Everyone was on high alert.

The barn was covered with heavy wood and securely placed plywood. Additional supplies and equipment were readied to be moved with the evacuation. They were as ready as they could be for the storm. The relief barns were ready to accept them. The morning weather reported that the storm speed increased and was moving faster. They told everyone who needed to get out start going now. The roads and highways would be jammed. It seemed that overnight the storm had blown up into a full raging nightmare. Winds were gusting at one hundred and fifteen miles per hour. That was a category three storm. Evacuation plans were in being activated. Everyone worked together. The older horses went first, then everyone else. Moving twenty-two horses in a rush was actually working out well. The horses seemed to understand that they needed to cooperate with the move. A few acted up and others didn't want to go along with the plan but in the end they all were loaded.

Lee had Cole and Chip in one trailer and all they had to do was load the last two thoroughbreds. They both were very easily agitated and at times hard to manage. They come in weeks ago off the racetrack heading to the auction house. They were doomed if they made it to auction. The only thing both horses knew was to run and they wanted to run. From the day they arrived they ran all over the pastures. They never tired of the running games. Everyone loved to watch them. They were the attraction at the moment. Jack and Lee were ready to go. All they had to load was the thoroughbreds. Kate and Debbie walked them both together, thinking that they would go in jointly it would be safer.

In the process of loading them one horse pulled back dragging Kate to the ground. The other one did the same with Debbie. As they bucked wildly, everyone scrambled out of the way. Within seconds the horses turned and ran. One jumped the fence to their pasture and the other ran through the open gate. They were out of control and gone.

All four of them ran after the horses, knowing that it would be a lost cause. They could never get the horse in the trailers without sedating them and the medication was on the other vehicles already on the road.

The wind gusts were picking up. Tree's swayed to the breaking point. An occasional downpour left everyone soaked. The wind bands exceeded sixty miles per hour. Rain pelted their faces and hands. Mud slid under their feet creating slimy quick sand. Both ladies faces blackened with mascara running down their cheeks. The storm worsened every minute. Time was running out for a safe evacuation.

Debbie yelled to Lee to go ahead, she would stay behind and hide in the medical barn. It was remodeled to withstand heavy winds in the event of a hurricane.

Another gust pushed them around. Lee argued with her to leave the horses. Debbie was not leaving them.

Jack and Kate were having the same disagreement. "You're both crazy to do this Kate, I understand your love for these animals but you can't get killed trying to save them."

Debbie was yelling at Lee that if he didn't get on the road they could get stuck and then have a worse problem.

There wasn't time to argue. The husbands left and they would have the argument at a later time.

Kate ran for longer lead ropes and Debbie found two long lines. The chase was on to find and capture the loose horses. The winds were blasting the area. Neither one of them could run into the wind. Debbie started laughing at Kate trying to face the wind. Kate joined in laughing. Debbie wasn't any different.

A break in the wind allowed them to search for their lost horses. They had a good idea where they would be. Hiding in the cove of trees on the opposite side of the pasture. They could feel protected, however, the horses didn't understand that the trees could crush them.

The winds speeds were increasing. They had to get the horses into the barn before they were picked up like Dorothy in the Wizard of Oz and flown into lands unknown. When the winds slowed down they saw both horses trotting toward them.

Kate hollered, "I guess they figured it out how to get home."

It took no time at all and the horses were happy to see the two ladies. They walked back to the barn without needing halters. The horses followed them straight to the medical barn and without an escort walked into the stalls. Inside the barn of leftover hay was piled against the walls. It took both of them to close the heavy doors and even then the doors banged around. At least they were inside away from the angry weather.

Kate found the old radio and batteries. They listened to the reports, they didn't need to know how hard the wind was blowing they could hear it. The horses would circle every time the metal roof shook. Kate reported "They just said the winds were about one hundred miles per hour and expected to increase in the next few hours. I think we're in for a wild ride this afternoon."

Breaking up a bale of hay to sit on, Kate offered the horses something to eat. They were not interested in food.

Debbie took another bale and set herself up. "You didn't happen to find a deck of cards anywhere?"

Kate shook her head.

Both ladies ducked when they heard the pounding of the metal roof. "It sounds like it's ready to cave in," Debbie said. "I'm hungry. I'm going to the office and see what I can dig up for us. You want to tie a rope around my waist in case I get blown away?"

"Not a bad idea. I'll go with you as long as we have a short break in the wind. I have a bad headache. I need a couple of aspirins and it's going to get worse as the barometric pressure drops."

In the office they found the pain relievers, a half-finished bottle of wine, along with hard rolls, butter, and a bag of chocolates. A heavy band of wind whirled and the power went off. With the little daylight they had left they made sure to grab if there was anything they might need. The safest place for them was back at the other barn. Walking back, the mud sucked their feet and Kate started to fall. She reached for Debbie and they both went down in the mud. Trying to stand wasn't working for them. They crawled back. Locking the door they knew that it would be the last time they left their safe bunker. They checked on the horses, who seemed to be taking the whole thing in stride. They would act up, when the wind shook the building. Every now and then they would hear a loud bang against the side walls.

Eventually the eye started to pass and this was their chance to get out and look around. Tree limbs, shed doors, trees fallen over, fence boards scattered throughout the pastures. The metal strips from the barn roof were wrapped around the gate. Debbie walked down to the front gate and found it gone. All that was left was two mangled metal posts. They tried to use their cell phones and couldn't get through.

Darkness set in making it hard to see all of the damage.

"Kate, I hate to see this place when this is over. We have the back side of the storm to battle yet and that's the worst part. Can you think of anything we need in the office or try to save in the office? I think it might be gone when we get back."

"I know. Look at the mess around here. I'm nervous for part two of the storm. The office was stripped when we evacuated. They were smart to take the computers and all the electronic gadgets. As the second round hits us, it might be a good time to finish that wine." Debbie spoke so softly as if she didn't want to hear herself.

In the medical barn they propped wood beams against the sliding doors to prevent them from opening. The horses started to be agitated, circling in their stalls and snorting in the air.

Debbie looked up at the roof. "I think it's back. Kate, lets pull more bales around us in case this place comes tumbling down on top of us."

"Good idea," Kate nervously answered.

They piled bales of hay higher to make a wall around them. They had a tarp to drape over it and moved it all closer to the inner wall.

The storm returned with a vengeance. The metal roof shook, doors slammed in and out against the opening. The ground rumbled beneath them. For hours they were tortured by the wind and rain. It was a relentless beating. They would get a few seconds for a reprieve. But it returned and beat on the building. The horses started to frantically kick the walls.

Debbie opened the stall doors and they dashed out, running up and down the aisle. Both ladies crawled into the stalls to hide. The horses were in a panic and they nearly ran into each other. One bit the other one on the neck. They swung around each other.

Kate screamed, "They're going to kill each other! We need to open the doors, let them out!"

Debbie screamed back for her to stay in the stall, they might settle down. Worried if either one of them left the protective stall the horses could kick or bite them. Within a few minutes the panicked horses quieted down. As quickly as the winds quieted down, it heavy wind bands blasted the barn again. This time part of the roof started to peel back the metal roof shook and rocked in the wind. Heavy bursts of wind lifted the roof and dropped it. The horses found the bales of hay to graze on. While the two women cowered in the stalls. Rain poured in through the roof opening. The sound of a freight train rumbled from the ground beneath. The winds shrieked and the walls of the barn groaned. More of the roof peeled back like an open can of vegetables. They were being attached from every direction. Both of them could feel the pressure of the storm in their heads. The wind continued to pummel the barn, tree limbs clawed the sides. Debbie looked over the top of the stall door and both horses had lain down together. Crawling out of the stall to where Kate was cowering in fetal position. The wind sounded like a monster chewing the building. Kate felt the side of the barn shake as if it was leaning toward them. Debbie could feel the same thing. Wriggling out of the doors they stayed close to the ground and made their way to the horses. The horses didn't move. They kept their heads up and ears pointed into the bashing wind. Without fully understanding it, the ladies inched between the horses, cuddling with them. The horses remained on the ground, allowing the four of them to hold on to each other.

Kate called out, "You know what is going on here? They are staying down and protecting us. I owe them an apology for cussing them out when they ran away." Debbie reached over to Kate's hand, tapping it." I know this is something nobody would believe unless they saw it for themselves. This is the most remarkable feeling I've ever experience. I never want to move away from them".

The four remained motionless and quiet. Debbie could hear the sound of the horse's heart beats as she lay with them. They drifted off to a light sleep for a short time in the comfort of their companions.

The wind started to shift away, yet sporadic torrent winds would rip open. The storm was moving away. It was almost over. Eight hours in the belly of a hurricane in a wooden, creaky barn was remarkable. The longest eight hours of their lives.

The horses started to get up and walk around, finding the hay they were content to eat. Not knowing what to expect and with much anticipation they took a quick glance outside at the damage. Looking up through the hole in the roof it was still dark outside.

Kate handed Debbie the spotlight. It glowed off the ground. Panning the barn from floor to ceiling, the place was unrecognizable. The main barn was half-collapsed. The roof lay in its side in the middle of the parking area. The rain continued for the next few hours. Knowing they couldn't do anything for the barn, they returned to a dry corner that was their shelter from the storm. Pushing hay around to make a bed, pulling the tarp over themselves they finally fell asleep.

# Chapter 27

The next day Lee and Jack returned home, finding the destruction, and never understood how the two of them had survived.

Days later volunteers returned to start the rebuilding process. Offers to temporarily care for the horses came in. The response from the community to reconstruct the damage was overwhelming. What wasn't covered by insurance was covered by the wonderful hearts those of the public.

Kate adopted the two special thoroughbreds. They would never want for anything. She vowed to protect them as they had done during the storm for them. Promising to give them a secure forever home.

Nobody understood how or why she did that. She told Jack the story and he was grateful to the horses. He would do anything to make them have a happy home.

Lee brought Cole and Chip back. Somehow over the last few days they had all become very attached to each other, creating a special bond.

For whatever reason the four of them returned to their homes sustaining very little damage. Kate and Debbie opened their homes to any volunteers who couldn't stay in their houses.

Over the next few months the rescue returned to normal, the damage was repaired and forgotten. The back five acres were donated and a new barn was erected strictly for horses that had been rescued from kill buyers. They named the barn Michael in honor of Michael the Archangel. To protect all those who entered. Three volunteers were hired on as permanent employees. Every stall had a small piece of the old barn attached to the stall doors. Amazingly, the only area not damaged by the storm was the Memorial Gardens. A beautiful picket fence from the old barn wood was built surrounding the special section.

New Years day the rescue welcomed everyone to the grand opening. People came from miles to see the new facility. It was a new start to an old idea.

If you save one you can save them all.

I would like to introduce my next book

## "Broken Eyes"
### 1

*"The best thing for the inside of a man, is the outside of a horse."Winston Churchill*he most humbling experience is to spend time working as a volunteer at a horse rescue farm. To witness the destruction of these beautiful creatures with their ribs protruding and fur gone, so weak they are unable to walk, is just too heartbreaking an encounter. Observing their daily struggle to survive and the fortitude they show to regain their natural character puts everything else in life in perspective. We, as humans, should be humiliated by the devastation we heap upon these beautiful horses. Yet, we think nothing of it, because we don't feel their pain. My husband and I adopted Obie from a local rescue farm. His history of abuse made him frail and fragile. His hips resembled a salad bowl on steroids. His ankles and knees were thick with calcified arthritis. The story narrated to us by the rescue volunteers was that he was a trail horse and someone called the rescue service to report his condition. A witness observed a riding stable using him to carry heavy people on five- and ten-mile trail rides. Before his trail days, he was a training horse for jumping. As he got older, he couldn't carry an adult jumper, so he was used as a child's training jumper. He worked his whole life and beyond the age he should have. His past owners sucked the life out of him and used him until he was liberated by the rescue team. His final job with the trail-riding stable completely ruined him.

Volunteers from the rescue facility arrived without notice to follow-up on the anonymous call. They found Obie on a trail ride with a two hundred and fifty-pound man on his back. Adding a saddle and in the dead, humid heat of Florida, he had the equivalent of three hundred pounds on his back, which was like wearing a heavy fur coat. That is equivalent to putting a two hundred-pound backpack on an eighty-year-old, five foot two man. By the grace of God he was rescued, and they took him away, and we fell in love with him.

While he spent his days at the rescue facility, Obie was classified "unadoptable" due to his age and because he was lame, arthritic, and had an exceptional, cranky disposition. The unadoptable status protected him; the rescue farm didn't want anyone to adopt and use him again as a working beast of burden. As for his cranky disposition, it all depends on how you interpret Obie's tale. I can't imagine not being cranky at his age, and how his delicate, old body must have ached. My husband Brad and I volunteered at the rescue facility and we fell in love with Obie. He wasn't cranky with us once we proved ourselves to him, and he allowed us to enter his world. Obie was noble and wise. In our hearts, we felt he was better than the world champion horses such as Zenyatta, John Henry, and Secretariat. Although he is only 14.2 hands in stature, to us he was the size of a Clydesdale. We knew his twenty-eight years of hard work were taking their toll on him, and we wanted a better life for him; we never knew how long we were going to have him, and we wanted every moment to count.

We offered him green pastures, plenty of food, and tons of spoiling; we felt we owed it to him. I had often wondered how he survived all the years of abuse he had endured.

One lady said to me, "I think Obie made it as far as he did because he was waiting for the perfect herd, and he wasn't going to give up until he found it, and I think he found that in you." It was a tall order to fill, but he deserved it.

After the adoption was finalized, we boarded him at a property recommended to us by the rescue volunteers. For awhile, life at the new barn was good, but it turned sour for him. The other horses dominated him; they would kick and bite him—he was the barnyard punching bag. I couldn't believe how he would not move his legs, allowing the other horses to bully him. He stood still and refused to back down, even if it was hurting him. He started to slow down again, and we couldn't bear to watch him deteriorate. We had the owner of the barn move him to a protected area away from the other horses. This seemed to stop the other horses from bullying Obie.

As much as we tried to ease his pain, it was easy to see he tried to please us and go along with everything we asked. Every day, we would rub his legs with arthritis cream and massage his hips. We walked him all around the property and on the dirt road to strengthen his muscles; slowly, we saw a new horse start to develop. His hurting days were less or at least bearable. The walks kept him from getting stiff. In the pasture, he would roll his toy green gym ball toward us, and we would play a game of walking soccer. His cranky nature vanished; instead, he gave us kisses and affection. We brought our grandkids to come to the barn and walk Obie. He seemed to find the kids fascinating; his head would follow them, and he would get dizzy watching them. We considered ourselves a happy, content herd. But the bullying from the other horses was not acceptable. We had to find a new home for Obie.

I made an appointment to inspect a new barn for Obie. This place was only a few miles away and close to the horse rescue facility. We drove into a long driveway, hidden and very private. Tall oak and pine trees canopied the property. The overgrown foliage kept the summer heat a few degrees lower and provided nice shade.

The owners seemed very nice. They were older gentlemen, and from first impressions, they had good hearts. The barn had sixteen horses at the time, and most importantly, it was quiet. Obie would have a large pasture and paddock area with a sweet, quiet Appaloosa mare as a pasture buddy. We made arrangements quickly, and the following Saturday morning we moved Obie to his new home.

The day we arrived, as Obie backed out of the trailer, I thought the owner of the property was going to faint. I saw his hand reach to cover his open mouth; his face turned ghostly white. His eyes fixated on Obie's mutilated hips. I could tell he was just mortified. I felt embarrassed that I had allowed this to happen.

I put my hand on Obie's hip and said, "This is why we moved him; he needs to be safe." His hips looked like ground beef. The bites tore his skin, and it looked worse than it was. I had been treating his wounds with an antibiotic cream.

He just nodded his head and walked away. We followed him to Obie's stall and paddock. The barn housed five separate stalls with three large pastures. On the back side were two large stalls, and each one had its own paddock area. They decided to have Obie in the second stall from the front. He would share a pasture with an Appaloosa mare who seemed eager to have a roommate. There was enough grass to comfortably split up between the two of them. Obie confidently walked in his new pasture as if he knew he wouldn't be bullied any longer.

While Obie wandered around in his new pasture and introduced himself to his pasture buddy, Brad put shavings in his stall and hung his water bucker and salt lick. Obie rambled into his new stall and inspected his new home. We all went into the stall and just sat with him for the rest of the day. Obie turned toward the corner of his stall and within a few minutes he put his head in the corner; he needed a nap. I sat on the ground, watching him as his breathing became a soft rhythm, whispering to him, "I am so sorry, Obie; I failed you and failed to protect you." He opened his eyes and slightly turned his head. I walked up to him, squeezed his neck, and gave him a kiss. He went back to his nap; I left him alone.

I went to help Brad unpack the rest of his supplies and his food. Obie's feed was in a tub; we prepackaged it from home. We didn't want to burden anyone with extra work, and this way, we knew he was getting everything he needed. Obie's daily diet consisted of rice bran to keep his weight up, and because he was missing so many teeth, we had to soak his food. He started to choke on his hay, and we tried soaking it; however, it didn't help him enough. We replaced the hay with soaked alfalfa pellets.

Immediately, I could see Obie start to thrive again, and we resumed our walks. We had a special gym ball to play soccer with Obie. We would lightly kick the ball to him, and he would push the ball with his nose toward us. Once he rolled the ball to us, we would raise our hands in the air and yell, "Score." Obie rewards us with a kiss, and we returned the reward with an apple slice. He put the weight back on and was looking like he should have. His wounds healed, and his coat was back to its copper color. The old Obie we knew and loved was back to his old, affectionate self.

A friendly relationship started to grow with the owners of the property. Brad and I are not super friendly folks; we have always stayed to ourselves and family. I had a policy to always stand back and watch to see if people were as genuine as they tried to be. This was a business deal, not a match-making affair. We both wanted to keep it on a business level.

While at the horse rescue farm, I had heard horror stories about owners and boarders not getting along—barn managers, property and horse owners—all failing their responsibilities. Nevertheless, the horse always is the one to suffer in the end. We wanted to avoid drama and conflicts with everyone.

From the beginning, I was seeing a few things that made me uncomfortable. I saw the warning signs and red flags started to flap lightly in the wind. We all got along peacefully; we respected them as property owners, and as the saying goes, "My Barn, My Rules." We had to respect that. They seemed to return the respect.


## 2
*"You have to take risks. We will only understand the miracles of life fully when we allow the unexpected to happen." Paul Coelho*

Within a few months at the new barn, I noticed a dark-colored horse all alone in a dusty, back pasture. The horse was circling in the center of the pasture and appeared very agitated or frightened. I stood at the fence, watching this strange behavior for about fifteen minutes until the horse stopped and faced toward my direction, with its head tilted to the side. The horse just stood there with this intense gaze in my direction, as if it were looking right through me. Our eyes didn't meet. Then the circling started up again. This was a very peculiar thing to watch.

There were sixteen other horses at this barn, but this horse captivated my attention. Over the next few days, I watched it perform the same pace, circle, and stare. I didn't understand what was going on with this horse. I felt a twinge in my stomach when I looked at it: its hooves were overgrown; it pranced like it was wearing scuba-diving flippers; it had learned to live with this. Somehow, something was wrong, and my gut instincts told me to listen.

It; I kept calling it "it"; IT had to be something; was it a girl or boy horse? "IT" was not correct. I felt coldhearted, calling this beautiful horse "it." I climbed through the pasture fence, trying to get a closer look at "it." I needed to know… and as luck would have it, *she* went to the bathroom. Ah, a mare. I giggled out loud, and my laugh caught her attention. She faced my direction and titled her head. Again she stared straight at me without looking; it didn't make any sense. I was intrigued by this dark horse.

 I had to touch her, and I wanted to make friends. I introduced myself. She kept a safe distance from me, yet her head followed my footsteps.  Her gangly legs were spread apart, as if she were trying to balance herself, and she had a little rock to her stance.  This was a curious process.

I couldn't help endlessly staring at this dark horse, and for a short time, it seemed as if she were staring back, yet she had a huge stay-a-way-from-me look mixed in with another look of who-in-the-hell-are-you? She wasn't my horse or my business, so I kept my distance from her.

But I was drawn to this horse, and every chance I got I would walk to the pasture fence to watch her. While standing on the edge of her dusty pasture, I tried to figure out her breed. I knew she had to be some sort of gaited horse, but my knowledge of breeds was limited. Her coat was black, but I had to look again; was it black, or was this horse just filthy dirty?

She reminded me of the Helen Keller movie—Ann Bancroft trying to teach Patty Duke to understand sign language. She was a survivor. This horse was also a survivor. No one had taught her to turn and face in my direction. I wasn't sure if it were her self-protective instincts to face her threat or a form of body sign language. She had to do it on her own. I wondered if she were trying to analyze me. I couldn't take my eyes off of her; she was amazing. She had an inner, independent strength that defied anyone to approach without her permission. I was starting to admire the tenacity of this beautiful animal.

The Florida heat was well into its usual pattern of heat and heavy afternoon rains. It was an exceptionally hot and extremely humid afternoon that particular day, standing at her fence.  I yearned for Mother Nature to give me a cool, pre-rain breeze to blow through the dusty pasture.  The property owner walked up behind me without warning and said with a deep southern drawl, "You watchin' her?"

He startled me; I wasn't expecting anyone. "Could you give a warning before you scare the pants off of me?" He just looked back at me. I wanted to ask him, if he smiled, would his face crack? Nodding my head and not taking my eyes off her, I said, "Yes, she is beautiful, although she could use a bath." I didn't want to bring up the condition of her feet. But I wanted to ask him why any horse would have overgrown hooves. It looked painful to walk, with her hooves long and ragged.

"Before you ask about her hooves, let me tell you somethin'; she can't be caught. Even if we could halter her, she would kick the dickens out of you. She is a stubborn one and besides, she ain't worth getting knocked around. I ain't gonna spend good money on her."

Looking at the other horses at the farm, I wanted to ask him what his excuse for the other horses was. There were others who needed care, too, although none were in as bad shape.

He must have read my mind, because without my asking how she got to this barn, he turned toward the mud-filled pasture, waving his cold hand and heaving an exasperated sigh in the direction of this magnificent living being.

"Her name is Miracle. I ended up with her when the owner walked away, and she was abused by an evil bitch. She is about eight years old, an Andulusion Paso Fino. This is a wild one; trust me, she would be better off put down. She's crazy wild, and won't allow anyone to put any hands on her. I'm afraid of her; she will run a person over. She bites, kicks, and she has a wicked attitude. I don't think she could be tamed. We had thoughts of having her put down, or when the one guy comes around looking to buy horses, we could sell her."

I slowly turned to face him. "Are you telling me you would sell her to a kill buyer? Have her taken to an illegal slaughterhouse?" I couldn't believe what I was hearing. I wanted to pick up a chunk of manure and throw it at him. I just sighed. "Then why keep her?" I asked.

He gave me a stern look, which I clearly understood as "mind your own business." I had learned in a short time what both the barn owners' facial looks meant. Knowing and thinking it was for the best with the bleak situation, I left it alone. I would find out for myself sooner or later.

While we booth hung on the fence watching Miracle, I wasn't sure I really wanted the answer to my next question, but… I asked what the previous owner did to her. Assessing her, I noticed her tail and mane were cut—more like butchered? The story was: they had placed a rope halter on her and held her down to cut her mane and tail because it was a hornet's nest. Another story I was told was how they haltered her and performed a water burn; that is, they used a high pressure hose and placed it directly on her skin and forcibly rubbed her skin to remove any dirt to deep-clean her skin to make her coat shine. She was used for sympathy to gain money for the owners. They ignored her and fed her whenever they felt like it. They hid her food and let her search for it.

I tilted my head, "Why hide her food; she could find it, sympathy?" His hand gestured again and with an additional sarcastic *hmph* in his voice he said, "She's blind!" as if I were stupid and didn't see it.

All I could say was, "Oh."

I turned back in her direction and stared at Miracle. Total silence; there wasn't a sound coming from anywhere. Birds, horses, tractors, and wind, everything was completely silent. I was thinking that she doesn't look blind—she has beautiful eyes—but that explains the head tilt. The word "blind, blind, blind," kept going over and over and rolling around in my head. The instincts of this horse must be tremendous, and I just had a revelation of how much enormous respect I had just developed for her.

He walked away and I stood at her pasture fence. I called to her, "Miracle, Miracle come over here." I extended my hand across the fence. She moved slowly toward me with suspicion. Reluctantly, she walked to the fence. I put my hand out closer to her nose; she took a smell then turned and ran off kicking.

She let out a scream as if to say, "I am warning you; I am my own boss."

Why the kicking? Why, why, why? Was all I kept saying to myself. "Okay, you can be the alpha mare; you have to be the one in charge."

I was speechless, confused, enthralled, fascinated, captivated, and mesmerized by this dark bay mare. Watching her circle with her overgrown hooves in her grassless pasture, she dealt with it as if this were normal. This was her life; she had to accept it because she didn't have a human to improve her quality of life. She had to survive. She adapted to the sad living situation of being hurt and lonely.

These abused, neglected horses adapt to their environment to survive. It made me think about Obie in the beginning, how much he had to endure to be in the elite survivor's club. My second thought was about all the horses unable to endure and who lost the fight to stay alive. What a cruel world we have for such a respected animal. Over the next few weeks, Obie settled in. I put all my time into him. We walked and played with his green ball. We spent whole days together, and Miracle was not my immediate concern.

Over time, though, I started to notice her more and got interested in her again. I had to see what she was capable of. I had heard that when you lose one sense that the others become even stronger. I wanted to test this theory out. Her senses of hearing and smell must be phenomenal. With her grazing a good quarter acre away, I wanted to test her hearing. I stood at her pasture fence facing her, with a light wind blowing at my back. My scent was carried on the breeze blowing in her direction. In almost a whisper, I called her name, "Miracle, Miracle can you walk up to me?" I repeated this again. Her head went up and to an angle; she stared in my direction. Her ears pricked up; she took a few steps toward me. She stood still, as if waiting for me to ask her something. I didn't have the right question at that time. I started to have a one-way conversation with her. I talked about anything and everything that came to my head. Her ears never moved off of me. Her whole head froze at what I have come to call the "blind horse tilt." She could zero in on just about any sound as long as the wind was in her direction. I stood in awe of this horse. It seemed like every time I went near her, there was something new to discover.

I continued my one-sided conversation, and she slowly walked over to me. We stood muzzle to face. I kept talking, I couldn't shut up. Miracle sniffed my face, hair, ears, neck, as if she was taking me all in, or was she making a picture of me in her mind? I couldn't or wouldn't move until she was done. My conversation turned into idiot babbling with a lot of *ers, ahs, ums, heys, ohs*…. Miracle backed away from the fence as if dismissing me.

Reaching into my pocket for a treat, I called her back in my normal voice to come get a treat. She walked up and took the treat from my hand. Her head followed my hand as I reached for a second treat. Her nose went to my pocket and she wiggled her soft muzzle at the hidden treats. Ha, her treat scent works very well. I gave her all the treats in my pockets.

I was determined to make it right for this horse. I wanted to know why she was blind. Watching her, I couldn't figure out what it was about her, but she had my heart. I had to hug her, maybe not right at that moment, but one day I would. I knew I would never know or understand the answer to my "why" question. It wouldn't matter how hard someone would try to explain "why" to me. Why didn't anyone see how special this horse is? I wouldn't, couldn't accept any cheap rhetoric or reasoning. This horse is all alone in a pasture, blind, dirty, fearful, and confused. What kind of reasoning would anyone have to justify this mess I was looking at?

Her breed as an Andulusion has a history as far as noblemen and kings of Spain. They are one of the greatest, ancient breeds. The Andulusion horse has been highly regarded since the Middle Ages. They are known to have a high-stepping gait. However, Miracle couldn't perform a natural gait because of the dreadful conditions of her hooves, ruined by stupid humans!

I turned and looked toward the owner's house; he lived with this every day. These are the same people who told me how much they loved their horses, pledging their undying care and bragging about the endless hours of work they did for all of their animals, with their heartrending, sob story about the expenses they had to suffer to maintain a peaceful and good quality of life for these discarded horses. All I could do was shake my head and think, "pitiful people."

I was standing with my arm stretched out and my hand open over the fence. A slight breeze rippled over the pasture. It was so quiet; the only sound was a few far-off birds.

I saw Miracle stand very still with the unusual tilt of her head and look in my direction.

I started to talk to her, "What are you going to do, little girl?" She was owed an explanation of why her life was this way. But yet, she might have accepted it better than I did. It was me; I had to understand. I wanted to tell her I was different. Would she understand me?

"Miracle, they are probably not bad people, they are just stupid. I don't understand the human race myself." Suddenly she stopped rocking and just stood and stared at me.

"Miracle, I don't want to be the kind of person who does the chest-beating mea culpa, I saved a horse. I think you are very strong, but even the strongest creatures do feel pain and loneliness." I stood looking back at her and let my mind wander.

"Miracle, are you getting any of this?" Her ears where pointed right on me.

With my silence, her rocking started again. "Miracle, if I talk, will you stop your rocking?" The sound of my voice stopped the rocking action. My silence reactivated the heavy sway.

"Miracle, please, come here, feel my hand, give me another sniff." It sounded as if I were begging her. She turned away and the circling began. This conversation was over as far as she was concerned. I left her paddock and walked over to Obie. That was all she was going to give me today.

I stood in Obie's stall, putting my face to his neck and inhaling his aroma. He had a special smell, and I loved to hug him, taking it in. But I smelled something else while standing there. Looking around, I saw he left me a present on the ground to pick up. Patting him on his neck, I said, "Thank you, baby boy; as silly as this sounds, I am always glad to see that."

While mucking out Obie's stall, I started thinking that Miracle needs someone. She could be an awesome horse. She was very smart, kind of like a runaway kid, street smart. I would have to enter her world. Would I do more damage to her? My skills with horse training were limited, and my confidence to do the job was even more limited.

The following afternoon was excruciating humid and hot. I mucked out the stalls and pastures, washed buckets, mixed Obie's food, and groomed him. Grabbing a bucket of water and towel, I walked into Obie's stall to cool him down, staring at his face. I kept dipping the towel into the cool water and draping it over his body. He rubbed his face in the towel and wiped his own eyes and forehead. He wasn't much of a sweater; at his age, his body thermostat didn't work as well as it should. I added a can of sugar-free lemon-lime soda to his bucket with water to dilute it; I held it, and he drank it completely. It must have tasted delightful; he seemed to enjoy it as he licked the bottom and sides of the bucket.

### 3

*"When something poses as an obstacle to you, surmount it and use it as a miracle to move on to greater heights."* ❧ *Ifeanyi Enoch Onuoha,*

There wasn't any escaping the heat. Perched on the fence attached to the side of the barn, a small crescent of the overhanging roof gave me a slight shadow for little relief. I couldn't move anymore. My body was soaked in perspiration, my face burned, and the heat just kicked my butt to exhaustion. I was watching Miracle in her near, grass-bare pasture, while in another pasture the other horses were standing under a water sprinkler for relief.

Shaking my head, I thought back on my life and how I got to the point when I first encountered horses. I don't know how I ever became excited about horses. I do remember that anytime I got close enough to a horse, I couldn't walk by without having to reach out and touch it. Movies like *Black Beauty* and TV shows like *Roy Rodgers* had me captivated. I didn't watch the actors; I watched the horses. I have pictures of me as a little girl wearing a cowgirl outfit—it was blue with plastic fringe on the dress and vest. I can't pinpoint when my love for these splendid beasts came to be.

My family was not interested in horses; they were truly the definition of "city folk." Especially my mother; not only did she dislike country life, but she didn't like animals. My dad was mean to our pets, and I always wanted to protect them from him. He would get jealous if I would spend more time with our dog then with him.

He would say to me, "They are animals. You don't treat them like humans, and you don't put humans before any animals."

Being a stubborn ten year old I just heard him but didn't go along with his thinking. I couldn't understand my parents, and I really didn't care or want to figure them out. I do remember a neighbor girl whose parents took her for riding lessons every Saturday morning. I would ask every Saturday if I could tag along to watch. Her mother always said yes, but I needed to get permission from my parents. Of course, they always said "no"; Saturday morning was chores before going anywhere. On Friday nights, I would scrub the floors, dust, clean my room, and get all the tasks done. I can recall one Saturday morning, I was up at 6:00 a.m. and started to vacuum the house. My parents came flying downstairs and gave me hell about the racket at "this ungodly hour." Finally, my dad convinced my mother to let me go to the stable and finish my house responsibilities when I came home. I agreed to the deal, and off I went every Saturday morning to watch my friend go through her lessons. It seemed as if she were gliding on the back of the horse. It was something out of the movies to actually watch a horse canter and maneuver over the jumps.

Every week, I would come home and beg my parents to give me lessons. I wanted to run with the wind and ride like I was a part of the horse, to feel the rhythmic hooves hitting the hard ground and the sensation of flying on the back of a horse. Every Saturday afternoon, I had the same dialogue with my parents, telling them all I had seen, and finally the question was, when can I ride? I begged them to come out and take a tour of the stable.

My mother's answer was, "You don't need to ride a horse," and my dad followed up with, "It's a waste of money to have you break your neck falling off a horse." I promised to not break my neck, and that "Yes, I needed to ride a horse." It was just as important to ride as it was to breathe. The answer was always, "NO!" Then, I wasn't able to go along on Saturday mornings because of my stupid begging about the riding lessons. Knowing that they wouldn't let me go to the stable or take lessons, I devised a plan to get the money on my own.

Coming home after school one afternoon, I dragged all my dolls, stuffed animals, toys, and clothes to the front lawn. Laying everything out on a blanket, with my crayons, I composed a "For Sale" sign. My business venture didn't last long; the nosey neighbor lady called my dad at work. He called my brother who was supposed to be watching me and had me clean everything off the front yard and go to my room until he got home from work. I knew I was a goner. I would be grounded for life, and my butt would be sore for a good, long time.

I sweated it out until I heard his car pull into the driveway, then I waited for my bedroom door to open and face the wrath of the almighty deity. I braced myself for the impact. I kept saying to myself I needed to think faster, to come up with a good reason I embarrassed him in front of the whole neighborhood. As a good Catholic child, I tried to make a deal with God. If he got me out of this, I promised all sorts of things. I would end world hunger, eliminate disease, and bring world peace. The only catch was I had to live long enough to fulfill my promise.

I heard the back door close; it didn't slam, it just closed. Was this a good thing or a bad thing? The anticipation was excruciating, waiting for the sound of my father's footsteps on his way up the stairs and the dreadful warning snap of his belt. It never happened. I waited and waited, then I heard my mother's voice, and I thought this was going to be a tag-team effort. It was worse than I originally thought!

"I'm dead." I wouldn't live to see my eleventh birthday in a few weeks. People would talk about how I could have lived if I only had behaved myself. They would say things such as, "She could have had a bright future, but she couldn't learn to behave." Then I heard my name rattle throughout the house.

Passing my brother in the hall, he gave me a mean smirk and said, "You're dead meat." My whole body trembled as I reached the kitchen. Here were the two of them, and they were not smiling. My mother had a look on her face as if she couldn't wait to get a hold of me. My dad had a funny look I couldn't read; he seemed almost amused with my escapade. My mother went first, with her arms across her chest, holding a wooden spoon. I offered to stir the food on the stove, thinking I could disarm her of the wooden spoon.

"How could you embarrass us, young lady? The whole neighborhood got the impression we are penniless, selling your things, which were not yours to sell. We bought it all for you. As long as we buy your things, you don't have the right to sell them. You will go door-to-door and tell everyone it was your idea, and that we are not broke or paupers." Her voice meant business, and I wanted to crawl into a hole, having to tell everyone we were not bums."

"Okay," I humbly answered.

Turning to face my dad, I looked at him just below his eyes. I had always heard to never look a crazed person in the eye; it can set them off. "What were you thinking? I don't care what the neighbors think. You can't sell your stuff, but seeing how you think you don't need any of it. You will pack it all in a box and take it to the basement. I will figure out how much it all costs, and you can earn it back with work. This will pay for your stupid horse lessons."

I couldn't move. Did I really hear him say, "My stupid horse lessons?" I am getting to ride a horse! I didn't want to smile for fear he would take it back and call the whole idea off.

"You won't have to go to all the neighbors and tell them we are not penniless, just Mrs. Wagner across the street; she'll tell the whole world. You will work around the house and the money for the horse lessons will come out of your chores. You will donate to the church all of your toys you dragged out front. Say 'thank you' and go to your room for the night."

"Thank you and I bounced all the way up to my room. Passing my brother in the hall, I jumped up and down in front of him, saying, "I am going to ride a horse, I get to ride a horse." Sticking out my tongue, I ran to my bedroom, slamming the door. I followed the orders to pack up all my stuff to donate to the church, dragged the boxes to the basement, and returned to an almost empty bedroom. With a big sigh I said to myself, "Now I have room for horse stuff!"

My parents bought me my first lesson as a birthday present. This stable taught only English with the expectation to develop only blue ribbon winners. They taught jumping, show, and dressage riding. Every girl arrived to her lessons with the proper attire of breeches, blazer, and tall, shiny black boots. At eleven years old, I wanted to be those girls, to look like them. The outfits made them all look like sophisticated and experienced riders. However, this was not ever going to happen with me and my riding outfit. I showed up wearing boy's blue jeans, tennis shoes, and whatever shirt that I could wear that was not for school. Needless to say, I didn't make any friends. If the saying is that "the clothes make the person," I truly was *not* made for their lifestyle.

My lessons were basic walk, trot, and canter. I didn't have a desire to train for the shows. I wanted to ride. Getting bored with the lessons, I moved to just riding on Saturday afternoons. This disappointed my mother. She wanted a showstopper, and again I had failed her blind ambitions. Riding was very simple and easy for me; I relaxed in the saddle and rode a horse for an hour. It was all I needed until I could find a horse to call my own one day. I rode the trails and in the arena when the others were done with their lessons. The stable owners and workers understood I wasn't in it for the show, but in it for the horses. There were about thirty-five horses, and I learned each one of their names. The privately owned horses were boarded in a separate barn away from the rentals. I didn't venture into their world, and they ignored me.

When new horses arrived, I was first in line to take them and walk them around, introducing them to their new home. I couldn't touch the horses with private owners; the barn hands were the only ones privileged to handle them. I would watch as the young girls arrived, following their horses to the exclusive barn. Walking past the barn doors, I could see and hear them giggling and sitting on their horses. Talking about how their "daddy" had bought them the best steed in the world. I was envious of them being able to have a horse to call their own. On the other hand, I had a barn full of horses to call my imaginary own.

They were held captive in their world, and I was in my separate world—we all had our own calling. I knew in my heart one day I would have a horse and when I did, I wouldn't wear the silly clothes or have the pressure of shows and didn't need the privileged life. Having a horse put all of us on equal ground; the common denominator is a horse.

As I grew up, horses and riding became less and less a part of my life. I made every effort to ride when I had the time, but high school life and marriage and kids kept me out of the equine life. At some point, I did fall back into it, and would ride just to feel the wonder of a horse beneath me.

## 4

*"The horse though all its trials has preserved the sweetness of paradise in its blood    Johnannes Jensed,*

Sitting on the fence mulling over the future with Obie and Miracle, my daydreaming ended when
I felt a nudge on my thigh. Obie was reminding me he was waiting for his dinner. I needed to think about this whole situation. I was very confused about me and Miracle. Was there a reason for me to be in this place? As I watered and mixed Obie's feed and pellets, my mind reeled, as if there were something telling me I had to do something about Miracle. Dragging Obie's heavy buckets to his stall, I sat back up on the fence between their pastures. Not trying to think so hard, just watching the slow-passing clouds. It was better to stare into space, let the dust settle, and follow the path and see where it goes.
I wanted to connect with this horse. She needed more than what she had in her muddy and grassless pasture, all alone.

I didn't want to make an emotional decision. Miracle didn't need to have anyone who could fail her and leave her. She had had enough disappointment and loneliness in her lifetime. Making a decision about this horse was something I had to totally be committed to. She would be mine no matter how things turned out. Even if she never learned to trust me and was unable to love me, I would love her. I had to accept it as it was. I had to trust that whatever came our way and whatever path we went down, it would be together. We would be in it mutually for a long time. Our relationship might have limits, and she would be the one in control of the constraints or letting go of the boundaries. Miracle understood what she needed more than I did, and I had to allow her to release her inner feelings. Was I prepared to do this and not do more damage to her?

I tilted my head to watch this mysterious and strong, dark horse. I tried to analyze her; I could see weak muscles. I knew her insecurity was masked with a protective shield. She allowed only a small light shining from her heart.

The second guessing had to end. I understood I had already made the commitment in my heart. The deed was done; I had to have her. Standing in the pasture, talking to myself, "Did he say she was blind? Is she totally blind?" All at once, my talking to myself became actually aloud. I had a sudden thought, "Oh shit, I will have to discuss this with my husband Brad." He went along with one horse. Two might be a maximum stretch, and I knew what he would say: *"Not a chance!"* I looked around to see if anyone was watching me talk to myself. All I could do was look intently at her.

In my daydream, I could picture her standing in front of me and accepting my hand, accepting me. I wasn't very optimistic about it; the damage might be too much to repair. Only time will tell how this will work out, then wishing I could see the future. I said to myself, "Be careful what you wish for."

I went back to Obie and asked him if he wanted a little sister. Obie gave me a look that said, "I'm an only child, and let's keep it that way." I understood his animated looks; he said a mouthful with just the look in his eye or the way he turned his head at me.

Every day I spent with Obie, I stole a few moments to introduce myself to Miracle. She was very guarded as she walked toward me. Her shyness became a bit daring each time I extended my hand. We both were uneasy with each other; Miracle didn't trust, and I didn't want to land in the emergency room.

Day after day, I tried to introduce more of myself. I thought a sprits of perfume would help her to remember me, along with the treats. She became more familiar with me every time I walked to the fence. It was time to let the games begin and open the door to the unknown.

Meanwhile one hot afternoon, I watched how the owners treated Miracle. Just before the evening feeding time, I watched as the younger of the owners threw her hay in the pasture. Miracle heard it fall to the ground.

He said to her, "Go find it."

Stretching her neck to the ground, scanning for the hay, she eventually found it.

I was thinking about how this owner told me the previous owners did the same thing. Watching them, it seemed strange how the story sounded a little bit familiar.

Mumbling under my breath, "Hmmm, were you telling me about someone else who did the same thing as you just did, or were you just tattling on yourself?"

Miracle finished her hay and rocked for a few minutes. She was searching for something; I didn't understand what she was doing. Suddenly, a light went on in my head, thinking that she can't find her feed. Grabbing her feed bucket, I stepped into the pasture, shaking the bucket. Miracle's head lifted. I quietly called to her, "Miracle, here it is, here's your food, come on, girl, come get it." She slowly approached me. I walked backward, tapping the side of the nasty, dirty feed bucket. I reached the door to her open stall and said, "Follow, follow." Lightly tapping the bucket, she followed me in. I hung her bucket on the inside fence. Her neck stretched to test the area and feel for her bucket. Tapping the bucket, I said again, "Follow." Miracle walked to her feed bucket and started to eat.

www.ingramcontent.com/pod-product-compliance
Lightning Source LLC
Chambersburg PA
CBHW072137170626
46813CB00004BA/1601